MADE OF

STEEL

The Autobiography of
Sir Oliver Marsden VC,
Marshall of the Royal Air Force

DICK CADEN

APS Books
YORKSHIRE

APS Books,
The Stables Field Lane,
Aberford,
West Yorkshire,
LS25 3AE

APS Books is a subsidiary of the APS Publications imprint

www.andrewsparke.com

First published worldwide by APS Books in 2023

A catalogue record for this book is available from the British Library

MADE OF STEEL

CHAPTER ONE

I served in the military, one way or another, for almost fifty years. The majority was within the RAF, with a little of it outside in civilian flight testing. I fought and lived through two world wars, crash-landed at least three aircraft, got married, made a home, and enjoyed the comradeship and friendship of some of the finest people ever to grace our planet. I also lost many of those dear friends. But in the end, I'm just like everyone else who takes part in noteworthy activities, whether it's military, scientific, engineering, or whatever; I'm just a normal, everyday bloke who happens to have a story to tell, or at least, a story that some people might want to hear.

By the time I was born at the Royal United Hospital, Bath on the morning of 27th March 1920, my dad, Randolph, who had inherited an acceptable fortune in his early twenties, and my mum Charlotte, lived a very comfortable life in a very comfortable world. Despite having owned a massively ostentatious twelve-bedroom pile in north Devon, Dad had wisely chosen to downsize, at a time when downsizing only happened if you fell on hard luck. He had, however, foreseen the benefits of a smaller property with a significantly larger bank balance.

He bought a decent-sized farm in Kelston, just outside Bath, where he bred sheep for wool, and kept hundreds of chickens on the ten acres of land. My mother was in sole charge of the house and oversaw the work of the cook, the maid, and the shepherd. She also spent time each week assisting at a poor house on the western outskirts of Bristol and was an avid churchgoer. Dad, on the other hand, was, according to his own accounts to me many years later, a rather lapsed Christian. He had been highly decorated during World War I, having volunteered for war service during the very first week of hostilities at the ripe old age of 25. As a Captain in the Infantry, he was never far from the front line and narrowly missed a most awful fate when his Regiment's trenches on the Somme were gassed whilst he was at GHQ receiving the news that he had been accepted for training with the Royal Flying Corps. Dad had first returned home in January 1919, and now a Major in the newly formed Royal Air Force announced to my mother that he had accepted a permanent commission and was to be based at a secret location in Southern England (which turned out to be Old Sarum). He now had two month's leave and used this time fruitfully by getting heavily involved in the workings of the farm. Even after his new job as Second in Command at the airfield began, during the post-war period, the RAF was cutting its fleet size significantly and he was able to spend many weekends at home.

I was educated at home by a private tutor until the age of eight and, after that I boarded at Clifton College. To be totally honest, I would describe this period of my life as acceptable but little more. I had few really good friends and didn't enjoy being away from home one bit; especially as home was so near.

I left the college in 1938 with a Higher School Certificate and a burning desire to follow my father into the sky. My aim was to be a fighter pilot and I had read just about every book written about those knights of the sky, and wanted to be a part of it. What's more, I knew I could do it. I so wanted to swoop through the clouds in a Hart or a Gladiator, but my dream was to get my hands on the beautiful Hawker Fury. Even though the Hurricane was coming into service now, the biplane Fury was everything that an aeroplane should be.

Whilst Germany's resurgence was apparent to the British government of the day, the common man had little knowledge of their intentions. So, when I was attested into the RAF in January 1939, I had no idea that I was entering an Air Force that would be at war within a matter of months.

At Brough in Yorkshire as an Under Training pilot, I went solo in a Tiger Moth at 8 hours. On completion of the basic flying phase, and expecting to be passed onto single-seat fighters without question, my instructor was of the opinion that 'Marsden possesses neither the nerve nor the spirit required for a pilot of fighter aircraft in the modern age. His pure flying skills are, however, above the average and I would recommend him for an eventual posting to either Bomber or Coastal Commands.'

I was utterly devastated; I was going to have a career flying about in great big lumbering targets. However, Service rules stated that I was duty-bound to accept this assessment, even though I felt the instructor was talking out of his arse. How dare he say that I couldn't be counted on to fly fighters effectively. After all, his experience only extended to post-war Avro 504s and then Tiger Moths. He hadn't even seen a Hurricane, let alone flown one. He became one of the very few people in my life for whom I genuinely wished bad luck would befall them. Nothing dramatic of course, just a bit of ill fortune; maybe a small crash or two.

I was sent to Boscombe Down to fly the Avro Anson and then converted onto the Whitley bomber; an ugly brute, but actually I rather liked it. It was streets ahead of the Hendon and Heyford which it replaced. It had an extraordinary nose-down attitude in flight and was long and thin but it carried a very useful 7,000lb of ordnance and wasn't particularly difficult to master. I only ever flew the version fitted with the Armstrong Siddeley Tiger engine which were quite unreliable. I never did get a chance to fly it with the Merlin engine which, by all accounts, made it a superb machine. By the time that Mk III version was put into service, I had converted to the Wellington, which wasn't any bigger than the Whitley but looked very different. It sat close to the ground and was magnificently rugged. Its very clever construction meant it could withstand unbelievable amounts of punishment, it was good to fly, and with improved engines on each new marque, it got better and better. I first flew the Mk IA and quickly got to go through the ritual of putting together a crew. The early variants had five on board, so I had to find a radio operator, navigator/bomb aimer, observer/nose gunner and tail gunner. You were on your own in those days. No such luxury as a copilot. My observer had applied for pilot training though, and he would have had no trouble getting a Wimpey down if I had been clobbered.

I remember the Declaration of War as if it was yesterday. I was at Marham and we were in the mess, but hadn't turned off the radio for days. When it finally came, my stomach sank. I even felt a little bit sick. There was none of the cheering and bravado you might have heard of, at least not in my mess. To this day, I don't understand how our government could have been so utterly unprepared for it all. This was the beginning of the so-called 'phoney war,' but for us, there was absolutely nothing phoney about it. The CO called us to a briefing after lunch and as we all settled into our chairs, the Intelligence chap pulled back the curtain. And thus my war began.

To be honest, those of us who were flying in the early days of the war really had it very good indeed. There were, of course, a number of bombing raids where we couldn't find our target, dumped our bombs in the sea and flew home for tea and buns without ever seeing an enemy aeroplane, but with each new mission, the danger of fighter interception or being hit by flak grew greater. By the time I had completed my first twenty sorties, we were into May 1940 and things were hotting up no end. I was then told that I was to go to the operational Conversion Unit at Scampton where I would learn to fly the recently completed second prototype of the Short Stirling.

We were walked around the aircraft by one of the engineering officers and there is no doubt that she was an impressive beast. She was very long, quite spindly and immensely high off the ground when you got to the cockpit. Sitting for the first time in the pilot's seat was a dizzying experience. Apart from being totally surrounded by plexiglass, the overall feeling was of being on a grand verandah in some vast house overlooking a valley. The ground seemed to be miles below and you got absolutely no impression of the scale of the rest of the aeroplane or where on earth the undercarriage was in relation to you. It felt intimidating and, I thought, rather a lonely and exposed place.

There were only two Stirlings on the base and the rest were very slowly being brought in from the factory by the girls and boys of the Air Transport Auxiliary. Some in the RAF called them the Ancient and Tattered Airmen, but I never saw them as anything other than a bloody godsend. They had pilots from neutral countries as well as the allies, and one in eight of all ATA pilots was a girl. Handicaps weren't a problem either; if they could fly an aeroplane, that was good enough. We had peg-legged, one-armed bandits, and there was even meant to be one chap who only had one eye. It was an incredible sight to see a huge bomber swoop in over the field, make a perfect landing and then for a tiny weeny girl to climb out and disappear off in a jeep to go and get her next aircraft. Sometimes a whole lot would be delivered all at once and on those occasions, an Anson would take all the pilots back.

After conversion onto the Stirling, I was posted to 26 Squadron at RAF Coningsby. It was during my twenty-seventh sortie overall, and what turned out to be my seventh operational flight on the Short Stirling, that my luck ran out. It even started badly. There were three Stirlings, all really not much more than preproduction models, taking off from our aerodrome that night. There were also twenty-four Wellingtons. We were the tenth aircraft to go, and as we were taxiing out from dispersal, there was an almighty flash of light and a bang from somewhere in front of us and a cry of 'There goes one!' The aircraft two ahead of us had failed to get airborne and had run off the end of the runway and hit a farmhouse where it exploded. I believe one of the boys' actually survived, having been thrown clear. I was expecting the op to be scrubbed, but far from it; within a minute or two, I had her lined up and opened the throttles. The noise and vibration seemed to me to be greater than ever, and it took ages to get airborne. The tail wheel kept bouncing us about and it was very uncomfortable as the aircraft already had a tendency to swing about anyway. Once airborne, it was quite dark, but I had a lovely view of the countryside slipping away beneath.

All too soon, we were crossing the English coast.

The gunners tested their weapons and the remainder made final checks of their equipment. The engines were running nicely and the temperatures and pressures were behaving. We had barely reached the French coast when the rear gunner, Don MacStravick came onto the intercom 'Are there Spits or Hurribags with us tonight?' But before any of us could tell him that we were definitely unescorted he yelled 'One Oh Nine on the port beam!' followed immediately by his guns firing and a thudding sound as the Messerschmitt's bullets tore into us. I could feel the aircraft responding through the controls and it was immediately obvious that one or more engines were in trouble. To confirm this, the port outer exploded, and by the feel of it we had also lost a good portion of the port wing as well. I throttled back the starboard outer slightly in

5

an effort to trim us but we were already going down. There was an almighty flash and a dull thud as one of the other aircraft received a direct hit and disintegrated off to the right. I didn't have time to look for chutes, but doubted anyone had time to get out. The altimeter showed we were already down to twelve thousand and there was nothing I could do to get more altitude. The port inner was coughing and I had shut down what was left of the number one engine.

The Radio Operator Marty, shouted out that the port wing was flapping rather more than one might expect and it looked as though it was probably going to fall off. I ordered 'Bail out' and checked my own parachute was secure before calling on the intercom to see who was left. There were no replies but as I was about to nip through the fuselage for a final look-see, Marty popped up next to me. 'They've all gone skip except Don. He's copped it.' 'Off you go then, old man,' I replied and he disappeared. Having unharnessed myself and struggled out of my seat I just had time to catch sight of Marty as he slipped through the hatch in the floor. I didn't hang about and was out myself within a few seconds. The instant I left the aircraft I was smashed by the slipstream, blinded by the smoke from our damaged engines and then became aware of the unbelievable cold. As the Stirling slipped away in front of me I thought about poor old Don and said a little prayer. I pulled the cord, and was wrenched to what felt like a standstill in the freezing air.

The sound of the aircraft receded but I could just make it out as it disappeared into cloud. After that, it was just me and the sky. I could see absolutely no sign of the ground and couldn't say for sure what altitude I had bailed out at but before I had time to take stock of my ever-worsening situation I broke through the cloud base and could see that the ground was very close indeed. I stiffened up and smacked into the ground with tremendous force. The chute didn't deflate and I was being dragged along without any control at all. I was banging on the quick release but it was a good thirty seconds before the bloody thing opened. The parachute was whisked away by the wind and I could hear the harness tinkling its way across the French countryside.

It was dark and windy and the ground was sodden, but at least it wasn't raining. I appeared to be in the middle of some vast flat meadow and it was a good twenty-minute's trudge before I could make out any features around me, and, even when I did, it didn't immediately click as to what it was I could see. I was sure it was an upturned boat and, sure enough, as I got closer that's exactly what it turned out to be. An upturned rowing boat in a field. There was a substantial hole cut in one side at ground level and it resembled an outsized dog kennel, albeit for a very large dog indeed. It was going to start getting light soon and I had little alternative but to clamber in. There was what felt like straw on the ground inside and the sound of deep breathing and an interesting smell. As I squirmed about trying to get comfortable, I touched the bristly flank of my boating companion, a great big dozing pig. It didn't seem particularly put out having a human bed down next to it and as the night wore on into an increasing light dawn, I was able to manoeuvre myself so that I was the other side of the beast and effectively hidden from casual outside view. I then fell into a deep but very troubled sleep.

I woke to the sound of a loud snort but I can't say for sure whether it was me or the pig. It was daylight now and the animal was wriggling about irritably trying to get comfortable. At one point it turned its head and regarded me with its beady eyes but then nodded off again. I leaned up onto the animal's flank to peer outside but could see little other than a field and a line of trees about five hundred yards away. There was no obvious habitation anywhere in sight. Needless to say I spent an uncomfortable day with my new companion but did find it a rather distracting creature to be with. I even took to scratching its neck, and each time I stopped, it nudged me to carry on. It was two in the afternoon, according to my watch, when the pig finally scrabbled to its trotters and wandered outside to do its business and have a snuffle around for grub. It didn't stray far from the sty, and when it returned half an hour or so later, it made a great big fuss of lying down and getting comfy.

By the time a miserable soggy dusk hove into view I was utterly bored, but ready for the undoubted excitement of my fist full night in enemy territory. I left my pig friend and walked through the field for over an hour before my feet suddenly touched what was quite obviously a metalled road. Keeping very close to the edge at all times I came across a house. It was just gone one in the morning. There was a barn nearby, but this was a good two hundred yards from the main house. I made my way to it and was delighted to find that not only was it bereft of smelly livestock but it also had a hay loft with a ladder. I climbed up, covered myself with a good sprinkling of hay and fell into another restless sleep. At some point, my fretting must have melted away because it was nine o'clock when I woke. I could see that the sun was shining and the whole barn was warming up. Footsteps were coming my way and I had a dreadful sense that mine was to be one of the shortest enemy evasions of the war. The door to the barn swung open and I heard someone walking towards where I was hiding. The bottom rung of the wooden ladder creaked ominously but it wasn't the Jerrys; it was a little Frenchman who I could see climbing the ladder as I eased myself back as far as I could go into the depths of the hay. Creak. Creak. And then there he was looking straight towards me even though I had squirmed backwards and was hidden. Straight into my eyes. He reached the top rung and walked over to where I was hiding. I got up hoping I wouldn't terrify him. He stopped and smiled. 'English?' he asked.

I said yes and he offered me a muslin bag that, due to the smell and the lump of bread hanging out the top could only mean food. I thanked him and shook his hand. He gave me a little embrace. Then he said 'German' and swung his arm in an arc. He just smiled wistfully and began climbing down the ladder. I walked to the edge of the loft and looked down as he reached the bottom and there was someone I supposed to be his wife. They both waved.

I examined the contents of the bag. I had some cheese, bread, and a giant tomato. I ate the flipping lot and felt pretty content. Then climbed back into my hide for a rest.

By the time I awoke this time, it was already getting dark but I simply couldn't face striking out for freedom just yet. Besides it was now pouring with rain and I was warm and relatively comfortable. I decided that tomorrow would be the start of my escape home.

The next day passed monotonously slowly and I was relieved when dusk finally came. The farm yard was very quiet and there was absolutely no sign of life. I peered into every outbuilding, not really knowing what I was looking for and tried the doors of the house. They were firmly locked and there was no evidence of recent habitation. I have no idea where the farmer and his wife came from or how they had any idea I was there. So after little over fifteen minutes of investigations I broke every rule in the enemy evasion manual and set off up the road. I could only have walked for about twenty minutes when I came to a roadside hut; a place that I presumed was set aside for construction workers or their equipment and was utterly astonished to find a family of four nesting inside. Unlike my visitors to the hay loft, these people reacted very badly to my arrival. The woman, who looked most unwell, wailed and hid her face and the man began what sounded like pleading. My mother and father had never been impressed with my foreign language results at school and I admit to not enjoying Latin or French, so all I managed was, 'Je suis une aviateur Anglais.' This stopped them dead and they motioned me to join them in their little hovel. I declined and struck out along the road with great urgency. Quite what those poor people hoped to gain by hiding on what was obviously a main road escaped me. Suddenly, there was a car engine. Without looking, I threw myself into the ditch at the side of the road and held my breath as the vehicle passed by. Then I heard it stop by the roadside hut. I waited for perhaps a minute before I even dared inhale, and then I attempted to peer over the edge of the verge. I could make out a figure who was shouting into the hut, and as I craned my head to try and hear what was being said I heard a throat being cleared behind me. I spun round and there, less than two yards from me was a German officer in a grey greatcoat, with Wehrmacht brevets and a Luger hanging lazily at his side.

'You, young man, are a very nice addition to my collection of English airmen. Come on please, onto the road. ' His command of English was almost perfect, and I expected him to tell me any second that before the war he had studied at Oxford or Cambridge. But we never got to that conversation. I scrabbled to my feet and onto the road where I did the only sensible thing and put my hands on my head.

'Do you have a sidearm please?' asked my captor.

'No' I replied.

'Then hands down, thank you' as he leapt across a small stream and joined me on the roadside. 'Now my friend, you are my prisoner'

'Oliver Marsden. Pilot Officer Royal Air Force. Service num…'

'Yes, very good. Come please'

By now we had been joined by two very burly and serious soldiers. One carried a submachine gun and the other a rifle. I was ushered towards their little Kubelwagen. A third soldier stood near the hut and I had a sudden dread that before we drove off they would execute the poor people cowering within. Far from it; they left them where they were, climbed into the vehicle and off we went. My captor told me that I had landed just to the north of Saint-Omer and that we were now heading to a holding facility near an airfield to the southwest of the city. On arrival we drove into the entrance of a large metal hangar inside which were a group of four Nissen-type huts. Outside there were a couple of Me110s undergoing maintenance and a Do17 doing engine runs. I presumed the rest were away shooting up and bombing our airfields. I was ordered from the vehicle and escorted into the nearest hut. It was cold and entirely empty of people.

'Now it is eleven thirty. You will remain here until one o'clock when your lunch will be served outside your hut. Then we will speak some more. Good day' And with that, the officer walked off and I was shown to my accommodation by one of the soldiers.

'Where do I sleep' I said sweeping my hand in an arc around all the rows of unmade bunks.

The soldier shrugged and left. I bagged the bottom bunk nearest the small coal heater and proceeded to get it lit with the kindling wood, fuel and a large box of matches that lay nearby. I made up the bed and rested on it until a soldier came in and motioned for me to get outside where I realised I was far from alone. Milling around, waiting their turn for food, were over a hundred other men in a variety of uniforms. Some were quite clearly RAF types, others were soldiers. There was very little conversation and barely a glance between them. I said hello to one chap and he just nodded and offered me a cigarette. This was not what I had been expecting allied POWs to be like at all. I imagined that there would be high spirits and chumminess and a willingness to get back indoors and continue burrowing under France.

I took my fag, my bowl of stew and my piece of bread back to the hut and perched on the side of the bed.

'I imagine there are many lumps of fat?' I spun around and saw the officer from the field sitting up on the top bunk next to mine. 'Please continue your delicious lunch.'

'Can I help you?' I replied. Feeling immediately inane, 'Why am I in this block on my own?'

'Because the others are very full and we need to keep you apart from the others.'

'Why?' I asked

'Because you are a surprisingly important man.'

'You do know that I'm only going to tell you my name, rank and number don't you?' I blurted. The food was lying heavily in my stomach and I put the bowl to one side.

'It doesn't matter who you are. It is what you are. At six this evening I will send for you and we will talk a lot more. Goodbye for now, Oliver.' He got to his feet, straightened his uniform coat and walked towards the rear door. It was opened as he approached and I saw a guard outside who saluted as the officer passed.

So I pondered the question until six o'clock arrived when, almost to the second, the rear door was unbolted and a soldier appeared. He motioned for me to follow and we walked out the back of the hangar, across a parade ground and into the rather plush reception area of what was clearly the officers' mess. An orderly approached and dismissed the soldier and I was then led into a most luxurious office. It contained all the paraphernalia I would have expected in the inner sanctum of a committed Nazi. A swastika flag on a pole to one side of the desk; what appeared to be an original oil painting of Herr Hitler, and a photograph of soldiers looking heroic and very pleased with themselves. A door opened, where I had not noticed there was one, and my captor entered. He was dressed in a suit and tie, and smiled warmly.

'Please sit,' he urged.

He then offered me brandy and cigarettes, and being a prisoner of war with quite possibly a limited lifespan I accepted both. He sat behind the desk and made himself comfortable and then produced a briefcase which must have been on the floor under the desk. He laid it on the tabletop and extracted a folder. I opened the first few pages and immediately realised what it was. I was being shown a dossier drawn up by a group of senior Wehrmacht officers who were fervently opposed to Hitler and the war.

'A balanced text isn't it?' I said, and he looked at me, with a hint of a smile. He got up and left the room and almost instantaneously a soldier appeared and ushered me, with far less grace than before, back to my billet.

After a terrible night's sleep, and as soon as it was light, I could hear from outside the usual rattling and murmurings that accompanied mealtime, so I rushed out and joined the queue of cowed POWs. As before, no one spoke. I collected my meagre ration of bread and some very weak coffee and returned to the hut. On entering, the door was slammed shut behind me. My interrogator stood framed in the dim light at the far end.

'You slept badly, I imagine,' he quipped.

'Yes,' I replied sipping the horrible drink.

'Not to worry. Tonight you will sleep much better. Tonight you will sleep in Berlin' and with that he actually slapped his left thigh and smiled broadly.

Not quite knowing whether his interpretation of sleep meant death or he really meant Berlin I asked, 'Why?'

'Because some important people want to talk to you.'

'Honestly, I don't know anything,' I said miserably.

His smile faded and he turned, talking as he went, 'Ten minutes and we depart, Marsden.' And the door slammed behind him.

True to their word, within ten minutes, I was herded out of the hut and made to walk a good mile or so to the main gate of the airfield where I was ordered up onto a canvas-sided lorry. I had no idea if this was my mode of transport to Berlin or if I was being taken to a field somewhere to be shot. But thinking about it, why would they go to the trouble of that when they could simply garrotte me in the hut? We lurched off across the last few yards of uneven ground to the gatehouse and then out onto a road. Although the truck was noisy as hell and was clearly being driven by a drunk, the motion quickly sent me to sleep. My last thought as I nodded off was to hope that this would be a long journey. Barely had that thought entered my mind than we came to an abrupt stop.

I didn't need to look outside to know that we had stopped at a railway station or siding. I could hear an engine simmering away, and there were voices and the sound of goods being manhandled. The rear canvas covering was whipped back and an extraordinarily burly soldier jabbed his thumb back towards some rail carriages. I jumped down and looked around. I was in a small marshalling yard with one train in a siding, and another on what appeared to the main running line. About a hundred or so yards away was a small station. I heard a car door slam and turned to see my tormentor strut from beside the vehicle. His uniform was immaculately pristine and he carried his. smart tan leather attaché case.

'Come now Marsden. We are going on a train journey' and with this, he walked towards the nearest carriage, and after passing the case to an aide, he boarded. Presuming I was to follow, I too boarded the train. The inside of the coach was supremely luxurious. Not quite Pullman standard, but marquetry inlaid walls, beautiful mirrored engravings and exceptionally plush upholstered seats. The aide showed me to a seat and I obediently sat.

'Remain seated Marsden. If you require the lavatory, you will ask my man. You will be refreshed later,' was shouted from further up the coach.

Moments later the train began to move and before we had passed the little country station, I had wedged myself against the side wall and began to doze. Now I don't know whether I actually slept or if it was some sort of daydream, but I imagined I was in a room with lots of people. They were all staring at me and getting closer and closer. I jumped and was immediately awake, and there opposite me, was my erstwhile captor.

'I made you jump. You do seem to have an uncanny ability to sleep almost anywhere' Then he laughed.

His lackeys were buzzing around, and brought a selection of nice looking biscuits and coffee for both of us in fine china cups. I tucked in without asking.

'Oliver Marsden, you may possibly be the most important English prisoner in Germany. '

'How can that be?' I asked, concentrating on shifting as many biscuits as I could before the good times came to an end.

'Let me tell you, Marsden. Before your arrival I was just Ernst Huber, a Hauptmann of the Wehrmacht. A captain, equivalent to you in rank and with a high expectation of being killed in Russia. But now I am not going to Russia for a little while. Instead I am travelling with you to Berlin where you will meet very important people and I will end my days as an Oberst or even a General-major. ' He was grinning almost inanely and then offered me a cigarette from a beautifully engraved silver case. He was almost beside himself with glee and patted my arm as he lit my fag.

Since I was clearly, and bafflingly, very important I said, 'Hauptmann. If I might be so bold, what on earth makes me any more special than the other officers at the airfield camp?'

Huber looked away.

The train rattled onwards passing station after station across the flatness of Belgium and onwards towards Germany. The only truly common feature throughout was that at every station and every halt there were German soldiers. There was a rather impressive map on the wall by the coach vestibule and I realised, for the first time that Berlin is almost at the far end of the country.

As it got dark, I was presented with my dinner. The main course was lamb with fluffy mashed potatoes and some odd pickle, all followed by a sort of meringue. It was utterly gorgeous. After I had finished, a liveried steward approached and indicated, by the use of hand signals, that I should follow him.

We walked back two carriages and then he stopped, opened a door and revealed my cabin for the night. More inlaid wood panels, a lovely soft looking bed with crisp white linen a fluffy pillow and a basin. He closed the door behind me and it was then locked from outside. I wasn't really expecting that, but the bed was so tempting, the prospect of having to piddle in a sink didn't bother me at all. On the bed was a note signed by Huber which informed me that I was to dress in the clothes that were in the wardrobe, and that my uniform would be collected in the morning for laundry purposes. The cupboard contained a rather nice business suit, a white shirt, a tie, two pairs of underpants, two pairs of socks, a black belt and a pair of very shiny black leather looking shoes. Not wanting to dress in fine new clothes whilst smelling rather horrible and looking worse than I had for years, I used virtually all the soaps, shampoos and other treatments to be found in the basin cabinet and set about a very close shave, and an all over body wash, aided no end by a new flannel. I went to bed feeling refreshed and smelling very fine.

That night I dreamt of the hayloft and I imagined I had climbed in amongst the straw. Then there was a grunt and suddenly I was back in a field with a pig in the upturned boat.

I woke as the door of the cabin opened. The steward held a piece of paper in front of him and announced, 'Hauptmann Huber requests your company in the dining car in ten minutes. ' He then closed the door and left me to dress. Once fully attired, I checked myself out in the finely engraved full-length mirror, and aside from a few rather nasty shaving nicks, I reckoned I passed muster. I had no idea that Speisewagen meant dining carriage, but as it was the only sign outside my cabin and had an arrow pointing away from my seat of the previous day; I thought I'd give it a try. It was the right choice, and as I entered, I was greeted by a beaming Huber who gestured me over to his table.

'Soon we will be in Berlin. Isn't this exciting?'

Simply saying 'No' probably wouldn't have been sensible so instead I replied, 'Yes, very'

'And my, don't we look smart in our new civilian clothes?' and he laughed out loud.

Resisting the urge to tear out his throat, I smiled weakly, and was then distracted by a steward who brought us coffee and pastries and cold meats, cheeses and fruit.

'I thought I had to eat at my table?' I said.

'Only for the one night. Now you are one of my elite, and so you will dine here with me' Huber was twitching around his left eye and he could barely hold his fork. He noticed I was staring.

'You are hoping that I am going mad? I'm afraid it is simply nervousness. I have never been so excited. ' And by the looks of him he could have exploded at any minute.

'Hauptmann, can I ask one thing?'

He placed his china coffee cup in its saucer and looked me in the eye. 'You may try'

'Why am I here?'

He merely stared at me.

We finished our food in silence and Huber seemed flustered and a little angry. I rather thought that whilst he was content for me to be there, he didn't want to actually talk any more.

The train journey took on a familiar pattern. Sleep in a locked cabin, breakfast, a restless morning back in the cabin, lunch, restless afternoon, dinner and then bed. Huber barely spoke to me, but I still had to sit opposite him at every meal. I reckoned I was the best fed and fattest prisoner of war in history.

It took three days to reach the outskirts of Berlin, with long periods of the journey spent in sidings, and little country stations and halts. Eventually, though, we seemed to have reached the end. The train was being shunted into a big marshalling yard and I could see a small convoy of staff cars and trucks parked nearby.

After breakfast, Huber left the carriage and I was told to follow him. We walked briskly towards a waiting car and I was ordered into the back. I sat in the middle between Huber and another officer who I had not seen before. As we moved off, Huber leant across me and shook hands with the other man. They spoke briefly and were then silent for the entire trip, which seemed to take an age.

CHAPTER TWO

We arrived at a very grand castle-like house, and swept through the wrought iron gates and up to the fine front entrance. I was ushered out of the car, marched inside and shown to what I presumed was the library, where I was joined by Huber, the officer from the car and half a dozen other men, variously dressed in uniform or civilian clothes. The room was very beautiful and the enormous table in the middle was laden with cold meats, cheeses, a variety of breads and odd looking vegetables and pickles. There were carafes of wine and spirits, and all the assembled Nazi worthies tucked in as if it was their last meal.

Huber was the first to speak even though he was clearly not the man in charge of this gathering. 'General, esteemed guests and gentlemen, I would like to thank you all for attending this historic meeting, and I wish to take this opportunity to introduce you to our courier, Pilot Officer Oliver Marsden of the Royal Air Force'

They merely looked at me. I wasn't expecting a round of applause, but they did seem rather detached. And then it struck me. A courier? Of what?

Huber continued. 'Marsden will be taking our proposal document to London, and he alone will be our conduit for any and all responses. '

Some of the men were receiving translations, others clearly had no idea what was being said. Huber continued in German and went on for about forty minutes. I stood for the whole time, trying not to catch the gaze of any of them. When Huber had finished, all the others left, withoutfarewells or hand shakes.

'Drink Marsden,' he shouted, which made me jump. He poured an enormous glass of red wine for me and motioned towards a chair. With glass in hand, I obediently sat.

'I presume you speak no German?' he asked.

'Not a word'

'Then I shall tell you what will happen. Tomorrow, after a fine dinner here, you will put your uniform back on, you will be taken by train to eastern France and you will be flown to England where your pilot will invite you to parachute out of the aircraft. You will have about your person a document which you must take to Mr Churchill. After he sees this document, he will want to speak to you and he will then want you to come back to see me. That, I am sure is something he can arrange. '

'But…,' was all I managed to say before he continued.

'You will no doubt be tempted to go straight home, to climb back into a bomber and resume your career, but when I show you the document, you will agree that you have to speak to Mr Churchill and you will want to come back to Germany'

Before I could explain that me gaining access to the Prime Minister was as likely as Huber being granted an audience with Adolf, he took a sheaf of papers from inside his jacket and passed the top sheet to me.

Te High Command of te New Reich
Wishes t inform te Prime Ministr, te Government and te people of GreatBritain of teir intnton t cease al hostle acton against tem and te ttal witdrawal of al German military forces fom France, Belgium and Holand on a dat t be agreed. Te existng High Command of Germany wil be arrestd and brought before German civilian courts t answer charges against te Geneva Conventon. Te High Command of te New Reich wil instuct te army, navy and air force of Germany t contnue t push eastwards where we wil achieve our avowed aim of ridding te world of Soviet Communism.

That night, I thought it would be a good idea to plan my escape, but of course, there was no escape. I was almost in Berlin, and had an almost certain expectation of death if I even set foot outside the building. Apart from my night with the pig, this was the nearest I actually came to feeling like a prisoner of war. However, on this night, rather than being billeted in the main house, I was locked in a tin hut which held a small bench, a blanket and a bucket. On the bench was my own flying suit so I ditched my German civvies and put it all back on. Even though there were quite a few layers and it was nicely warm, I didn't sleep a bloody wink. I couldn't even lie down properly.

19

At breakfast the next day, Huber sat with me. I knew I looked ridiculous sitting at a beautifully set dining table dressed in RAF Bomber Command issue clobber surrounded by high ranking German officers and officials, but it didn't seem to matter. 'Now you understand Marsden. We will lock up Adolf and his cronies and then we will send the Russians to hell, where they belong,' he said.

'There's an awful lot of Russians you know?' I replied

'They are Slavs, Marsden. What is more, they are brainwashed Slavs. The filthy Stalin fellow has led them to believe that communism is their saviour. But of course, all it achieves is very big houses, gold bars and limitless prostitutes for the party leaders, and a handful of grain for the peasants'

'That is simply not true,' I said.

Huber ignored my comment. 'When the Russians realise that their leadership is so corrupt, they will cave in and surrender, and then we will use them to build the new Reich that will stretch from the border with France in the west to Omsk in the East,' and he waved away his grand plan with a flick of his hand.

'I'm not particularly good at geography, but isn't Omsk somewhere in the middle of Russia?' I asked

He didn't answer my question. 'Your Prime Minister hates the Soviets as much as we do. He will see the sense in our proposal. There is no question. I also think that in due course, you may find yourself helping us out. I think the British and the Americans will be quite keen to assist with the extermination of the communist.'

'I don't understand. The Russians are not all that bad,' I said.

'Not to you English perhaps. But to us, to Germans, they are the lowliest creature on the planet. Their leaders are parasites and the people are like snails and slugs,' Huber replied, quite angrily. He was chewing on a runny egg that now dribbled from his mouth, and his expression was not at all happy. 'Will you let me eat please!' he shouted. Within the hour, Huber, myself, a guard and our driver were on our

20

way. I guessed this was my trip to the aerodrome for my one way flight to see the PM. Huber turned to me and handed me a folder. 'Do not open this until you get to London, Marsden. Guard it well, and give it to your top intelligence people. It states that only you will be accepted back into Germany to offer Mr Churchill's reply. There is also a list of our agents and their radio frequencies, callsigns and codewords. It is everything you will need to end the war for England.'

When he turned to me again, he had a slightly deranged smile spreading across his mouth. 'Now I will answer your rude breakfast-interrupting question. Omsk will be the eastern border of the Reich. Our little Japanese friends will be taking everything from the Sea of Japan right up to the Irtysh river,' he announced.

'You've done a deal then? With the Japanese?'

'When Hitler is dead or gone, we will do a deal. The Japanese are already getting rid of their Chinese foes. Then they will invade the Korean peninsula, the Malay peninsula, Mongolia and Russia. There will be a glorious German and Japanese empire stretching throughout Europe, Asia and the far East' And at this, he slapped his knee.

'Mr Churchill won't agree to anything if the Japanese invade India,' I stated.

Huber's eyes narrowed and he moved very close to me. 'Did I mention India, Marsden? Did I? No I didn't. '

I just looked straight ahead. I could tell that he was trembling.

'It is in the papers that you have. If Churchill agrees with us, your Empire will not be touched. Do you understand. Do you understand, bastard?' he almost screamed. I continued to look ahead. At which point Huber grabbed my chin and turned my head towards his. 'Do you understand?' he shouted. Then he let go.

'Yes,' I replied. But I couldn't leave it there. He hadn't killed me so far, and I didn't believe he was going to now either.

'What if Churchill doesn't agree. What if he tells you to take a running jump?' I knew I was pushing it, but it just seemed to be such a fantastical proposition.

'Oh my God Marsden! If Churchill disagrees with our proposal, we will annihilate England, starve the French, the Belgians and the Dutch and then we will kill all the Russians anyway. The Japanese will kill every Chinaman and then they will burn their way through all of Asia, including India. And then, and the main reason we want Churchill to say yes, is that the Emperor of Japan thinks that they could also invade America. And I don't just mean Uncle Sam. I mean Canada and all of the South as well. That is simply ridiculous. If that happens, the silly Japanese will all be dead and our plan will not work. Churchill must agree, you see.'

At that point, mercifully, we turned into a lane and approached a brick-built guardhouse. The soldiers on duty saluted, and lifted the barrier for us to sweep through. Then the tree-lined lane gave way to a wide open space and we were on the perimeter of an airfield. We drove straight towards what I identified as a Junkers Ju52 and we stopped beside it. The guard grabbed my arm and ushered me out of the car and then followed me with his machine pistol pointing generally at me.

Huber climbed out and walked up to me. 'Now you will go home for a little while, and then I will see you again to shake your hand and eat a fine meal with you. England will be free, your British Empire will be free, but the new German Reich will be the greatest empire the world will ever see. Go now, Marsden. Go'

And with that, he and the guard turned away, got back into the car and drove off at speed. For a moment I just stood there. I honestly thought I was on my own but a second later, I heard a click and turned to see a very dangerous looking soldier in the doorway of the aeroplane. He was pointing a pistol at my chest as he waved for me to climb aboard.

I had never been very impressed by the look of the Ju52. It looked like, and in fact was, a corrugated shed with wings. What I was now also finding out was that it was extremely loud and extremely cold inside. The burly guard sat opposite me on the bench seats that were attached along the length of the fuselage, and next to me was a less dangerous looking chap who was my parachute instructor for the day. However, despite Huber's, so far, meticulous planning, he had overlooked a critical part of my instruction. The parachute expert spoke only German. And he spoke it very quickly, very loudly and in a very high pitched voice. He would occasionally point at a strap or punch a quick release thingy, but I had no idea what he was saying or what I was meant to do. Now, I hadn't exactly been expecting to have a kip on the way but I had imagined that I might at least be a bit comfortable. But because the little German man had put my chute on me as soon as we were airborne, I now crouched forward like an expectant mum. After about an hour or so, one of the pilots came out to talk to me. I wouldn't normally notice such things, but this chap had the blondest hair peeking out from his leather helmet and the bluest eyes; I was quite taken aback. What's more, he spoke perfect English.

'Your little friend will tell you to get up in about two hours time. He will take you to the door and he will then very likely push you out. You must count slowly to three and then pull this,' at which point he indicated the ripcord.

With that, he turned and went back into the cockpit. When the time came, it felt more like it had been ten hours aloft. But as promised, the annoying little Jerry grabbed me by the parachute straps and led me to the door of the aeroplane. It was a very big door, especially designed to allow dozens of rotten German stormtroopers to exit in quick order. The burly guard opened it with little effort. I was about to ask where we were when I received a huge heave, and was then tumbling out into the slipstream. There was a short period of indignation, followed by a very quick moment of utter terror as I realised that I had already been falling for around ten seconds. I immediately pulled the cord and mercifully the chute opened almost straight away. I couldn't hear the aeroplane any more but I could hear rain battering onto my helmet. It was bloody dark and all I could think of was what was lying below me. I could have landed in the sea, into a lake or river or, it crossed my mind just for a second, the lion enclosure at London Zoo. And just as these thoughts were spinning around in my mind, I saw the ground and

23

thumped into it. I remembered to roll and started bashing away at the quick release button. I was suddenly relieved of the crushing weight of the damn parachute, and lay on the soggy ground panting frantically. My ears were ringing, my ankles ached like hell, and I was soaked to the skin, but I was alive. I was probably in England and despite everything I had imagined, I hadn't broken so much as a leg, ankle or toe.

I had convinced myself that I had landed on flat ground, but as I gingerly started walking, it became obvious, very quickly that I was on dramatically downward-sloping ground. Because it was so wet, every second or third step I slipped onto my arse. After a short time, I decide to give up and sat under the first tree I came to. It afforded almost no protection from the weather but I didn't care. I fell almost instantly asleep. When I woke, there was the faintest hint of dawn's light and the rain had stopped. It was bloody cold though, and I hoped I could just curl up again and catch a few more hours kip. But after a minute or so, I got to my feet and started off down the hill. I eventually came to what looked quite a well trodden path and followed it. When I got to a junction in the path, the ground became quite flat and after about half a mile I came to a wooden sign that read HASTINGS. I made a little high-pitched noise and my shoulders shuddered. I could feel tears welling up. But then I thought, 'You're British. Get a grip and go and find a pub.' And that is exactly what I did. By accident of course. There were no more signs along the way. There were lots of posts that used to have signs on, but now they were all stored away so that the Jerries couldn't follow them. I would love to have had a set of German binoculars; if they could see a little road sign from two thousand feet.

I had only been walking another ten or so minutes and there it was. It was as wonderful a thing as I had ever seen. The Royal Oak A Free House. As I stood outside I tried to make myself look a bit more presentable and once I was satisfied that I wouldn't be too terrifying an apparition, I knocked on the door. I heard a creak up above me but before I could even look up, whoever was there shouted down, 'We open at twelve!' and then slammed the window shut again.

As I sat on the bank in front of a hedgerow just opposite the pub, I thought that this was the rudest landlord I had ever encountered. And then I thought, maybe they don't get many downed airmen passing by, so I settled down and had a little nap. It was quite a firm nudge that woke me. There was a man in a suit standing over me. 'They're open you know. If you're coming in'

And then he strolled off into the now open door of the pub. It did occur to me that if I had happened upon a man sitting on a grassy bank who was obviously wearing military clobber, that I might just have said things differently. I dragged myself up and walked into the bar. It smelt of yesterday's beer and fags and was quite the best thing in the world at that moment. There were four chaps already hanging around the bar. Two of them seemed oblivious to anything but their conversation, which I think might have been about a tractor or hay or something like that. The other two and the barman were looking at me as I might have expected.

'Well, what have we here now?' enquired the barman.

An awful lot of things went through my head in that split second. Should I affect a ridiculously upper-class 'Hello chaps, just got shot down, don't you know' voice, or would they run me through with a pitchfork as soon as I started supping my ale? And then I thought no. To be honest they looked a little spooked by me.

'I would quite like a beer and then to use your telephone, if you have one please' Which I thought sounded much better.

As the barman pulled my pint, one of the two who had been in deep conversation before spoke. 'Are you an airman then?'

'Yes, I am.'

'Are you one of us. You know, English?' His voice had a certain strain to it.

'Yes. Of course I bloody am,' I replied.

At which point, the weight of the world seemed to lift from all of them, and they offered to buy my pint and the barman shot off to get me some food. He returned moments later and placed a large plate in front of me on the bar. 'Bloody well done, son. There's no restrictions on onions you know,' which was a reference to the biggest pickled onion I had ever seen that now adorned the plate between some rather nice-looking bread and some decidedly off-looking cheese. 'We'll have to go and get the constable I'm afraid because the 'phone doesn't work anymore' announced the barman.

'Right ho. That's fine,' I replied, eagerly tucking into my first normal food since the French barn.

The police station must have been miles away because it took more than an hour for anyone to turn up. And when he did arrive it was as I had surmised. He was quite old, puffed out from the walk up the hill and half grabbing for his notebook whilst keeping a firm grip on his truncheon handle. He tried to say something, stopped, cleared his throat and then said, 'Identity card please'

So I fumbled around like a fool because it had not occurred to me for one moment up to now whether or not Huber had even given it back. But it was there, exactly where it always was. The constable clearly also had trouble with his eyesight. He squinted at the ID for quite a while before the barman lent over and snatched it away from him.

'Oliver Marsden, Pilot Officer. Here you go, Stan' And he handed it back.

The policeman struck up an authoritative stance and announced, 'The LDV boys are sending up a truck to take you into town. They shouldn't be too long now.'

'Why the hell didn't you come up with them then, Stan? All this is no good for your ticker, you know,' said the barman.

Twenty or so minutes later a creaking old truck, that appeared to have been hand-painted a sort of dark green colour, pulled up outside. A corporal and two soldiers got out and tried to be both chummy and serious at the same time. The NCO and one of his men both looked to be around fifty, whilst the other chap looked about fourteen. The corporal had a Webley pistol in a holster and the other two had shotguns.

We drove down into Hastings, or at least I presumed it was Hastings. There were no road signs, but it was by the sea and it looked quite grand. There was an awful lot of military activity. Some other LDV sorts, but also quite a lot of what appeared to be Regulars too. I was taken to a nice looking building called the Majestic Hotel and into an office just behind what had once been the reception area. Before I had even sat down, a door opened opposite, and an army officer burst out. He had his right hand stretched out way before he got near me. He shook my hand vigorously and even slapped me on the back a few times.

'Come on, come on. Come in. It's marvellous to see you,' he enthused.

We strode into his office, which was a terrible mess, and after he had beaten a chair a few times to raise some dust, he signalled for me to sit down. Then he scrabbled around with some papers, offered me a cigarette, which I accepted, and after he lit us both up, he finally sat back, sighed and then looked at me with a smile.

'What a palaver eh, old chap?'

I didn't know whether he meant me or something else. 'Yes'

'The war I mean. You and I should be working in banks or solicitors offices, not trying to kill people eh?'

'Um, Yes,' I offered.

'So, you're Oliver Marsden, a Pilot Officer and you were shot down by the bloody Jerries and now you're back. Spiffing, simply marvellous. How did you manage that then?' And I immediately knew I might be in trouble. I realised that, once again, there had been no preparation by the Germans for my return to England at all. It hadn't crossed my mind that I would be interrogated by my own side. I thought I would be welcomed home, promoted, given a week's leave and a medal from Winston, and could then live out my life rearing sheep at home whilst Moscow burned. It was time to think very quickly.

'I mean, take your time old chap. I'm not busy or anything like that,' and then he blew a most amazing smoke ring and grinned as it wafted across the table towards me.

'Do you think I'm a spy?' I asked

'You tell me, old man. We'll find out who you are alright. It's just easier if you tell us. Saves a lot of bother.'

At which point there was a knock on the door and after the officer yelled 'Enter,' a soldier walked smartly in, stood to attention, handed him a sheet of paper, about turned and left. As he began reading I said, 'I am not a spy you know. I am an RAF officer who has escaped from Germany' I had thought that up very quickly. The rest was already forming in my mind.

He waved his arm at me and said, 'Good, sshhh.' So I sat like a lemon, puffing away at my cigarette and wishing I could have another pint. After about five minutes he threw the paper onto the desk and stared at me. 'An Oliver Marsden, Pilot Officer went missing on the 7th July and is Missing Believed Killed along with his entire crew. What do you say to that?'

'I say. Oh. Bloody hell, my parents must think I'm dead.' It had finally hit me

'What are you saying man?' said the officer.'

'My parents. My parents think I'm dead?' I felt terrible. It hadn't crossed my mind once since I was shot down. I hadn't given my mum or dad a second thought. How utterly terrible is that?

'Oh well, yes They will very definitely think you're dead. Or at least missing. Which after what - eight weeks - probably means you are dead.'

'Then I need to tell them. To see them. They need to know. My mother…'

'Swales!' yelled the officer.

Within a matter of seconds, the NCO re-entered the room. He snapped to attention at the table.

'Would you please take Mr Marsden to Charlie wing and show him his room,' said my interrogator.

I realised there was no point pursuing the point. He had lost interest in me. I got to my feet and followed the soldier out of the room across the corridor and through some guarded doors where I was shown into a small but comfortable looking bedroom.

'Used to be hotel staff quarters sir. Night, night, sir'

And with that, he shut the door and locked it from the outside.

It wasn't particularly dark and it was definitely not bedtime. The room was depressingly small, and had a little window that looked out onto some very large rubbish bins. The bed looked nice though, and despite it only being time for babies and toddlers to nap, I lay down to practise the military art of kipping anywhere, anytime.

I woke with a start because there was a key rattling in the door. Just for a moment, I forgot where I was and was half expecting some burly damn Jerry to waltz in. But it wasn't a stormtrooper. It was Bertie Wickstead, my Squadron adjutant. 'Oh bloody hell! Ollie!', he shouted as he strode towards me. I jumped off the bed and we shook hands firmly.

Bertie and I remained in the hotel until the morning, and then took the train to London and onward to Coningsby. The biggest disappointment for me about this whole affair was that I never got to meet my army interrogator again. I have fostered a deep loathing for him that remains to this day, even though I know he was only doing his job. It was one heck of a long journey back, but it gave us plenty of time to catch up. Bertie told me that my parents didn't yet know that I was alive and I asked him to leave that to me. He had smiled and asked if I really thought that spending eight weeks in occupied Europe, and then escaping warranted any sort of leave. We then got to the more sombre matter of my crew. Only Martin Kimber was confirmed as being a PoW.

The remainder were Missing. I liked Marty very much, and hoped he would either have a pleasant internment or would manage a daring escape.

It was a beautiful day at Coningsby when we eventually arrived. I wasn't expecting a fanfare, but was genuinely surprised, and a little disappointed, that not only was there no obvious excitement at my return, but I hardly recognised a single soul on the airfield. Bertie explained that half the chaps were dispersed away to other airfields and rather a lot had bought it on raids. There were two chaps in the mess who greeted me warmly and the station chaplain was most kind, telling me that I was blessed.

Squadron Leader Brian Morton was recently promoted and new to the post. He seemed a nice sort, and told me that I was going to be promoted too. He congratulated me and then shook my hand. He told me I could have four days leave, if I wanted it, but that I was to be back for ops as soon as I returned. No one had asked me how I survived, how I escaped or how I got back. I was bloody surprised. Then I was taken to the Intelligence Wing.

The Intelligence bod's office was adorned with huge linen sheets over what I presumed were highly secret maps and lists. He sat me down and then asked me all the questions I had been expecting. His face was a picture as I told him exactly what had happened.

'This isn't right, Marsden. Just not right. How on earth can you prove any of this,' he said, with a huge ladleful of disbelief. I fiddled around inside my tunic and retrieved the folder which felt a little damp and smelled rather nasty. I handed it to him and he sat back and started reading. I have never seen the colour drain from a man's face before, but now I did, and it was a picture. There were little beads of sweat forming on his forehead as well, and he began clearing his throat; quietly at first and then increasingly loudly. In fact, I thought he might die at any moment.

'Bloody well sit there. Don't move. Do you understand. Don't move' and he shot out the door. Seconds later, he retuned and scooped up the folder which he had left on the desk.

Squadron Leader Morton came back into the office first followed by the Int. chap. Morton sat at the table and then looked at Int.

'Where is it?' Morton asked Int.

'Oh, sorry sir,' said Int and handed him the folder.

I then watched as Morton read the contents. Every two or three seconds he would look up at me before returning his gaze to the German proposal. 'Is this true. It's not some stupid joke is it?' he asked.

'Completely true sir,' I replied.

Morton left the room with Int, and shortly afterwards they both returned and told me to stay put. They would return in due course having decided what to do next. They didn't lock the door from the outside after they had gone either. So, for the next hour, I smoked Int's cigarettes, drank his water and flicked through a couple of Operation reports lying around on his desk. When they returned, they had two Provost Branch soldiers with them and without a word, we all left the room, then the admin. block and then the airfield.

The car was a new Humber and very comfortable indeed. We drove for absolutely hours and eventually arrived at what I later discovered was Bomber Command Headquarters in Uxbridge. The two Provost chaps remained outside the main building whilst Morton, Int and I were shown into a very fine anteroom and offered tea and cigarettes. Then I was left alone again after the other two were called into an adjacent office. I was idly smoking yet more of Int's cigarettes, and then wandered over to the door of the main office. There was a very beautiful name block at eye level, and it appeared to be burnished mahogany. It read, Air Officer Commanding-in-Chief Bomber Command Richard Peirse. The outer door to the anteroom then opened and a Flight Lieutenant entered.

'Flight Lieutenant Marsden, come with me please,' he barked.

For a moment I thought he had made a mistake. Had I been quietly promoted? Was I now a Flight Lieutenant?

I walked with this chap into the mess which was an awfully long way from the main building and he sat me down and arranged for lunch to be served. The steward brought me fish and potatoes, peas and a sauce, all washed down with nice strong tea. Then I was given a whole packet of cigarettes and a box of matches. It was whilst puffing away and swigging my tea that I noticed I was the only soul in the mess. What's more, I could just make out the two Provost chaps standing by the main entrance. The steward then came and stood in front of me and cleared his throat.

'If you could follow me sir, I'll show you to your room,' he said. I was bright enough to realise that Huber's document had obviously got the high-ups into an absolute tizzy of excitement, and also that the whole thing was most secret. I followed the steward and kept quiet. The Provost men followed us and stood guard outside the room that I had been allocated. The steward then produced two new pairs of pants, two pairs of service socks, two vests, two new service shirts, tie, highly polished shoes and trousers. 'If sir could change into these, I will get your uniform cleaned and your new rank attached. There is a bath through there for you,' said the steward. With this, he left and closed the door.

I was a bloody Flight Lieutenant!

I had a good shave and a long hot bath. It took ages to get all the grime off, but eventually I think I did a decent job and got dressed in my new clobber. It may seem inconceivable to nonservice types, but catching a nap is as important to the military man as food and drink. Needless to say then, when Morton knocked on my door, I had nodded off again.

He entered and sat on the chair by the little writing table. 'Oliver, the Air Officer C in C has seen your proposal and is taking it to London. Now, we know that it states that you alone must speak to the Prime Minister, and if it is felt necessary, that will happen in due course. In the meantime, you are to stay within the confines of this camp. You may dine with others; you can even sit with them if you wish. But you can say absolutely nothing of the document and you most definitely cannot use the mess bar,' he stated.

'Careless talk sir?' I said.

'Quite,' he replied. 'You cannot discuss this matter with anyone. At the moment the only people who know are the three officers who have seen the document and you. No one else must ever know. Is that understood?'

'Completely sir,' I replied. 'And sir?' I added

'Yes, Marsden'

'When can I go on leave, please?'

I stayed at RAF Uxbridge for four more days with absolutely nothing to do. Everywhere I went, there were guards watching me, and almost everyone I spoke to spent large amounts of their time tapping their noses with their fingers and telling me that they understood everything was 'hush hush.' Bloody idiots. On my fourth miserable dull day at Uxbridge, I was in the mess nursing a beer when Sqn Ldr Morton came in, and told me I had been summoned to London. I wasn't at all surprised to find myself waiting in the reception area of the War Office main building. After all, it was I who was meant to have hand-delivered the German proposal to Mr Churchill. I hadn't for a moment thought that things would work out that way. But here I now was, watching all the highest ranking military and civilian bods in the country wafting from one office to the next sorting out how we were going to broker a peace deal with Jerry. I half expected to see Winston himself. Considering the rank and status of most of the people I had already seen that morning, I didn't think it at all unusual when I was approached by an Air Commodore. He was a most cheerful looking sort, and spoke in wonderful Etonian tones. 'Flight Lieutenant. I wonder if I might ask you to come with me,' he said.

Having snapped to attention, I followed. 'Yes sir,' I replied.

He walked and I marched, rather well I thought, until we reached the Air Commodore's office. Once inside, I realised how marvellous it must be to get thrust this high up the chain of command. His desk was a picture. It was oak with a fine leather top and brass buttons all around the edge. His chair was brown leather, and looked supremely comfy. He motioned for me to sit. He sat too and then rested his chin on his hands and smiled.

'Firstly Marsden, I bring you the personal thanks of the Prime Minister for your courage and diligence in bringing the document to us. Your story is really very 'Boys Own' stuff,' he said and offered me a cigarette from a clever silver pop up device.

I accepted and said, 'Thank you sir'

'What you will now hear must remain a secret. No one can ever know. Is that clear?' His tone was exceptionally serious but he continued to smile.

'Yes sir, of course.'

'Marsden, the Prime Minister has stated to the Cabinet, and on occasions even to parliament, that he would never accept a peace deal with the Nazis that didn't include their complete surrender'

'Yes sir '

'So, even if the circumstances were different, he would had said no to Huber and his merry men'

'Yes sir.'

'But the whole matter is now entirely academic. You see, Huber and his co-conspirators have been found out and, as we speak, they are doubtless being tortured and butchered in the time-honoured Nazi tradition.'

I knew that my mouth was moving but I couldn't get a word out. The Air Commodore leant forward. 'All that effort for nothing, it seems.'

'Oh my God!' was all I could muster.

'Quite,' said the Air Commodore. 'Now. What to do with you eh?'

CHAPTER THREE

Being a truly decent man, Air Commodore David Percival Smyth made hasty arrangements for my leave to commence with immediate effect. But before I left London, I had to sign a document that specifically excluded me from ever mentioning the German document, and it added that, if asked about my escape from occupied territory, I was to follow a particular storyline. The RAF High Command would confirm the facts to anyone who enquired.

It was quite extraordinary how the Chiefs of Staff all took the news of the German conspirators' capture with such everyday nonchalance. Perhaps such unbelievably complex decisions were being made every day, though I doubted it. I had got over my immediate shock, and also my momentary sense of pity for Huber. I also presumed that all the men I met at the conference in Berlin were also dead or being subjected to some sort of horror.

The Air Commodore was awfully nice, and rehearsed me in the splendid cover story that his chaps had dreamt up. We left his office and as he was handing me my travel warrant for my journey home, he took me aside. 'Marsden. You might become a bit of a movie star because of your heroic escape from the clutches of the Nazis, and because of that, I am redeploying you to a different squadron. You will go to 9 squadron at Wattisham. They're flying the Wellington at the moment but will be one of the first to fully transition to the Stirling, so you should be happy there. Alright, old chap?' It wasn't really a question, but I didn't mind, I hardly knew anyone back at the old place anyway.

'We're having all your gear packaged up and sent on. It will be there when you get back from leave. Goodbye Marsden.' And with that, he returned to his desk and the task of winning the war. A war that would now continue for God knows how long.

I was driven in a staff car to Paddington railway station and caught a train to Bath. Once there I took a taxi to Queen Square station and took the local passenger service to Kelston. Quite why it was called that is a mystery. It's a good mile to the village and was rarely used. But I knew it well enough and walked up the very steep hill until I reached the footpath that led to the house. I knew that if I simply turned up, I might well give them both heart failure, so I hid in the trees and peered through to see if I could spot anyone. I felt ridiculous, but also unbelievably nervous. My dear parents thought I was dead, and I was about to tear their world apart. In a good way, of course. To my great surprise, my mother was sitting on the terrace and appeared to be reading a book, so I walked up the side wall and sneaked in through the gate. I closed it very quietly and she didn't stir at all. It was a lovely afternoon and she had obviously dozed off. I hadn't really hatched a plan at this stage, but I decided simply to walk over and try and sit down before she noticed me. Quite amazingly, I was able to get onto the terrace and sit, ever so slowly in the chair on the other side of the table from her. And then I just looked at her as she dozed. The woman who had brought me into the world was so utterly lovely. My beautiful, kindly mother. I had looked away for just a moment and when I turned back, her eyes were open and she was staring straight at me. I just smiled at her. I think that just for second she thought it was a dream, but it didn't last.

'Oh Ollie!' It wasn't a shout or even very loud, but it made me jump just the same. She shot up, as did I and we hugged for a long, long time. I was jolly surprised that she didn't cry but that was absolutely fine, because I did. I think I had lost track of just how much I missed her. Stuck in enemy territory and swanning around in London, I had forgotten my responsibility to my parents. But now I knew I wouldn't leave them like that again, and I certainly wouldn't take them for granted.

My conversation with mum was very much along the lines of 'where were you, why did they tell us you were dead, how did you get back?' but I just shrugged it all off saying, 'I'll tell you both once we see dad.' Which was okay with her. My father was over at a friend's house apparently, so mum and I decided to go around and surprise him somewhat. He was only five minute's drive away so I started up the Triumph Twelve and we motored over to the far end of the village. I could see him standing with Mr Dolland at the front of the house and they appeared to be inspecting a motorcycle. Dad saw the car approaching and waved as he recognised it. I suppose it was then that he must have thought it was rather odd, because mother didn't drive. As we got closer I saw his legs buckle a little bit, and fearing that the shock of seeing me might kill him, I slammed on the brakes, jumped out of the car and ran over to him.

Mr Dolland was standing there with his mouth open and was saying, 'Oh my God, oh my good God!'

I hugged my dad, as much to keep him standing as anything else, as he was shaking quite violently. Mum came over and said, 'It's all right darling, Oliver's back. Why don't you have a little sit down? 'Mr Dolland dragged over a big old bucket and he turned it upside down so that dad could sit. I held dad's hand as he breathed deeply. Eventually, he said. 'Why didn't they tell us you were alive, Oliver. Why?'

I explained that I had only just got back, and that it was quicker for me to come over rather than sending a telegram. Mr Dolland, a sweet man, asked us if we would like to have a cup of tea at his, so I said yes and we went into their garden. Mrs Dolland cried as soon as she saw me and she was still crying when we left an hour later. Mum was much calmer by then, and even dad had settled down. I had told them all about my miraculous misadventures; obviously, the new official version from HQ. I had been shot down by an Me110, baled out over France, hid in a pig sty, then a barn. I then made my way, on foot and occasionally on a borrowed bicycle through the occupied area until, after many weeks of dodging the Germans, I came across an airfield. Here, I stole a German transport aircraft and flew my self to England. Not wishing to be shot down as I landed unannounced at an RAF station, I pointed the aeroplane out to sea, baled out over the Sussex coast and found myself, by God's good fortune, very near a pub just north of Hastings.

And who wouldn't believe that! To this day, I don't know who dreamt up my little story, but I very much owe them a large drink. I would hate to think it was that miserable, suspiciously untrusting Army bloke.

Over the next two days, I was the village celebrity. I didn't have to buy a single drink in the pub or fret about lifts to and from wherever I wanted to go. I also didn't feel in the slightest bit ashamed of my subterfuge. I had been shot down, and I had parachuted into Sussex. It was just the bits in the middle that were different. I wished I could have told mum and dad the truth, but I suspect they would eventually have blurted it out and I would have ended my days locked up in the Tower.

By the third afternoon of my leave, things had quietened down no end and I could walk to the grocers without ladies bursting into tears or hugging me or the men slapping me on the back and offering to buy me dozens of beers. On that third evening, my parents and I were sitting on the terrace overlooking the garden and the valley below. I heard a train passing on its way to Bath and decided I should tell them what was happening next.

'Unfortunately, I have to leave tomorrow at lunchtime. I have been posted to a new squadron at a new aerodrome' I announced.

My mother had tears in hers eyes but she bravely sniffed just once and then said, 'We knew you would have to go back soon darling. It just doesn't seem very fair after all you have been through.'

'You will be back sooner this time won't you old boy?' asked dad.

'I absolutely promise you that I will. I promise,' I said. Leaving them was horrible, and I couldn't really give any true indication of when I would be home again. I just knew that I wouldn't let them down again.

So, I toddled off to my new squadron and was relieved to find that all my kit had successfully arrived ahead of me. I was warmly welcomed by everyone I met on the airfield and the station commander, Squadron Leader Benjamin Denton, gave me a whole extra day to settle in before I had to return to operations. Then, on the 15th September, I was given command of my new aircraft, a Vickers Wellington. I gave her a walk round and she looked to be in fine fettle. I was very much looking forward to meeting my new crew as well, but as I was walking towards the crew room to find out who the lucky boys were, a guard fellow ran over and informed me that the Station Commander wanted to see me immediately. I was pretty certain I hadn't done anything wrong, so I was fairly upbeat when I was called in. He was a nice bloke and I could tell that he had something unpleasant to tell me. After we had lit our cigarettes, he breathed deeply and said, 'The chaps at Uxbridge were on to me last night. They wanted me to know that as you had already done twenty seven ops, you were only going to do three more, and then you were to be rested and sent off to an OCU to train new blokes to play with the Stirling. But then they rang back and said that I was to hold on as they were sending a dispatch rider. So this chap arrived this morning and I have received a bit of a briefing on what happened to you in Germany'

'Oh,' I said.

'Quite,' he said and then continued, 'It seems that one or more of the German conspirators mentioned your name and it is thought that if you were to be captured, they would be less than kind to you. So, in essence, you're off ops and training and instead you're going to Vickers at Weybridge. A chap I know down there called Joe Summerfield will help you out no end. You leave in the morning, old man.

Forty-eight hours after arriving in Wattisham, I was off again. I knew it was wartime, but this was bloody ridiculous. This time I had to take my kit with me, and I had only just flaming well unpacked it all. An orderly helped me put it in a car, and then I was driven down to Stowmarket to catch the fast train to London. I then took the Underground across to Waterloo and caught the stopping service to Weybridge. I had been booked into the Hand and Spear hotel which sits on the roadside right by the railway and was an easy stroll to the airfield. A young chap met me at the station entrance and handed me a sheaf of papers; some to read and some to sign, and then he informed me that I was due to start the day after tomorrow. I was pretty bloody miffed at all this. If I had known, I could have spent another three days at home.

Anyhow, it was nice to have a comfortable bed and nothing to distract me. It was also nice to be able to go straight from my room to the bar and sip a beer in the garden whilst listening to the Wellingtons at the aerodrome. At 9 o'clock on my first morning, I arrived at the heavily guarded entrance and was then shown to the pilots' briefing area. A very crusty old chap introduced himself as Timothy de Boultaire, and announced that he was the chief pilot! I thought he must be in his seventies, but it turned out he was 56 and had had a difficult Great War. It also turned out that he was very funny and good to be around. That same morning, he and I strapped ourselves into what looked like a Wellington and shot off towards the Isle of Wight. This heavily modified Wimpey was a prototype for a new civilian airliner and it had more powerful engines and a bigger undercarriage. It performed quite well and he let me land back at Weybridge, which was quite a treat.

That evening in the mess, I was introduced to a lot of the other pilots and also to the Wattisham station commander's chum, Joe Summerfield. He was a good bloke who had attracted the nickname 'Mutt' from some of the others on account of his rather odd habit of piddling on the tailwheel of every aircraft he flew for good luck. His argument, it seems, was that crashing a kite with a full bladder and then lying around injured could kill you. Most just thought he liked marking his territory.

Now, there had been women in my life from time to time, including an ATA girl who I first met when she and a few others stayed over at Scampton because of terrible weather. She had been exquisitely beautiful and when she first spoke to me I had hardly been able to reply. My mouth went dry and I could feel my ears were reddening up. She said she found that both funny and rather endearing. It turned out she had got her pilot's licence when she was about seventeen and when she invited me round to her place, I understood how she had been able to afford it. Her parents' house was just outside Mablethorpe and was just completely enormous. It turned out she was the sole heir to the estate, even though she was already loaded. I had liked her very much, but in the end, I don't think I was quite what her parents were hoping for.

Anyway, on my second night at the Hand and Spear, there was a ravishing beauty at the bar. She was smoking a cigarette in a small holder and was sipping a gin. I had gone to the bar to order a pre-dinner beer, and she and I got talking and it turned out she was a nurse based at the small medical infirmary at the Vickers factory. Her name was Anna, and she was four years younger than me. She had dark hair and she looked like a film star. She wore the most mesmerising pale red lipstick and the tightest jumper imaginable. Whether it was a wartime thing, or whether it would have happened anyway, we went to bed on that first night.

At breakfast the next morning, I half expected her to ignore me, or that I might find her with a group of girlfriends, and that they would all be laughing at her tales of my inexperienced love making. But far from it, she was delighted to see me and we sat together for quite a time. She held my hand and asked if I would like to go out with her. I said that I very much would. From then on, whenever we both had a break at the airfield, we would go behind one of the huts or hangars and smoke, talk and very often kiss. On one occasion during lunch, we slipped out and climbed the very steep racing track banking and, having climbed over onto the level ground on the other side, we made love. It was exhilarating.

As we lay there afterwards, I asked her how many men she had known.

'Known?' said had replied in a slightly miffed sort of way.

'You know,' I prompted, pointlessly. 'Oh, you mean done it with,' and she laughed.

'Yes, alright. Done it with.'

'Oh dozens,' and she fixed me with a steely gaze. I was flabbergasted.

'Oh,' was all I could say.

She laughed like a drain. 'Don't be a bloody idiot, Ollie. Who asks a girl that sort of question anyway?'

We agreed not to discuss it again.

Even when it became patently obvious to everyone at the factory that Anna and I were now a couple, we still slipped off at lunchtime and found ever more ridiculous places to, as the Americans called it, 'fool around.'

I was loving my time Weybridge but, aside from my blossoming relationship with Anna, I always felt a bit inadequate. Not because I couldn't fly as well as my colleagues - I could - but rather because I always felt they were asking themselves quite why, at my age, I wasn't flying operations on a squadron. They knew of my escapades, but I never truly felt one of the team.

During my time at Vickers, I managed to get home on six occasions. On the first, I didn't even mention Anna. On the second, I took her with me. I was quite nervous that mum and dad would find her rather 'modern.' Far from it, as it turns out. Mum absolutely adored her and dad found it difficult to take his eyes off her. I could understand why.

In July 1941, nine months after I had arrived at Vickers, I was called to the communication room and took a call from Squadron Leader Denton at Wattisham. He asked me if I would like to come back onto an operational squadron. I told him I very much would.

Within five days, I had completed my assigned tasks at Weybridge, and after a rather boozy night in the mess with Anna and some of the chaps, I had a lovely last night in her room at the hotel. We promised to write as often as we could, and when I left the following morning I told her that I loved her. She half laughed and half cried and told me that the feeling was mutual. I felt like a little boy who had just been told he had inherited an ice cream factory.

When I got to Wattisham, Sqn Ldr Denton made it clear that I was now on my second tour of ops and I would be expected to completed the full thirty before being sent off on more instructional flying, testing or grounded as 'time expired.' He also reminded me that it would be ill-advised to get shot down and captured again as I would very likely be strung up. I told him that I would be careful.

My new crew were quite a mixed bunch. My copilot had sixty hours on Stirlings and my navigator had an impressive twenty ops in his logbook. The remainder were very young chaps and I was quite worried for both their well-being and ability.

Our first missions were over France, which I didn't like very much. I always felt so terribly sorry for the locals down there and the fact we could never guarantee to only hit the Jerries but my crew were lucky; we rarely got fired on from the ground and hardly ever saw a German fighter. Not so the other aircraft on the squadron. On July the 9th, we took off to pound Brest and our squadron was one of ten or so that were on the raid. Almost as soon as we crossed the French coast we were attacked by dozens of Luftwaffe fighters. I saw a number of our aircraft go down. One just exploded and disintegrated in front of my eyes. Not a single aircraft from our squadron got back to Wattisham without at least a bullet or flak hole. We lost five aircraft, and overall RAF losses for the night were thirty two. It was a terrible night and morale was at rock bottom. And it went on like that for months.

Every single time I went up, we would meet some form of resistance. Sometimes fairly light, other times it was like flying through hell. And every time, I would get my Stirling home in one piece, yet the losses around me could be extraordinary.

Denton told me that other crews were clamouring to get aboard my kite because of a seemingly guaranteed safe return home. I reckoned I was just very, very lucky indeed.

Very early in January 1942, I managed to catch some sort of influenza and was totally incapable of moving from my bed so I was placed in the sick bay for two days. My temperature was incredibly high and I actually don't remember much about it. I wasn't the only one by any means, and on one night, only eight aircraft got up due to incapacitated crews. Those chaps that were okay were being swapped around until they had the requisite number, and half my boys ended up with other skippers.

My aircraft was being flown that night by a chap called Gerry Grant, who was a Canadian. Early the next morning I felt pretty much okay, or at least well enough to get up. I padded around the sick bay kitchen and made tea and toast for some of the chaps and then heard the first aircraft returning. I couldn't make out who it was but it was trailing smoke from somewhere. Eventually, it hove into view and it turned out to be a Wellington from another squadron that was just trying to find anywhere to land. Once it had taxied in, I could see that the rear turret was gone and so was half the tail. But it still flew on. A wonderful aeroplane. I went back inside and dozed for a while and when I awoke again it was eleven o'clock. I wandered out to dispersal and discovered that only three of our eight had returned to Wattisham. One other had somehow managed to get down at Eye. One of the four that were missing were my entire crew and my aircraft. I was sick as a dog. Right there on the apron. The medical orderly thought it was some sort of relapse. But it wasn't, it was shock at the loss of so many magnificent blokes.

A day or so later, and I was well enough to leave the sick bay and I returned to my room in the mess. Before my illness, I had been sharing with two other skippers. Both their bed spaces were empty when I got back. The sense of misery was palpable throughout the whole airfield. Not just pilots, but engineering, admin' and the rest. We were all down.

The one thing that didn't change though, was the war. So, within six hours, of getting back into my room, I had met with a new crew, been allocated a new aeroplane and taken it and them up for an air test.

The following week, my room was filled back up with two new boys. One truly was a boy and the other looked to be early thirties. Also in that week, the squadron went out on three sorties and all our aircraft returned safely. On the Sunday, half the squadron were given 24 hours leave, and just after Denton had announced this, and we had been dismissed, he called for me to stay behind. When everyone else had gone, we sat on the edge of the stage.

'Oliver, I have been asked to inform you that you have been promoted to Squadron Leader. You're going to 3 Group at Mildenhall. You start at 0900 on Monday. So if you wanted to pop home for a night, I can get you a travel warrant,' he said matter of factly.

'Thank you, sir,' and briefly considered my options. 'I think I'll stay here and enjoy a day of total peace.'

We stood up and he shook my hand firmly. 'Well done Ollie, richly deserved.'

'Thank you, sir,' I replied.

'Ah-a,' he said. 'We're the same rank now.' And I smiled.

I was twenty-four years old and had been made a Squadron Leader. For a moment it seems ridiculous. Then I recalled that there were quite a few Royal Flying Corps Colonels who were barely into their twenties during the Great War. Conflict can do funny things to the world.

During the following eighteen month period, I completed 36 further ops. Even though the maximum was meant to be thirty or a total of approximately 200 hours operational flying, five of my sorties were either scrubbed at some stage during the flight, or our bombs missed their target. In a cunning bit of creative accounting by the thinkers at Uxbridge, these efforts were not counted towards a crewman's total. Still, in the end, I had 58 bombing missions under my belt. Remarkably, most of the sorties had gone well and squadron losses were low. It actually felt as if we were getting somewhere at last.

Also during that eighteen-month period, I got home to Kelston on two occasions, and to see Anna in Weybridge on three. It was on that third trip down to Surrey that I plucked up the courage to ask her to marry me. She said she would, and asked if we should have an engagement party. I thought that was a splendid idea, so she promised to arrange it in time for my next bit of leave whenever that would be.

I was told, years later, that stories of my so called, extraordinary good fortune in keeping my aircraft and crew safe were becoming the stuff of folklore around a variety of stations. As far as I was concerned, it remained nothing more than bloody good luck, with perhaps a touch of decent flying. Nothing more. On some occasions, I would sit in the briefing room, and if any of my crew were sick, had completed their appointed flying times or were posted elsewhere, I would watch as most of the spare parts gravitated towards me. Not only was it extremely embarrassing, I know that it made the other skippers damned angry.

There is definitely a lot of distortion of the truth regarding my apparent ability to avoid death at the hands of the Luftwaffe. It is certainly true that I got the aeroplane back safely, but hardly ever in one piece. Numerous engine fires, flak damage and cannon holes were testament to this. Besides, there were plenty of other skippers who were in the same boat and appeared 'untouchable.' Some of the criticism of my rather blasé approach to post-operation reports might include a raid we flew on the 23rd November 1942, when my squadron of fourteen Stirlings and sixty-five other aircraft from other stations took off to bomb industrial areas around Lille in northern France. I remember that at the time, I wrote it up as 'one of my shortest.' The facts are that our bombers were attacked by thirty-six Bf 109s and twelve of our aircraft were shot down. Once we reached the target, heavy flak destroyed two more and damaged another three. The Luftwaffe lost seven fighters to our Stirlings and Wellingtons. I flew home with the number one engine feathered and a severely injured navigator.

Because so many sorties were disastrous in one way or another, 'one of my shortest' is no more or less of a good description than one in January 1943, when I wrote it up as, 'Twelve out. Nine back. On target. A/C had two damaged engines. Two crew injured. Not bad. A good one.'

There. What more could they want?

In July 1943, because I had done my second tour, and because they asked for me, I was seconded back to Vickers for three months. I spent a very enjoyable time flying newly built airframes from Weybridge to Wisley for final fitting out, and sometimes even onward to squadrons. During this time, Anna and I had a wonderful time, and even managed to get up to London on a couple of occasions. We talked about the wedding a lot, but decided that we couldn't contemplate marriage until after the war was won.

In October '43, I was posted to the Avro factory near Manchester to quickly convert to, and then carry out experimental flights on the Lancaster. A lot of my early flying on this type took place out of

Woodford Aerodrome in Cheshire. The aeroplane wasn't as large as the Stirling, but it could carry a much bigger payload and was much more forgiving during take off and landing. It was generally a rather delightful machine, and I knew of very few pilots who didn't like it. Its one major deficiency was that it was very difficult to bale out from.

In March 1944, I was informed that I was to be promoted to Wing Commander imminently, so I asked for an immediate move back onto an operational unit. I was very aware that my life in the future was likely to be behind a desk, so I was keen to get some more hours under my belt. After a week or so of frantic telephone calls, I was posted to 40 Squadron at Binbrook. The idea was that I would be allowed to complete three sorties whilst my new job was being handed over to me but then that would be it for flying. I would then take command of Binbrook, two surrounding squadrons and three satellite landing grounds. Very cleverly, I had wangled it so that my promotion got a bit 'lost,' and I managed to squeeze in a total of six bombing sorties before the piece of paper caught up with me, and I was shown to my new, ground-based office. One useful feature of my elevated status was that I was duty-bound to visit my other squadrons regularly, and the best way to do that was by air. It is true that they were both within only forty minutes driving time of Binbrook but it meant I could drop in with a skeleton crew on board whilst keeping up flying hours.

I quickly learned that command can be very lonely. Of course, I had lots of administrative support and the engineering team were excellent. The ground-based gunners were a splendid bunch too. They were itching to let off rounds at the Luftwaffe, but during my tenure the enemy never attacked our aerodrome. My days consisted of the flight briefing, seeing the chaps off, writing letters to Anna and mum and dad, visiting various sections around the airfield, and then waiting impatiently, and very often in a state of dread, for my squadron to come back. In the first eight weeks, I lost seven aircraft across the three squadrons. It meant that I spent a great deal of time writing letters to parents and loved ones, an emotionally-fraught task I hated.

On 17th May, my fellow Wing Commanders and I were called to Horsham St. Faith near Norwich to receive a briefing. Nearly all of us flew in, and there were an awful lot of aeroplanes on the apron. Coastal Command chaps had arrived in a B24, which looked very impressive, and other types included Stirlings, Lancasters, Halifaxes, Mosquitos, Beaufighters, Typhoons and Spitfires. It was like an airshow, but without the ice cream.

We were told that in a couple of weeks, tens of thousands of allied troops would land in France to begin the final push towards Berlin. It all sounded very straight forward. The war would be over by Christmas. The Germans were on the run. The Red Army were pushing the bastards out of Russia and the High Command was in disarray. Naturally, we were to tell no one what we had heard, and the whole thing was most secret. In the coming days, all of our Stations would receive deliveries of black and white paint that we were to liberally daub over the wings of all our aeroplanes for identification purposes. It sounded like a great deal of fun. And what's more, we were warned that due to manpower shortages, many of us Wing Commanders would be expected to fly some sorties. I was delighted. By the looks of some of the chaps around me though, it wasn't an opinion that was generally held.

Once back at Binbrook, we set about painting up the aircraft that would be involved in the great invasion, and I offered a prize to the crew that gave their kite the straightest stripes. The prize was a chicken. A live one. Flight Lieutenant Carl Wilson (Canadian) and his crew on Lancaster 'H' Henry won, and they decided that rather than kill the chicken, they would name it Herman and take it on ops with them. Due to its regular gift of eggs, it was clear this was a female chicken, but Herman seemed an appropriate name. Carl came to my office, and asked if I could write him a dispensation to allow livestock on board a bomber. I told him to get out.

On the Sunday evening, I called all the crews from my three squadrons to Binbrook. Firstly, I informed them that on return to their respective aerodromes, they were confined to base and that no one outside the aircrew element was to know of the operation until it was over. Normal ops were now scrubbed and they were to concentrate on their precision bombing practices. I did not tell them when the balloon was going up, nor what the target was.

On the Monday afternoon, I flew a Wellington to each of the two other airfields and presented the senior man present with the maps and briefing packs. Then, in the evening, I briefed my pilots on the mission.

At 2230 on the 5th June 1944, we took off and after joining up with the other two squadrons, we set off for Normandy. There was quite a lot of bimbling about, to ensure that we all arrived on target at the right time. I believe that there were somewhere in the order of two thousand aircraft aloft that night, and it certainly was a crowded sky over northern France. However, because the mission had been kept so very secret, the Luftwaffe either didn't show up or were very late into the fray.

In essence, we bombed the hell out of the beachhead areas until around 0130 when we began our respective returns to bases. By now, the Germans had woken up, and dozens, if not hundreds of Bf109s, Me110s and Fw190s were swarming amongst us. Some of the Focke Wulfs had long range tanks fitted and were able to chase us all the way back to the English coast. Losses weren't at all bad that morning, but from within my squadrons, two aircraft were lost. One of those was 'H' Henry, along with Flt. Lt Wilson and Herman.

During the next four weeks, we were airborne every day, sometimes even twice a day. We were either supporting the ground troops or softening up the Germans further to the east, and it was tremendous, morale-boosting stuff, and we felt we were making a real success of things.

CHAPTER FOUR

On the 8th July, I took off on what turned out to be my final sortie of the war. It was also one of my most hair raising. I suppose that it comes second only to being shot down on my list of flights I would rather have missed out on. We had flown towards the central region of France with a target to the northwest of Paris. We were to bomb from twelve thousand feet and the resistance from the Luftwaffe was expected to be fierce. As it turned out, the bomb run and most of the flight back were perfectly calm and bereft of any sort of enemy. We had crossed the French coast just to the north of Le Havre, and I was already imagining a plate of bacon and eggs, a nice cup of tea, some bread and butter and then a lovely long kip.

Now, I don't know if the Germans were just being very slow off the mark or it was their new tactic, but as soon as we were over the Channel, they came at us. We totalled over four hundred aircraft that day; mostly ours, but also American B24s as well. You would think that we were pretty safe, especially as Fighter Command had promised hordes of Spitfires and Hurricanes for the trip back. They arrived all right. Just too late.

I heard our tail gunner yelling that the Germans were coming in from above. Immediately, lines of tracer were passing over and to either side of us and then, the unmistakable sound of cannon shells ripping into our aircraft. The tail turret was firing, and as the enemy overtook us, the upper and nose turrets would open fire as well. The noise was absolutely bloody deafening. I saw 109s, Focke Wolf 190s and Messerschmitt 110s, and they would flash by us, then either lock onto some other poor bastard, or roll over and climb hard to come at us either head on, or weave round for another side or rearward attack.

My instinct was to dive down out of it, but the whole purpose of formation flying was that with all that concentrated fire from our bomber gun turrets, we were in better shape than if an individual aircraft broke out and tried to go it alone. That way, you're just a sitting duck.

My front gunner was yelling, and as he did so, shells started smashing into the cockpit. I could just make out the muzzle flash from the enemy's guns, but I couldn't see the aircraft. The front turret was now silent and I guessed the bomb aimer must have been hit. But my main concern was that half the glass in the cockpit was gone and the slipstream was now battering my face. As I was trying to think of clever ways to plug the gaps, I heard and felt the thud, thud, thud as cannon shells hit the left wing. The engines immediately started losing power and by craning my head, I could see that the port outer was now on fire.

Now we were going down. I had dropped out of the formation and knew that it was only a matter of moments before one or more of the enemy pilots saw us and decided to finish us off. I was desperately trying to shut down the number one, whilst reducing power on the vibrating and failing number two, at the same time putting full power on the right engines. This meant that we were now beginning to yaw horribly to the left, so I had to make sure any avoiding turns I made were to the right or I would surely lose control and we'd spin. I shouted over the intercom for the crew to prepare for either a ditching in the sea or a very rough landing somewhere in Sussex.

'There's a strip at Ford, skipper,' the navigator yelled back, giving me a new course to steer.

'For God's sake keep your eyes open and shout like hell when you see Jerry,' I exclaimed.

The aircraft was behaving like an absolute pig with the right wing trying to rise up and roll me over. I had a go at reducing power a little on three and four, but as soon as did that, I could feel that she wanted to stall. Even though the English coast was looming nicely, I didn't think for a minute that we were going to make it. The aeroplane was mushing down all the time and I was expecting a half dozen German bastards on my tail any second.

'Fighter Command's woken up!' was all that the mid-upper gunner said. But it was enough. Dozens, perhaps a hundred or more, of our little fighters were streaking straight towards us, and one Spitfire waggled his wings as he whooshed over the top of us. 'Useless bastards,' exclaimed one of crew.

'Shut up boys. They're here now,' I shouted. Now I was able to concentrate solely on landing, I prepared the aircraft for what was, inevitably going to be a crash.

With Littlehampton on my right beam, the runway at Ford, just to the left of the estuary, was visible from quite a way out. But I was rapidly losing sight of it now as we were constantly sinking down towards the sea. Thankfully, the coast is gently sloping there, and I got over the beach with about a hundred feet to spare. However, there was now no way I was getting onto the runway.

'We're going down!' I screamed over the intercom, and then again over my shoulder. I could see the navigator was already holding on for dear life. I kept the undercarriage up and didn't bother with the flaps because I was sure they were either buggered or that only one side would actually come out, tipping me over and killing us all. I could see the top of the lorry that was used as a mobile control tower, but little else of the airfield. We were down to just a few feet when the perimeter fence appeared directly in front. I pulled back the starboard throttles and cut the engines. The aeroplane ploughed through the fence, and I felt the tail strike the ground. It was fairly gentle to be honest until the propellers dug in and then we started sliding. The ground wasn't particularly rough and after a hundred yards or so, we ground to a halt.

The mid-upper gunner came forward and I told him to get out, which he did, very quickly. The Radio Operator and the Navigator helped the Flight Engineer out of his 'dickey seat' while I went down to see to the Bomb Aimer. It didn't require a doctor to tell me that he was dead. His right shoulder seemed to be hanging from his torso and the right side of his face was shot off. I hoisted him to one side as best as I could, and then, with the help of the others we chucked the Flight Engineer out through the forward hatch. They followed, and once they had got themselves out of the way, I went out too. I walked around the aircraft and was astonished to see that the rear turret was missing. Whether that had happened on landing or earlier, I couldn't tell, but the lower part of the rudder was missing as well, so I guessed we had lost the gunner as well.

The people at Ford were very helpful and looked after the Flight Engineer and made sure he went straight off to hospital. It turns out the mid-upper gunner had a lot of cannon shrapnel in the top of his right shoulder. I had lost my bomb aimer and my rear gunner, but the rest were at least alive. The aeroplane was a wreck, though. I got that breakfast in the end and whilst we waited for transport back to the squadron, we enjoyed copious quantities of tea and dozens of borrowed fags.

In the end, they sent an Anson down from Binbrook to get us, and the pilot filled me in on our losses. Our raid had consisted of four hundred and nine British and American bombers. Forty six were shot down, a hundred and twelve were damaged sufficiently to be later struck off charge. Thirteen made forced landings.

On the 9th July, I was informed that Wing and Squadron commanders were no longer required to fly on ops, and I retuned to the solitary life behind my desk. On this occasion, I wasn't too bothered because apart from my latest mishap, I had had a tremendous time throughout D Day, and now felt I could safely leave it up to others to finish it off. I did later hear that the mid-upper gunner was going to be fine. The Flight Engineer was immensely lucky to have survived. A cannon shell had torn through his right side and he had lost lots of blood. So, with an operational tally of 101 missions, I was finally grounded for good.

It had always been my secret aim to complete two full tours totalling sixty ops, so I was as pleased as punch. I spent the following four months at Binbrook, and had very much settled into the routine of being a ground-based Wing Commander. However, on 2 December 1944 I was asked if I would be prepared to return to Vickers, this time on an official secondment, to join Summerfield and Jack Bruce as one of the chief test pilots. I was at Weybridge right through to VE Day and beyond. I did call the brass at Uxbridge, and asked if they could wave my operational grounding and let me be deployed to RAF Pacific operations against the Japanese, but they turned me down flat.

On 3 September 1945, a matter of hours after the Japanese surrender, Mutt called Jack and I into the test pilot's office and told me that we were all off on two weeks' leave, effective immediately. Apart from guards and maintenance staff, Weybridge was closing down for a fortnight. I scooped up Anna and we took a train straight to Reading and then onto to Bath. It was a sweet moment when we got off the train as I hadn't been home since well before D Day, but I think that on this occasion, mum and dad forgave me. The day after I got home, I got a letter offering me permanent employment with Vickers.

It was clear that now the time was right for Anna and I to get married. I had been regularly corresponding with the vicar, the pub, the caterers, the dressmaker, the florist, the photographer and all the guests. We set a date in May.

I received a telegram at my parent's home, and I was told that once my wedding leave was over, I was to report to Farnborough for a couple of months detachment to assist with the testing of new types. I was thrilled to bits. In the coming weeks and months, aside from working at Farnborough, I was loaned to a variety of other manufacturers and flew some superb and less than superb aeroplanes including the Handley Page Hastings, the Vickers Viking, the Varsity and the sprightly little de Havilland Vampire.

On the 3rd May 1946, Anna and I got married at the parish church in Kelston, and it was a wonderful day. Anna looked as beautiful as anything I had ever seen, and the church was a picture. The ceremony was just long enough, and almost everyone cried, including me. The reception at the pub was everything I had hoped for, and was only slightly less than perfect because Anna's parents were still unaccounted for in Singapore. We decided to honeymoon near Farnborough so that we could spend as much time together as possible before I started my new posting. After four days of blissful inactivity, our honeymoon was over and I returned to my job.

It wasn't until the winter of '46 that I returned to my spiritual test flying home, and reconnected with my old chums. When it became obvious that I was going to spend a considerable amount of my remaining working life flying out of Weybridge, Anna and I decided to buy a little place nearby and she made it as perfect as any man could ask for. Even though she was always cheerful and optimistic about our future, I knew that our lack of a baby was eating her up inside. Anna had been terrifically patient with me because she knew my job was very important. But she was also desperate to start a family, as was I, so we endeavoured to conceive a new Marsden at each and every opportunity. It was like our early days together, and nowhere was safe from our amorous adventures. After a while though, we decided to go to the doctor and Anna's worst fears were realised. We couldn't conceive and it was mostly my fault. Naturally, she was wonderful about the whole thing and constantly told me not to fret because we were equally hopeless! But it was mostly me and I felt absolutely useless.

The next six months were very good at work and almost completely awful at home. It was patently obvious that we couldn't conceive a baby and it was a long time before Anna came around to a sort of acceptance. If it had been me, I would never have forgiven me. But she was different in so many ways. We had still heard nothing about her parents' wellbeing, and even though she was being very brave about it, I think even she now believed they were lost. We eventually settled happily into married life. I would leave for work at eight and on most days I could be home by six. Anna would spend her time looking for new houses to buy so that we could rent them out and make a tidy profit for our retirement years.

In early 1951, the government issued a request to aeroplane manufacturers to produce designs for an airliner capable of operating into and out of 'hot and high' airports across the entire 'Empire Route.' Most had come up with at least something, but it was Vickers' proposed VC10 that won the contest, and it was to this project that I was told to direct all my efforts.

Even though I hadn't flown the Avro Vulcan, I was well aware of its capabilities, and also the shortcomings of the Valiant and Victor V bombers. Even though these three wonderful aeroplanes were to be our future Bomber Command front line assets, I was fascinated by the possibility of either adapting airliners to tanker, transport or bomber roles. In the VC10, I saw an airframe that was capable of fulfilling all these functions. When I tentatively approached the Vickers management with a suggestion that they should offer the aircraft not only as a passenger-carrying vehicle, but also as a long-range strategic bomber, maritime patrol platform and a refuelling tanker, I was taken aside by a number crunching fools and reminded that such decisions were not taken by 'mere' pilots. I appreciate now that future events rather vindicated my arguments at the time, but they really did treat me rather shoddily after that. I was removed from testing the VC10 in November 1961, just a short time before the first flight, and was relegated to operating the Varsity variants. I didn't particularly mind, because it was still flying time, but I hadn't really appreciated quite how much I had put the cat amongst the pigeons. It seems that only the government and the Ministry decide what aircraft we fly and their decisions are based on what the big aircraft manufacturers wanted.

I carried on flying out of Weybridge and Wisley and was still enjoying myself when the Cuban Missile Crisis happened. Now, whether someone at Vickers had mentioned it in passing, or it suddenly struck somebody as a good idea, but the prospect of producing the VC10 as a bomber was now on the table. A couple of the chaps at Weybridge spoke to me about it and said that one of my old letters to management that had outlined the structural changes needed to create the bomber version, had mysteriously found its way to Whitehall. I have to say, I felt rather pleased with myself.

In February 1965, the British government conceded that it had been militarily unprepared during the Cuban Missile Crisis, and determined that the time was right for a significant expansion of the RAF's nuclear delivery capability. They asked both Avro and Handley Page to increase production of the Vulcan and Victor bombers. Both responded that they could only realistically expect to complete 30 additional airframes each in the first year and possibly up to a maximum of 45 a year thereafter. The Ministry of Aviation Supply had been hoping for an increase of up to 250 Vulcans and 250 Victors over five years. So, in March 1966, Vickers was asked if it could create a military version of the VC10. The specification required strengthened wings for the carriage of up to six Skybolt missiles each, with a build rate in the region of a hundred aircraft per year. The reply was positive and a preliminary design was produced within eight weeks, with a contract being signed in June for 500 new airframes. The aircraft was to be built at Brooklands, Bournemouth and Wisley. Once the VC10s were delivered, all Vulcan and Victor squadrons would reequip and retrain with the new aircraft.

By early June 1966, VC10 production was finally confirmed at 440, of which eight would be retained by Vickers. The aircraft would equip thirty squadrons. In mid-July 1966, Avro and Handley Page were ordered to undertake conversion of 38 of the existing 52 Vulcans to maritime patrol standard, and all 47 Victors to the tanker role. The final insult for Avro is that the remainder of the Vulcans would be stored with a view to eventual scrapping or sale. It was a terrible blow to both companies, and neither really ever recovered.

I was promoted to Group Captain in August 1966 at the age of 48. I remained with Vickers, but the RAF had made it clear that I could be recalled at a moment's notice, if or when required.

On August 15, late in the evening, and after Anna had gone to bed, I was in the study of our house reading up for the next day's flying when the telephone rang. I never got called at home and I was nervous as I answered it. Therefore, I was not in the least bit surprised to hear my father's voice. I knew it had to be bad news. And, of course, it was. Mum had apparently been home from shopping for a few minutes and had popped out into the garden. When dad went outside, she was dead on the lawn. According to the doctor, it was probably a heart attack. She was 72.

We buried her on the Friday at the little cemetery next to the church where Anna and I were married, and which was only two hundred yards from the house. It was tremendously well-attended and dad managed a wonderful eulogy. Even if I include the war that was yet to come, this was the worst time of my life.

I took a few more days off to be with dad, and then Anna and I returned to Weybridge, and I threw myself into flying duties.

In September 1966, despite assurances from the US that they would not object to the UK going it alone, the Pentagon announced the abandonment of the Skybolt programme in favour of a primarily submarine-based deterrent. The UK had, for a long time, wished to pursue its own aircraft launched system and now authority was given for English Electric, Armstrong Whitworth, Avro, Blackburn and Handley Page to proceed with tenders. Even though Blackburn pulled out, the best projected solutions of the remainder resulted in the acceptance for trials of the 'White Shadow.' Similar in profile to Skybolt, it had a single warhead at 1.2 Megatons.

By November 1967, White Shadow was showing considerable promise, and it was decided to adapt all in service and new build TSR2 variants to accept the missile as well as all our VC10s.

By January 1969, the first VC10 bomber rolled off the Vickers production line. Some aircraft had the Standard VC10 version's fuselage, but had the wing of the Super; the remainder had all the attributes of the Super. The undercarriage of all had been optimised for the heavier airframe and a new radar system had been scabbed onto the left side of the fuselage in a long pod. The aeroplane now also had an inflight crew escape chute almost directly under the front of the left engine cluster. So, if we could make it to the back as the aircraft fell to pieces, we had a chance to get out! I couldn't have been happier with the end result, or much more smug. Never once was my previous suggestion to create a bomber VC10 mentioned, other than in the mess and always out of earshot of management.

When you consider that a commercial airliner variant of the Victor had almost been allowed to get as far as being built, it isn't that unusual, or indeed complicated, for a bit of reverse engineering to turn a commercial project into a military one. And the VC10 was incredibly robust, which leant it to being a bomber. The truly fantastic thing was that after months of crisis in the programme and threats to scrap the whole project, the wonderful TSR2 had also finally gone into full production and by November 1969, the first RAF VC10 squadron stood up.

In January 1970, Anna and I moved into our new house near Chew Valley Lake in Somerset. I loved the countryside, and it was relatively close to dear old dad. It wasn't, however, close to Weybridge, but Anna had been very happy that I could leave work at the end of the week on a Friday at 4 o'clock, and be home by 7.30. She had successfully applied to be the chief nurse at Bristol Airport at Lulsgate and was kept very busy during the week. We had a rather idyllic life and thought I was very probably the luckiest man alive.

In June 1971, the government announced the complete withdrawal of Vulcans from Strike Command, much to the continued disbelief of their manufacturers. By the middle of 1975, the final domestic version of the TSR2 had rolled out at Warton. These 5a variants had uprated engines, new avionics, and additional self-defence capabilities. It was announced that all earlier models would be brought up to the 5a standard.

It wasn't until November 1977 that the final export TSR2s were delivered, and total sales were an impressive 553 for the UK, 142 for the US, 69 for West Germany, 177 to Saudi Arabia, 116 to Canada, 78 to Australia, 62 to New Zealand and 39 for Oman.

By December 1980, military production of the VC10 had ceased and all previously unconverted airframes had been brought up to MkII standard, with the addition of an internal rotary launcher and underwing fuel tanks for most examples. A hundred or so were going to be fitted out as very long-range versions capable of 26 hours of unrefuelled flight and these aircraft had only four external hard points for White Shadows, whilst retaining the six internally. The centre launch rails, under each wing on these variants now had a huge, dark green painted, fuel tank in addition to the outer droppable pair, and looked fantastically dangerous. The concept of a rotary launch system wasn't by any means new, but this project was a massive additional strain on engineering resources, and aircraft were being converted at twenty six different manufacturers sites. The dispenser itself was located over the wing root and contained six additional 'White Shadow' missiles. These were automatically loaded rearwards into a launch blister which would be depressurised before allowing each missile to drop free of the aircraft prior to motor ignition. Following conversion of the early marques, all VC10 bombers now had the facility to launch 10 or 12 'White Shadows' each, six internally and four or six externally. Twenty eight aircraft were modified differently. They were fitted with two ultra long-range fuel tanks, just outboard of the inner trailing edge flaps, and had four big hardpoints on the centre fuselage at the centre of gravity, for a single, massively adapted, Blue Steel missile. The boffins had increased and tweaked the warhead's yield up to a British record maximum of 12 megatons.

By 1981, RAF bomber strength peaked with 553 TSR2 5a and 432 VC10 MkII's across 60 squadrons. This enormous destructive capability was very nearly cut prematurely short when, in April 1982, the government announced that the Royal Navy would assume sole responsibility for the UK nuclear deterrent. Their ill conceived White Paper concluded that a reduction in airborne strategic defences of sixty percent would still leave the RAF with a world beating albeit conventional offensive capability. It added that the current fleet of 18 Polaris equipped submarines could be usefully reduced to twelve or possibly six! However, before the projected cuts could be made, it became increasingly obvious that the Eastern Bloc was bolstering its presence in East Germany with an unprecedented buildup of troops and armour near the border with the West.

The leaders of the NATO nations expressed their collective dismay at this unprovoked aggression and sought a UN declaration for the Soviet led Bloc to desist and return to their barracks.

On 6 November 1982, the Chinese government announced its full support for the Soviet stance stating that the 'continued expansionist policies of NATO and the West threaten the security of the world.' The world, I had decided, was going mad.

On December 1st 1982, it was announced that all mothballed and airworthy Vulcan bombers were to be removed from storage and quickly adapted to carry four external 'White Shadow' missiles. On that same day, I was in my office when I received a telephone call from RAF Northwood. It was Air Vice Marshall Sir Kenneth Farnsworth. I knew Kenny very well because he had joined Robby Belmont on the TSR2 acceptance trials, and they had spent long hours ribbing me about my lumbering airliner bomber. He was a fine chap, so I was pleased to take the call

'It's almost certainly going to kick off, Ollie,' he said.

This just seemed too unbelievable to be true. Why would the Soviets and their crazy Chinese friends want to incinerate the earth. Because that is what was going to happen. So, the feeling I had was like a mixture of every heart-stopping and horrible moment of my life. My mother dying, my pets dying; all of those emotions plus a sense of helplessness and deep, deep sadness.

'Are you there, Ollie?' he asked

'Yes, sir. Go ahead' I replied.

'Listen, I want you to command 617. If we go to war I want to be sure that our most important and famous squadron has got a top bloke running it. Look, I know you're a thousand years old but we're calling up all former bomber types and anyone under 65 who can still see and hear is getting the shout.'

On the 2nd January 1983, I hired a car and raced home to make sure Anna knew what to do if the balloon went up. We read the government leaflets, but quickly realised that they were pointless. There was a cellar and I spent a frantic day kitting it out for her. There was sufficient, food and fuel to keep her going for about three weeks. I only spent one night with her but it was wonderful. She asked whether I thought that it would be the last time. I firmly said that it was not. We talked about both retiring as soon as things blew over and then, after breakfast we said a very long and horribly painful goodbye. There was no time to go and see dad, but I made a mental note to call him as soon as I could.

On the 4th January, I shot back up to Weybridge and dumped the car in the station car park and boarded the first train to Waterloo. Once in London, I took the train to Kings Lynn and was collected at the station by an RAF car and conveyed to Marham.

It was late evening when I settled into the mess and I was surprised that I wasn't the oldest one there. Not by a long chalk. There was one chap who I bloody well knew was well over 65. In fact, I reckon he might even have been just tipping 70. But he looked sprightly and dapper and nobody seemed to be batting an eyelid in an officers' mess filled with old codgers. Sure enough, there were plenty of young chaps too but they all seemed to want to talk to us oldies about our wartime experience. They particularly focussed on two chaps who had both flown over a hundred bombing missions each during the last war. One of them, it was thought, may have managed 143!

After a couple of days of getting together with my crew whose average age was a surprisingly youthful 37 and being briefed on the situation, I was introduced to my aeroplane, VC10 MkII ZD243. It turns out she was one of the very long-range variants, so I had four 'White Shadows' outside and six in the fuselage. She had a darkish grey upper fuselage with the lower half being slightly lighter. There was a pale blue cheatline between the two different shades, and like all allied aircraft, she had a bold white stripe, with black edges prominently plastered on her roof and a similar one, but in dark red, on the underside. Our markers were, I guess, about ten feet long; on a Canberra or Lightning, it would have been much shorter. The idea was that we were all visibly goodies to anyone flying above or below us.

My aeroplane looked purposeful, if slightly scruffy, but I knew from first glance that she would do the job well. Her warlord was ten missiles, each with the capability of utterly obliterating a city the size of Bristol. On the 7th January I taxied her out for the first time. She was not armed at that stage, but she did have full tanks, both inside and in the wing pods. She felt very lively as we took off and flew west out over the North Sea, up over Rathlin Island and then down the west coast of Ireland before recovering to RAF Marham after two and half hours.

Marham was absolutely packed to the rafters with aircraft. There were fifty plus VC10s, including six of the very dangerous looking Blue Steel monsters, probably as many TSR2s, Hunters, Lightnings and Hercules' and there were helicopters by the dozen. Flying operations were going on 24 hours a day and there were no breaks for weekends. On the 13th March, all aircraft commanders were called to a briefing. There were probably two hundred of us in there and we were told that NATO was being placed on full war alert from midnight. Soviet forces were mobilising within a mile of the East German border with the West, their naval forces were at sea and their aviation assets were armed and preparing to get airborne. The Chinese were similarly on a war footing with huge concentrations of troops both at the border with India and moving northwest to join Soviet forces. This was either going to be the biggest military exercise in history, or there was going to be a war. Politically, it seemed to go quiet for a while and we all hoped this was just another 'phoney' war.

During the next few months we trained day and night, always with the same crew, and to and from a variety of RAF stations across the country and as far afield as Cyprus, Gibraltar and Ascension. We carried out air to air refuelling, fighter avoidance tactics and practised our low level target entry and exit profiles until we all knew our jobs inside out. We weren't allowed on leave, and were restricted to one telephone call a week.

It was on a training sortie that a Canberra flew alongside our left flank and took a cartridge full of photographs. It's an image I'd liked to have had for the cover of this book.

On the 30th June, all aircrew were called to a briefing. It was held in one of the very large hangars located inside a hundred foot security perimeter manned by the RAF Police. There were, I later discovered, seven hundred chaps listening intently as the station commander began. This was, he said, our last briefing before we would all disperse to smaller, less vulnerable bases, in preparation for an attack on the enemy. A political solution was, according to the British government, now highly unlikely. The Soviets and the Chinese had determined that they would attack the West and, if their manoeuvres were anything to go by,

India and most of the far eastern countries as well. The NATO response to any massed ground invasion would involve tactical nuclear weapons which would, in turn lead to a strategic nuclear deployment by the enemy. He reiterated that at the point the first Soviet soldier or tank entered West Germany, the war would have begun, and there could only be one outcome. Global nuclear war seemed inevitable and he cursed the politicians of all countries for letting it happen. He made it quite clear what we all already knew. There would almost certainly be no home to return to after a nuclear exchange, but that if we were still alive when all the bombs had been dropped, we should decide amongst ourselves what we wanted to do. So that was it. We were going to war and we were going to die. Quite a lot of the younger men looked quite keen to get going. Most of us older types just looked sick.

On the 3rd July, groups of pilots were called into the Intelligence Office and briefed on our attack profile. We were told that we were only permitted to inform our crews once we were airborne, outside UK airspace and had received the launch codes. Further, once we had all left for our dispersal airfields, Marham would be emptied of all aircraft and personnel and would be closed down. Hopefully, the Soviets would waste a bomb on it and avoid all the smaller bases where we were launching our attacks from.

We were then told to let our crews know that they had 24 hours off. The catch was none of us could leave the base. That evening, my crew and I took to the mess and we got plastered. I told them to regroup for tea the next day when I would reveal the location of our dispersal airfield and my plan for returning home, if we survived the war.

On the evening of US Independence Day 1983 we taxied out at Marham for a take-off to the west. I knew she would be heavy with her ten White Shadows on board but at least we only had the tanks a quarter full for our trip to the dispersal field. It was a full power departure and I was rather impressed how quickly we got airborne. As soon as the undercarriage was up I told the boys that we had been ordered to wait for war at our new home, RAF Wroughton in Wiltshire. It was only a short hop really, but the airfield looked rather nice from the approach.

As soon as I had shut down the engines, they took our White Shadows off and stored them.

By the end of that week there were eight VC10s, sixteen TSR2s and a host of Hunters and Lightnings with us at Wroughton. It was cramped and it was extremely busy.

In the weeks leading up to the war, we were airborne, on average, for five hours a day. I know that doesn't sound a great deal, but I was 63 and quite a lot of me ached quite a lot of the time. It wasn't only the crew that complained either. On more than one occasion, the aircraft refused to start on all four engines and on one particularly foul morning, the undercarriage wouldn't retract and we had to fly around for two hours burning off fuel until we could safely land.

I spoke to dad one evening just before it all started, and told him to get into the cellar and take as much and food and water down with him as he could manage. He laughed and said that he would just sit out on the terrace with a scotch and wait and see what happened. I wasn't in the least surprised at this either.

By the end of July it was apparent that war was inevitable. Western leaders were now using sabre-rattling rhetoric ahead of diplomacy. The US President was live on national television when he famously said 'Let the Russians and their puppet China take one step into the boundaries of the free world and they will reap a nuclear whirlwind that they cannot ever have imagined.' It isn't certain that this statement was the final straw for the Soviet-Chinese alliance, but it didn't flaming help.

On the evening of August 1, we were all ushered into one of the larger hangars at the airfield, and instead of the expected briefing, we were treated to a showing of Monty Python Live at the Hollywood Bowl, followed by a free bar and jacket potatoes with beans and corned beef. A very nice touch, and our last taste of normality before the whole world went mad.

On August 2, Chinese warships sailed towards the west coast of Japan and the north-western edges of Formosa while Soviet troops were poised on the borders of West Germany, India and Finland. At 11.30

pm on August 3 1983, the UK government gave the order for the mobilisation of all military assets to their designated launch areas. The army was stationed primary at the eastern extremity of West Germany, the ballistic submarine fleet was already on station and the RAF now followed suit.

By midnight, the Royal Air Force had 51 Vulcans, 47 Victors, 548 TSR2, 432 VC10, 194 Lightnings, 66 Buccaneers, 43 Canberras and 263 Hunters ready to take off.

CHAPTER FIVE

It was quite a hushed atmosphere as the pilots collected their respective launch code authentication packs. Once they were safely stowed, we all walked out to the fleet of Land Rovers and 4 ton trucks that would take us to join the rest of our crews at the aircraft. Once there, I told my boys that if they had any particular desire to piddle on any exterior part of the VC10 or stick a piece of gum on the fuselage, they were more than welcome.

We had ten minutes before we were due to take off so we all went and had a final wee on the grass at the edge of the taxiway and then we lit our last cigarettes. I looked at mine as it neared its end and I wondered if this truly was my last one. If not, I would definitely give up when I got back. Then I remembered that not only was I the captain of my aeroplane, I was leading the squadron. I would smoke whilst airborne. The take off rota was pretty simple and was determined by rank. Air Vice Marshall 'Dickie' Byrd was first to go with me second. By 0325, we were all strapped in and with checks complete, I started her up. Thankfully, all the lights were green and we taxied out behind the AVM to await our turn. We passed a fair few aircraft that were obviously near the back of the queue, because their crews were still having fags. One lot were playing French cricket under the wing. As my copilot pushed the throttles forward to the stops, I thought of dad and Anna. I closed my eyes briefly and hoped that were safely in their cellars and that whatever was about to happen either wouldn't affect them or that, if it did, the end would be quick and painless.

We took off for war at 0337 hours on the 3rd August and she felt tremendously heavy but not overly sluggish. We stayed on full power right through to flaps up.

I had experience of flying into war already, but the difference this time was that it was almost certain that I would be dead by the end of the day and that if I managed to survive, my homeland would be an irradiated smoking pile by the time I got back. As we climbed out over

Wiltshire, I wondered if anyone on the beautiful land below would ever see another dawn. None of us on board expected to be so lucky.

We flew north at 26,000 feet until we had passed overhead Aberdeen. I then dropped down to fifteen hundred feet and we set course for Norway. It was bloody bumpy down that close to the sea and it wasn't a particularly nice day anyway. We had our sandwiches about then but I don't think any of us were that keen on grub. I felt sick and I reckon the others did too. We then flew south of Kristiansand and then slightly north of Stockholm where we orbited for three dreary hours awaiting instructions to proceed. During that time I gave half the crew a chance to have a kip if they wanted. None did, so they went and played cards at the navigation station instead. They also smoked an awful lot of fags.

At the appointed time, it was onward towards Turku in southern Finland. Our flight plan then took us north east along the Finnish/Russian border. It was at Savollina, about fifty miles from the border, that the launch code device tripped into life. It was 0845.

The code display sat amongst the Weapon Systems Operator's instruments and was replicated on a box just below eye level on the captain's side of the flight deck. There were simply a series of numbers and letters. I snapped open the code authentication slip and checked it was the right prefix, suffix, day and time frame. Unfortunately, I was able to confirm with my copilot and then the WSO that we all agreed the sequence was correct. So that was it. The war was on and the bloody politicians had failed us; failed the world in fact, and now my crew and I were going to kill millions of people, and then die.

I made the announcement to the crew. 'Pilot to crew. Launch codes received and verified. We're going to war.'

My Weapon Systems Operator, or Bombardier as he preferred to be known, was called Steven Thorpe and he was a good bloke. He had hurried up from his position and was standing between me and my copilot, Nick Clarke. 'This is it then skip. I'll go ahead shall I?'

'Fraid so, old man,' I replied.

'Right ho,' said Steven and went rearwards to operate the rotary launcher. 'We're nearly on station, skipper. On your word, I'll be letting them go.' I had now turned us onto our launch course and we crossed the Russian border within three minutes. Shortly after, we passed over the northern shores of Lake Ladoga and I brought us down to one hundred and fifty feet and accelerated to full power. The waters were calm and we were flying in ground effect, but it was still hairy.

We had been promised a lot of fighter cover. But since almost every fighter the Americans had could also carry a nuclear bomb, it was likely that we were just being fed a lot of old bollocks. We had seen six Hunters and a couple of Buccaneers up until Ladoga, but they had now disappeared. Some of us were pretty sure that our Hunters had been adapted to carry nukes as well, and the Buccs already could, so I reckoned they were off on their bombing runs.

If you take into account all the allied nations, it would be reasonable to estimate that upwards of four thousand aircraft were in a position to launch on the eastern bloc and China that day. If you also take into consideration our Hunters, Buccaneers, and the American F4 Phantoms, Skyhawks and others, that figure could possibly have been doubled. There is little doubt that the enemy numbers combined would easily equal ours and were very likely much higher, especially considering that the Soviets could apparently even stick a nuclear bomb on a MiG17 and 19. However, with all that metal screeching around the skies, it felt, at that moment at least, as if we were entirely on our own.

So here I was, on the last day of my life, deliberately flying towards certain death. There was nothing that could be said. We just had our job to do and in a few minutes, the world and all its people would be changed forever. With 420 knots indicated, and the precise launch point confirmed by both Nick and the Nav, I hauled back on the column and climbed to five thousand. Even before I got to the apex I pressed the intercom button.

'Launch!' I shouted. I wanted it to sound as if I was in complete control. As if I wanted it to happen. I had to. I was the skipper.

'Up there, eleven o'clock!' shouted one of the crew. Quite distinct and flying very fast north westwards were six MIG 21s. They quite obviously hadn't seen us but I reckon they'd locked on to someone.

Unlike the airliner version of the VC10, the bomber variant didn't have a cockpit door and even though it was pretty noisy, I could hear the rotary launcher as it began to feed the first missile over the launching hatch. Then there was the clunk as it slipped inside and the door snapped shut. Next was the sound of the decompression and then a slight whistle as it slipped away. I didn't hear it ignite, but it soon flashed past in front and seemed to be settling nicely into its attack course. I had always thought Leningrad looked rather beautiful. I was about to turn it into a hole in the ground.

Straight ahead, and in the very far distance, I could see the smoke trails from dozens of Soviet SAMs as they hurtled skywards to intercept their targets. At that point, mercifully, it didn't seem to be us. Yet.

Just then, when our third missile was dropping away, we were completely blinded by a bloody terrible light. At first, I thought that was it, that we'd been hit, and that this is what your last moment looked like. But the light faded and it was pretty obvious that somewhere, probably behind us, had already copped a bomb. The Russians had always hated the Finns. I suddenly felt that we'd already been lucky to get this far, and made a decision to extend that luck a bit longer. 'Bombardier. Let the external weapons go now!' I screamed.

'Okay, skipper. Here we go!'

Oh my God! What followed in the next twenty to thirty seconds was a cacophony of noise, shuddering, and thick black smoke. I hadn't really believed that you could launch two at a time, but Steven had. Numbers one and four, then two and three. They all shot off and all headed obediently; most towards Leningrad, the last two as a present to Moscow. The smell of cordite and burning entered the aircraft and it was almost impossible to breathe without gagging.

'Bombardier, I'm turning away now, setting course westwards. As soon as I've completed the turn, get those last three away!'

'Wilco skipper.' Nick had just lowered the protective screens when there was another almighty flash. This time quite distinctly off to our left.

'Contact from the rear eight miles, closing,' exclaimed the excited voice of the radar operator.

'Okay, give it a mo and I'll dive away,' I responded.

'Number four and five gone!' shouted the bombardier.

'Two contacts now. Both closing. Roughly five hundred knots!' He sounded rightly agitated. We had no defensive capability. Sitting ducks! I tensed up. I suppose we all did, expecting a missile to tear us apart at any second.

'Christ. Look at that' shouted someone. Nick had raised his screen and we saw an aircraft flash by on our right side, going like the clappers and chucking our plumes of dirty exhaust smoke. A US Navy F4 Phantom.

'He's shot the fucking Ruskie down!' screamed Nick.

'Number six gone. All internal weapons gone. We're done skipper!. Dive!' shouted the bombardier.

I slammed the yoke forward and gated the thrust levers so we shot down. However, I barely had time to level out before I had to climb again as we passed over the northwestern shoreline of the lake and higher ground started appearing.

'Keep your flash screens down!' I yelled.

With mine down, I had about a two-foot square of darkened perspex protecting my eyes from the detonation flashes. It was difficult to see well, but it just about allowed me to do the job.

Then, another very bright flash. This time it seemed that maybe there were two. Then there were more. Many more. As if all the bombs and missiles were now finding and hitting their targets. I wondered if ours had impacted yet; the Leningrad ones certainly, the Moscow ones probably still on their way. I counted maybe twenty explosions. Some were very far away, others seemed to be very close indeed. There was buffeting too. It could have been weather, it could just as easily been shock waves. The world was going up in smoke.

I was trying to picture my mum and dad and Anna. I tried to imagine all of us sitting on the patio in Kelston, laughing and drinking a nice cold gin and catching the last glow of the summer sun.

'More contacts skipper. There's fucking millions of them....!'

So I began weaving and climbing then diving. I was tensing up, expecting in any fraction of any second a crashing sound, and probably a crushing feeling and then, merciful, final death.

'Where are they?' I yelled. 'Gone over skipper,' was the reply.

'What?' I exclaimed

'Passed overhead. Didn't see us.' Thank Christ again.

Before long we were out over the Baltic and I needed to get down again fast. This time I levelled out at two hundred feet and it was bumpy as buggery. I could see our aircraft's shadow on the surface below.

More flashes. More millions dying.

Up ahead was another aircraft, and as we drew closer I could see straight away that it was another VC10. Just in front of it, and partially obscured by the former's tail, was a B52. Our bomber was at about five thousand and the Yank at maybe seven or eight. The VC10 didn't look well, chucking out a lot of black smoke from her engines, but fairly soon we were closing right up on her.

I was thinking of climbing up to join them when it occurred to me that whilst one aircraft is a pretty enough target, three together could actually all be taken out with one well placed missile, or at the very least by a skilled pilot in a single fighter. As I pondered this, the B52 exploded and seemed to collapse in on itself. Whilst I was still taking that in, the other VC10 was hit and its left wing folded up over the top and it just rolled on its back and started diving towards the sea.

I dived down, right to the wave tops, and at one point there was a bit of a bump because I think I actually skimmed the surface with the flap sponsons. Then I climbed up to five hundred and thought that this aeroplane was never going to get over this mission. How it stayed together is beyond me.

'Contact skipper!' was the shout.

'Where?' I yelled back

'Everywhere. I've got ten from the east and six or more from the west.'

So this was it. I decided to cause as much mayhem as possible. Even though I was jigging the kite around like mad, eventually I could make out aircraft coming from straight ahead. They were relatively bunched up, so I decided to fly right into the middle of them. It would be quick; the boys wouldn't know what was happening and I could probably take out two or more.

Nick obviously knew exactly what I was planning. I had looked across at him and gave him a weak smile. He just raised his eyes heavenwards. I began a slight turn to the right so that I could slice through as many of them as possible when Nick yelled.

'They're ours!'

And in a split second, I could see he was right. They were Lightnings and they were leading a couple of Buccaneers. I levelled out and dived down towards the sea at exactly the moment the Lightnings let off their Firestreaks and the Buccaneers let loose with Sidewinders and cannon. It was all streaming towards us too, but mercifully above us.

I stayed down low. Very low. And waited for either our boys to come alongside, wave jauntily and guide us home or for the Soviets to take us out. But nothing happened and we simply flew along happily, now actually believing that we might make it out. Then, in front of us was an island and quite a big one. I later discovered it was part of Estonia and is called Hiiumaa. It looked as if it could provide some much needed cover so I headed towards it and kept very, very low and followed the coast, jinking up to avoid obstacles before shooting down again to sea level. After about thirty minutes, it became obvious that we were passing places we had already overflown once and, as I decided to finally set course for home, there was another shout over the intercom.

'Aircraft on our port side skipper. Not locked on!' he exclaimed.

I was trying very hard to work out what this meant, when there was the rather beautiful sight of a Blackburn Buccaneer sliding past my window. It was keeping station with us but there was something very wrong. The rear seater's canopy wasn't so much gone, as destroyed; I guessed by shrapnel or cannon fire. The pilot waved to me and pointed in the general direction of home. He had just begun accelerating ahead of us when the whole rear of the aircraft disappeared in a huge fireball and the Buccaneer fell away to the sea. There was no ejection by the pilot. It just plopped into the water without much drama or pyrotechnics. A second later, a MiG 23 pulled alongside precisely where the Buccaneer had been only moments before. It had the red stars of the USSR on the fuselage and fin and the nose number 4 in blue. He was chucking out a lot of sparks from his jet pipe and I reckoned he was in big trouble too. As I watched, the pilot wiggled his fingers in a wave and then slipped behind.

I hoped he was about to eject or crash. But I was wrong. 'Missile skipper....!' But the radar operator didn't finish because a split second later we were hit. To start with, the yoke was torn from my hands. Then we began a dramatic roll to the left which I countered with right rudder and aileron. She levelled out a bit but was still lurching alarmingly to the left. I could tell that we had lost power and it is certain that if we had been in this condition with the weapons still aboard, we would have gone down.

It simply felt as if the aircraft's control cables and rods had been disconnected. There were popping sounds coming from the left engines and a bloody terrible tearing sound from somewhere down below the cockpit. My copilot was staring straight ahead and there was blood trickling from his mouth. 'Bombardier, are you there!' I shouted through the mic.

'Right here, skip' said Steven as he appeared from the rear.

'Can you check everyone for me. I think we're in big trouble'

'Wilco' he said and shot off.

I admit to thinking that worrying about what damage we had or who was and wasn't dead was all rather academic because I was sure that the bastard Russian jet would be along to finish us off any minute.

However, after ten or so minutes, no follow on attack happened. Maybe he did us in just as he was about to blow up or eject or perhaps he was clobbered by another friendly fighter or maybe he saw something better to attack or thought we were goners anyway. In the end, as I was battling to keep the aeroplane level and out of the water, Steven came back. He had a look at Nick and listened at his mouth then squatted down next to me. He was shouting over the noise. 'It must have been a missile skip, cos' there's a hole in the bottom left of the fuselage and the top right, just ahead of the wing. Comms is dead and I think Flight might have fallen out.' The Flight Engineer was a very nice Scottish chap called Robin, and at about thirty five, he the youngest on board. His station was half way between the cockpit and the wing root and had been right in the line of the Soviet missile. The Comms officer was called Robert and he was from Sussex, roughly late thirties and a Regular. He was very good too.

'Steve, get me a map and let's plot a course out to Ireland, I want to go somewhere where there won't be many bombs going off or Soviet fighters'

'Right ho,' he said and shot off towards the back. When he returned I told him to raise the flash blinds because I couldn't trust what the instruments were saying any more. As Steven was raising them, two massive flashes appeared right in front.

'Fuck that skipper, let's head home.' So we turned and headed out to the north of Poland. The VC10 felt as though she would happily rollover and die if I let go of the controls, and I had to grip the yoke with all my might.

Suddenly, Steve was there next to me. 'I don't think the copilot looks too great, skipper?' he said.

'No, not great,' I replied.

'There are still some sandwiches and coffee left if you'd like some?' he then bizarrely suggested.

I have never met a cooler man under fire than him. So, I thought, 'why not.'

'Couple of fags?' I asked.

'Right ho,' he responded, cheerily.

I couldn't believe what was happening. Now, we were over northern Germany, and I knew that Hamburg and Bremen would have caught a bomb each from the reds as well as all the East German cities that we would have pummelled. There was something really wrong with the port engines and I was now having to push the left rudder pedal almost to the floor. I stayed as far north as I could without getting too far off my course for home. Denmark would have been safer bet, but it would have used up fuel that I could no longer afford to waste, especially if it was leaking. I had no way of knowing though; all the gauges were now jammed hard over to the right, telling me I had full tanks. We crossed the North Sea at Husum, about 40 miles south of the Danish border and I turned slightly west, south west to keep us over the sea, but close to land. I began a slow climb without using any extra thrust. I couldn't afford to overtax whichever engines I still had left. As we skirted to the right of Den Helder, on the north western tip of Holland, and despite it being almost fifty miles away, I could see that Amsterdam was completely ablaze. I imagined that Britain was going to look much the same. The next decision to make was whether to now fly directly into UK airspace, across the Midlands and look for somewhere to put down, heading for Ireland, where we'd probably be locked up, or should I try flying along the Channel. Although there was a very real likelihood of Soviet surface ships in the English Channel, it just felt right to go that way. We skirted northern France at Calais, which was just a pall of smoke, and then turned so that we passed a couple of miles to the south of Eastbourne. Once almost overhead, at five thousand feet, It looked to be intact, but it was impossible to tell because the entire sky, in every direction was now filled with dense, dark grey smoke. It was all over. The world was on fire, nearly everyone was dead or dying and the politicians had got their wish. They'd done for us. I was buggered if my aeroplane and my crew, alive or dead, were going to add to the roll call.

I also imagined that the Soviets and the Chinese had already decided which, if any, countries they were going to invade, so I kept an eye out for flotillas of Ruskie landing craft heading for the south coast. I soon put that thought out of mind; it was a daft notion. Why would you bomb somewhere out of existence and then invade it. If they'd won, they would just bide their time and come when we were all rotting in the gutters.

Now, we were about ten miles offshore and just south of the Isle of Wight. Where Portsmouth had been was now a grey misty cauldron. I could see some fires, but it was mostly just dense, grey smoke. I suppose that seeing somewhere I knew destroyed and burning brought home the fact that we were still almost certainly going to die. Bristol would be gone, definitely Plymouth, possibly Taunton and even maybe Weston because of the RAF station. Perhaps I should try for the Scottish highlands, or maybe Madeira. Or just stick with Ireland. Then we lurched, there was bang and popping sounds from the left engines. I thought I could hear one of them running down. The controls didn't feel like that though, but something bloody awful had happened. Then Steve was beside me again, fag in mouth and map in hand. I'm pretty sure he also had a sandwich in his breast pocket.

'There's stuff on the shortwave Ollie; a morse message coming through that claims to be Exeter Airport and they say all aircraft should land there' said Steve as he battled to fold the map in line with our current position.

I didn't hold out much hope. It couldn't be that there actually were people alive down at Exeter, but it was the first radio traffic we had heard, and it was good enough to give it a try. I turned the aircraft roughly back in the direction of Devon and she creaked and groaned her way around.

'Get me there, Steve,' I said.

There was another bang from behind and the aircraft began yawing alarmingly to the left. This time it meant one or more of the port side engines had failed for certain, so I began kicking in rudder, but I could barely move my leg. I hadn't properly noticed it before but now the pain was so bloody intense. I reduced thrust on the two right engines very slightly to counter the yaw and also to give my sodding leg a chance.

'Is that you, Ollie?' Steve was looking down at the footwell by my feet and pointing at my leg. I leant forward a bit and saw what looked like hydraulic fluid all over the floor. It knew it was blood of course. My blood. That would explain it then.

Like all good military transport equipment, whether it's a Land Rover or a bomber, everything comes with a broom as standard. Steve got ours, snapped it in half and began jabbing at my rudder pedal until he was able to take the pressure off my bastard leg. 'That'll do it. Shout when you want it moved.' he said.

'Can you shift Nick and take his seat please.' Unbuckling the copilot took him an inordinately long time, and with his back to me I could see that Steve had a nasty ragged hole in his flight suit by his right shoulder. He looked at me and raised his eyes.

'At least we're both bleeding to death eh?' he said and laughed. Nick now lay on the cockpit floor and by craning my head back I could see that he appeared to be trying to move. Three of us were still alive.

'Can you put all your weight on your right rudder pedal for me Steve please?' I asked. Expecting immediate relief, I was surprised when absolutely nothing seemed to be happening.

'It's flat to the floor, Ollie. I think it's buggered,' he replied. I had a quick look and it was obvious that the copilot's rudder linkage had been severed by the missile blast. So I was stuck with having to fly an aircraft with a totally redundant copilot station.

'The brush is helping though, yeah?' said Steve.

'Yeah, I suppose it'll do,' I replied.

Steve was listening on the shortwave and reported that Exeter said they had two aircraft on radar and were sending course changes. Well, I assumed it was us they were talking to. I also imagine how very amusing it would be if the 'other' aircraft was a MiG or a Sukhoi and it was just waiting to pounce.

'There!' exclaimed Steve, pointing down.

'I can't bloody see that. You'll have to tell me what to do. What is it?' There was a high intensity beacon I guessed on top of the control tower and it was dead ahead. I was letting her down slowly and we were now through three thousand. At the mouth of the River Exe, I turned and we flew up the estuary until the point where it narrows. I then turned almost due north ready for finals into Exeter and as I did, I could hear that the engines on the starboard side were making a terrible noise. It was a sort of grating sound. Like a moped and electric saw all rolled into one. I had never heard it before, so I knew it was bad. When we were on the eastern fringes of the city, and at the point where the railway passes under the A30, I turned finals, lined her up, and pulled the flap lever back to thirty degrees. I could now finally see the beacon that Steve had described, and it was a beautiful sight. There was much less smoke around now and I could clearly see where I was going. I could also make out some other aircraft parked or taxying on the apron. There were also a couple of Bloodhound batteries, just off the centreline, at either end of the runway. It was now that I realised that the pain in leg appeared to have subsided. I pushed down on the rudder, but my leg just crumpled and gave way. My vision was beginning to blur and I was blinking frantically to clear it. As I pulled the undercarriage lever, the wheels sounded as it they were coming down, but the indicator lights weren't working, so I couldn't really tell. As for the flaps, I just had to pray they'd extended at least part of the way and in equal measure. As we passed through a thousand feet, control was getting very difficult and I was having to make incredibly exaggerated control inputs. Just to get the slightest response laterally meant turning the yoke fully in each direction. I put the right engines on full power throughout the whole descent but I knew she now wanted to stall.

'Kick away the stick as soon as we touch down!' I shouted.

'Righty ho, skip' replied Steve. I looked across at him to give him an encouraging smile, but he was preoccupied with the map in one hand and a jam sandwich in the other.

At around forty feet, as we passed over the runway, I pulled back the power levers and instantly knew I'd done it too soon, because we started dropping quite quickly and we touched down on the grassy gravel to the side of the tarmac. Steven hauled away the broom and I put in reverse thrust and stood on the brakes. We were now on the runway at least. My leg was quivering ridiculously as I strained to put weight on the right brake.

'Push the pedal right down!'

And he did, with the brush handle, and I could feel we were slowing. Then we were off the bloody runway and bouncing along the grass. We crossed a taxiway and then rolled to a stop.

'Flick those upwards will you?' and I pointed to the engine start switches.

'What about those?' Steven enquired and I looked to where he was pointing. The fire lights for engines one, two and three were illuminated. It hurt so bloody much to look up, my neck was agony.

'Pull them!' Three engines were damaged or on fire. That would certainly explain the yawing. I shut everything down and then thought I heard Steven say, 'Shall we go?'

I looked out the front and I was sure there was a big rain squall coming because it was very grey. I felt fuzzy and incredibly tired. I could see some vehicles heading towards us and I could now make out a Victor parked on the apron. It looked terrible. It didn't look like it had a vertical stabiliser anymore. I thought Steve was punching me at first, but then realised he was trying to release my harness. Then he was trying to drag me out of the chair and I thought I was helping. Obviously, from his cursing, I wasn't being much use at all. The next thing I remember is sitting in the jump seat at the rear of the cockpit and hearing lots of bells and there were blue lights swirling around the ceiling. There was a terrible smell of burning as well. Steve was yelling out of the window on the copilot's side. Something about 'Well bloody break it down then.' There was tremendous banging on the port side door and then light as they obviously managed to get in. There were a number of men in the cockpit now and they were talking to me. I have no idea what they were saying. The last thing I really remember was a fire engine whizzing by.

CHAPTER SIX

Apparently, as the ambulance crew were dragging me from the jump seat, I fell into unconsciousness.

Nicholas Clarke, Steven Thorpe and I were taken to a hangar at Exeter Airport which had already been prepared to accept returning aircrew. Clarke had suffered a collapsed lung from shrapnel penetration, lost the thumb of his right hand and suffered severe internal trauma from the blast concussion. Thorpe had sustained various cuts and lacerations from the missile's shrapnel, the most serious being to his right shoulder.

I remained unconscious for four hours. Shrapnel was removed from behind my right knee, which ultimately needed a replacement. They also picked ragged metal from my left thigh and buttock. I also lost most of the hearing in my right ear.

All of us, and a heck of lot of other chaps, were transferred to Exeter General Hospital after a few days at the airfield. That ambulance journey was a bloody nightmare. We bounced along until I thought my leg would explode. Quite how Nick and Steve didn't die of shock, I'll never know.

The morse message that had been relayed to returning allied aircrews resulted in the successful recovery to Exeter Airport of a Victor, my VC10, two Hunters and a French Mirage IV. The message had also been picked up by Soviet aircraft, and three of the buggers - two bombers and a fighter - were intercepted and shot down by RAF Hunters and Lightnings in UK airspace. Three further aircraft, two MiG 21s and a MiG 23 were destroyed by Bloodhound missiles located at Bournemouth and Exeter.

The RAF's damage report for my aircraft described it thus: *The underside of the front fuselage had fallen away. There is a six foot wide hole through the port wing. The No 1 engine was blown away. The No 2 engine was severely damaged, and producing less than 20% thrust at the point of landing. The No 3 engine was surging and producing less than 30% thrust at the point of landing. The tail cone was destroyed. The rear of the vertical stabiliser was blown away. Yaw was principally only viable through engine thrust, but there was limited authority through the yoke. The Flight Engineer and Comms officer were killed, the former's body was not recovered from the aircraft. This airframe holds the record for the longest airborne period of any RAF aircraft on that day and the most damage sustained whilst remaining airborne.*

On August 6 1983, at the point where Soviet forces were deemed to have been rendered as destroyed, and the cessation of hostilities by the cowardly, shitty Chinese hordes, an inventory of RAF assets was conducted. The number and type of surviving aircraft was shown, followed by the percentage that recovered to UK or allied airfields:

06/08/83 @ 0700hrs:A/C recovered to UK/Friendly airfields as follows...11xVulcan (21%) 7xVictor (15%) 106xTSR2 (19%) 31xVC10 (7%) 24xLightning (12%) 49xHunter (18%) 0x Buccaneers (0%) 0x Canberras (0%)'

The war had lasted a little over six hours. Soviet forces had entered West Germany, West Berlin and Finland. At the same time, Chinese ships had begun launching against Formosa, South Korea, Japan, Singapore, and their ground troops had entered India. Allied forces had responded with battlefield tactical nuclear shells and missiles. The Eastern Bloc and Chinese forces deployed their long-range ballistic weapons shortly thereafter. NATO and the allies then launched theirs. When we launched our White Shadows, the war had already been raging for two hours.

On September 6 1983 the US Secretary of State as acting President confirmed that the US Air Force, which had a prewar inventory including 667 F111, 58 TSR2 and 602 B52 now had an offensive capability located only at Barksdale AFB, Louisiana, where the combined SAC bomb wings have their remaining aircraft. 94 F111, 16 TSR2 and 71 B52 survived the war.

By the 8th September, a full inspection and assessment of surviving Royal Air Force combat aircraft had been undertaken, and allowing for cannibalisation of damaged or unserviceable aircraft, the RAF's new strength was 6 Vulcans, 4 Victors, 73 TSR2s, 18 VC10s, 24 Lightning and 41 Hunters.

I don't recall anything about being recovered from the aircraft, or of going to the hospital. I vaguely remember people saying nice things and I had a lot of very strange dreams. The only thing I can say anything about for certain is that I was in a very big, very dark house and I could hear my mother calling for me. Every time I went into the room where I thought she was, I would hear her voice again, but from far away. The other one was Norman Wisdom lying on top of an ambulance, his body revolving in time with the blue light. Don't ask me why.

I stayed in hospital for ten days. My leg was obviously bandaged and the swelling was ridiculous. It hurt like hell and being deaf in one ear was horrible and confusing and incredibly irritating because I had to consciously sit so that people who were talking to me were always on my left side, otherwise I didn't hear a thing. The physiotherapist started on me after only four days and had me desperately trying to move my stupid leg. It wouldn't budge at first, but with each day, I would be able to swing it a little bit more. They made me promise not to climb any stairs for at least a week and thereafter to only try ascending if I assured them that I would use my crutches. I became very good on them though and could quite easily bomb up and down the corridors to get tea and toast from the little kitchen. They had showed me the X rays of my leg and the repair was incredibly complex. I now had bits of metal and plastic where before there had been cartilage and muscle. It looked utterly revolting. And my leg, or at least the knee, hurt like hell.

It was on day six, as I was idly flicking through a copy of The Lady magazine, that I heard footsteps in the corridor. Anna popped her head round the door and cried out when she saw me. Now, I don't know if it was a yell of joy, or a yell of, 'oh my God, you look terrible.' She hugged me and bashed my rotten ear, for which she apologised. She then sat on the edge of the bed and managed to half crush my stupid, useless leg, for which she apologised even more profusely. God, it was good to see her. My first question was how had she survived. It seemed that there were no bombs on Bristol or the immediate surrounding area. She had stayed in our cellar for two nights and then emerged to find that quite a lot of people were going about their daily lives in a fairly normal way. There were reports that every corner of the world had received a dose of radiation, but that the contamination in the west of England and some of Wales was relatively low.

Anna looked fantastic and apparently caused quite a stir amongst the other male patients. I was so proud of her, not only for surviving so prettily, but also for having the gumption to call every airfield she could think of to see if I had made it back. She said that after I left the house for the last time, she hadn't ever expected to see me again. She took a room in an hotel near the hospital and visited every day.

On day seven, I had gone walkabout. Or more correctly, hobble about. I found Steve, my Bombardier, on a small ward with three other flyers who I didn't recognise. He was, as always, rather upbeat and thanked me for saving his life. I told him that if he hadn't been there, if he hadn't used his head and got the broom handle, we would now both be corpses in the sea somewhere. It occurred to me that I should put both him and Nick up for medals and a promotion at the earliest opportunity.

I then went and found Nick. He was in a single room and was wired up to a variety of terrifying looking devices. He was pale as hell, which isn't surprising considering his injuries. Yet, despite having lost pints of blood, suffered a collapsed lung and had most of his organs scrambled up, he was most concerned about his thumb. He said it had been his favourite digit. That same day, the station chaplain from St. Mawgan had come to see me and asked if I would be prepared to take part in the funeral and remembrance service for our lost colleagues. Rather like my dad, I had lapsed in my church attendances from quite an early age and had been having difficulty with any belief at all for many years. With the war, I rather felt my uncertainty had been vindicated, and I didn't feel particularly kindly towards the clergy. However, this was for the boys, and I couldn't let them down. After I had agreed, he told me that the Bishop of Exeter would take the service, if I would be kind enough to read the names of those who didn't return. A suitable plot for a cemetery was identified in the far western corner of the airfield that would be consecrated by the Bishop immediately after the service and before interment. There were obviously very few bodies to bury; this was mostly going to be a memorial ground.

On the appointed day, and with everyone from the airfield except the RAF Provost in attendance, we laid the eighteen boys to rest who had either died in flight or later in hospital. It was all very moving. It was hard reading out the names of those that I had known personally, and it was particularly difficult when I got to my Flight Engineer Robin Kirby and Comms officer Bob Hegarty.

About three weeks after the war, by which time I had been given a room in the hastily created Officers' mess at the airfield, the RAF doctor came to see me and informed me that having taken everything into account, he was going to have to consider grounding me for good. I was quite surprised he'd bothered; it was obvious to me. I was sixty three years old, half deaf and had a tremendous, painful limp. He added that he would monitor my recovery and let me know, one way or the other, as soon as he had made his decision.

Anna, who had been to see me every day in hospital and had been spending long periods with me in the mess, thought she ought to go back home, not least to make sure it was still in one piece. I promised that I would be there as soon as I could and, for once, saying goodbye didn't feel like the end of something.

The day after Anna left, I got a call from Air Vice Marshall Kenneth Farnsworth. He sounded a bit fraught. He told me that irrespective of what I said, believed or thought, I was now the highest ranking surviving RAF officer in the country. I told him that this was patently bollocks, because I was talking to him and he was an AVM and I was a Group Captain.

'But you see, I'm dying, Ollie, along with all the other people up here.'

And of course he was right. I hadn't really asked about what had happened in the war but I already knew that the south west was relatively okay but that the rest of Britain was ruined. Kenny Farnsworth had been up at Lossiemouth, and even though he'd survived the bomb, he hadn't avoided the radiation. Everyone above him, including the Marshall of the Royal Air Force were already gone.

'They're giving us about two weeks. You'll accept my apologies for not coming down to say goodbye' He had sent a telex to authorise my promotion and it was effective immediately. I was Marshall of the Royal Air Force.

I bothered a lot of people on the airfield during the next few days, trying to discover if it could possibly be true that I was the senior man alive. The Air Traffic Controller told me that they had been talking to AVM Byrd's TSR2 as he returned to the UK, but they had lost contact when he was still over the Channel.

AVM Farnsworth and everyone else on his base died within a week.

After a couple of days more mooching about feeling lonely and sorry for myself, I got the Intelligence people to come and see me at the mess and they gave me a very good briefing on the state of the world. Short of total annihilation, it couldn't have been any worse. They had a world map and it showed that south west England and north west France were relatively okay. We hadn't escaped radiation, but because of the prevailing wind, the worst had been swept away eastwards. They had a big map of Britain as well. There were big black circles pasted on the places where there was complete destruction and red ones where the radiation was merely fatal. London, Birmingham, Manchester, Liverpool, Belfast, Glasgow and Edinburgh and Faslane were black. London had copped two ten megaton weapons. The rest had got five megatons each. Coleraine, Norwich and Inverness were amongst those that got between 750 kilotons and 1 megaton. There were much smaller black patches on a variety of airbases; maybe 250KT. Portsmouth and Plymouth had not been clobbered but not because the Soviets hadn't wanted to; in fact the RAF had tracked inbound missiles for Bristol, Cardiff, Plymouth and Portsmouth, but they hadn't hit, or maybe our Bloodhounds had knocked them out or they just didn't make it. Pretty much everything north and east of Bristol was covered in red.

The rest of the world was decimated, but at least the Eastern Bloc and the Chinese got what they deserved, the bastards.

Most of the British government was dead, dying or missing. What was left was now operating out of Britannia Naval College in Dartmouth. Rumour has it that the remnants of the Royal Family were there too.

On the 12th October 1983, the day after I finally stopped using my crutch, the British Government announced that there was no longer any threat from Warsaw Pact or Chinese forces. The UN, which was regrouping its resources in Iceland, had completed its assessment of the human cost of the war and the damage inflicted. Medium to high levels of contamination persisted across the majority of the remainder of western and central Europe. Eastern Europe was largely uninhabitable. Large areas of the US were uninhabitable. Southern and western Canada were significantly contaminated.

On the enemy side, Eurasia had been rendered substantially uninhabitable. The area of highest contamination stretched at its western end from the east of Ukraine and Belarus to the southern extremities of Persia/Iran. In the south, the contamination had reached almost to the southern tip of India. In the east, all of China, the Korean peninsula and Japan were devastated. In the north, only the eastern fringes of Russia were relatively uncontaminated. These areas were now being occupied by NATO forces. The UN reported that the prewar global population was 4.9 billion. They say that based on weapon impact patterns and wind currents, they estimate that 2 billion have died in the war or as a result of immediate contamination. At least 2 billion more were refugees, stateless or homeless. Hundreds of millions more would succumb to radiation sickness and everyone left alive would have a significantly shortened lifespan. It was predicted that only 150 million people globally still lived in their pre-conflict place of domicile.

The only countries not to have received at least one ballistic nuclear missile strike were Ghana, Chile and Namibia. No country had avoided contamination. As the levels of global radiation subsided, it was anticipated that the countries offering the most likely opportunity for a survivable future were southern Chile, southern New Zealand, south western Norway, Hawaii, the South Sea islands, north western France, south western England, south western Portugal, southern Iceland and northern Morocco.

On the 15th October, I was summoned to the Naval College to meet the new Cabinet. The Prime Minister was, he told me, pleased to be alive and to have his family still with him, but was otherwise distraught and depressed. As a junior minister in the Department of Trade and Industry, he hadn't really ever expected to reach any top jobs, let alone that of PM. But here he was now asking me, a former Group Captain, how we should rebuild not only our armed forces but also the country. We had a fair few quite clever people with us who were his 'advisers' and they were banging on about consolidating manufacturing and industry as far south west as possible, and he looked to me to confirm that this was a good idea. I had just nodded. It seemed sensible enough.

He took me aside and said that he wanted me to go down and meet the captain of one of our very few surviving Polaris submarines to inform him that he was now promoted to Admiral of the Fleet, but that he would be subordinate to me due to my excessive years and greater experience. My mouth had opened but nothing had come out. I had just been made Chief of the Defence Staff. Then he announced that the King had approved a recommendation from AVM Farnsworth that I should be awarded the Victoria Cross. Amongst all the insane things that had happened in my life, this took the biscuit. My crew were much more deserving, I had said.

'That doesn't cut any ice,' he replied. I was getting it and it was jolly well deserved.

I made it quite clear that I would only accept the award if I could immediately promote both Nick and Steven and award them VCs. I then made it abundantly clear that if I was to be the senior military officer in the country, all future promotions, in all Arms of the Services, were to pass across my desk for approval. He agreed to my demands.

The very next day, which all seemed a bit hasty in my opinion, I returned to the college to receive my gong from the King. I had frantically telephoned Anna and dad and asked them if they could make it. I promised to send cars for them, if they could. Anna was game, but dad said that whilst he was immensely proud of me, he didn't feel up to making a long journey. I completely understood. Anna's car arrived less than ten minutes before the award ceremony, but I was so pleased to see her.

I must admit, I hadn't really given the Royal Family much thought during the post war period. However, now that his mother was dead, our King, the former Prince of Wales, cut a rather fine figure and spoke very kindly of my efforts and those of my fellow airmen and all the soldiers and sailors who had taken part in the war. After my whirlwind of medals and back slapping, I felt it was time to get down to the business of running the military. My first task then, was to meet the newly appointed Admiral of the Fleet.

It turned out I knew Commodore Maurice Bowen already, or at least we'd met. We had both been to a series of bloody hard exercise cum seminar briefings at the Intelligence Corps depot's Joint Service Intelligence Wing at Templar Barracks near Ashford in Kent some years earlier. He was a Captain then and he and I had stayed up quite late one night laughing at our combined ages. We should have been driving, or sailing desks even by then; now we should both be long retired from service.

It was bonfire night and he had docked the previous day. I had never seen a ballistic submarine before but it was just enormous and brutally, somehow beautifully, ugly. A launch took me out to it and I was piped and saluted aboard. All his chaps were smartly dressed up in No.1s, which seemed daft. After I had told him about his meteoric elevation to the top naval job and he had been quiet for several minutes, I told him we were going up to the college so that he could tell me about his war.

Maurice Bowen was sixty and had been appointed captain of the Polaris submarine (SSBN 03) HMS Valiant in December 1982. A career submariner, this was his fourth command, and his second of a ballistic submarine.

Valiant was the third of an eventual eighteen strong fleet of SSBNs for the Royal Navy and she had first sailed on patrol in August 1970. Bowen was to be her captain from her eleventh patrol, and because the crisis was deepening every day, when they sailed from Faslane, with him recently promoted to Commodore, they had a full complement of weapons comprising sixteen Sea Launched Ballistic Missiles (SLBM). Six of these were fitted with a single warhead device of 5 megatons each. The remaining 10 had three warhead Multiple Independently Targetable Re-entry Vehicles of 750KT each. They also carried 42 torpedoes, 12 of those housing 100 Kiloton nuclear warheads.

On the day of the Soviet/Chinese attacks, HMS Valiant was submerged in the Sea of Okhotsk off the eastern coast of Russia.

The Royal Navy also deployed 3 aircraft carriers, 2 cruisers, 31 destroyers, 44 frigates, 27 Royal Fleet Auxiliaries (RFA), 16 SSNs and 17 other SSBNs on the day of the war. Aside from torpedo boats and a few minesweepers, the entire strength of the Royal Navy was on war duty.

Over rather a lot of whisky, Bowen described receiving the launch codes, the authentication process and the launches themselves. Not hugely dissimilar to mine, but so much more destructive. He had launched all sixteen and he was able to track them all. They all hit their targets. 'You know,' he said 'there is nothing that can really prepare you for that launch. All the training, all the exercises, they come to nothing. We knew that things were grave, that the government, all governments, were racking up the rhetoric and the threats and I just had this feeling that this time, the Soviets weren't going to back down. But you've got to ask yourself, what is it that made them think they could ever win. Sure enough, they could launch everything they'd got but they knew, bloody knew for certain, that they would get wasted. We got the preliminary warning from HQ to stand by for possible launch, and I put us on the edge of a shelf about three hundred feet down. We sat there for around thirty six hours and then we got the 'Prepare' notification. Even then, when all your training tells you that it's going to happen, you still believe that at the last minute all those bastard politicians will decide to sit down and have a cup of tea and talk it over. So I took us out, and we sat at a hundred and twenty feet and waited. And then the 'Launch' codes came through. The Wizzo and I put in our keys, the hatches opened and as soon as the first tube was ready, I squeezed the trigger and off they went. '

'Is it all bangs and noises from then on?' I had asked.

'Not at all,' he replied 'The missiles leave the boat by compressed air that gets them up and out, and once they get clear of the surface, the motor engages. We could vaguely hear the ignition, but it's quite an anticlimax really. But once they'd all gone and we'd closed the hatches, emptied them and got underway, Christ the difference was amazing. It was like driving an MG. We went down hard and fast and stayed as deep as we could doing the old zigzagging. And we never saw or heard one ship or one sub. Nor did we pick up a single aircraft; ours or theirs.'

At the point of Soviet collapse and Chinese cessation of hostilities, Valiant was one of only four of the original 18 RN SSBNs remaining afloat, all the others having been lost. And she was the only boat that retained a fully functioning weapons system. After 124 days submerged, Valiant had surfaced off the west coast of Alaska for weapons and provision resupply from one of the three remaining RFAs and a US Navy support vessel. Valiant's 12 replacement SLBMs were those recovered from HMS Andromeda, which had lost its steering after an attack by Soviet fighter bombers. Andromeda had been scuttled after her crew were taken aboard the RFA. Valiant was then ordered by the remnants of the Royal Navy's Command and Control (which was based in Port Stanley) to sail towards northern Russia. US intelligence reporting had established that two Russian cruise ships, carrying between them an estimated eleven thousand troops and volunteers were about to sail from Syndassko, and were believed to be heading for an attack on Norway. Valiant launched a total of six torpedoes against the ships and both sank in 2000 metre deep waters. No attempt was made at survivor rescue. HMS Defiant one of the now three remaining SSBNs was on station throughout.

Bowen's war had been a thousand times more complex, dangerous and downright bloody awful than mine. But he had disagreed, saying that sitting snug on the bottom of the sea firing off missiles at an invisible enemy was a doddle compared to flying an old converted airliner against fighter jets and enemy SAMs.

He then showed me the inventory list of surviving RN vessels. It comprised one aircraft carrier, three destroyers, four frigates, one SSN, three SSBN and three RFAs. However, most of these would never put back to sea due to damage or chronic contamination. The aircraft carrier, one destroyer, and one of the RFAs were to be struck off charge and either scuttled or used as targets for my aeroplanes. Two surviving, but heavily damaged frigates had already been deliberately sunk way out to sea because of their high levels of contamination. Attempts had been made to make our remaining potentially serviceable SSBN, HMS Dauntless, seaworthy for the voyage home, but the decision was taken by her captain to scuttle her on the 4th November.

I was utterly astonished at how calm and relaxed Bowen seemed. In fact his crew were all in good spirits. And I had always thought submarine types were weird. Maybe they are. Maybe that's why they were cheerful when everyone else was suicidally miserable.

The United States' intelligence machine was still relatively capable, at least in certain geographical areas, and they had received reports that Russian troops and civilians had been joined by hundreds of thousands of Chinese soldiers and volunteers on the coast at Tiksi in the Lapdev Sea. Heavy armour had been photographed being loaded onto ships. The last vestiges of NATO ordered them to be stopped. The only remaining French SSBN, from a prewar fleet of sixteen, launched her missiles, and USAF B52s and F111s completed the destruction of the remaining enemy with conventional weapons.

After what was now hoped to have been the final conflict of the 'final' war, Bowen and I went to see the PM and his Cabinet members rather a lot over the coming days, and each time we went up to the college, we would receive further information from around the world. I also pestered the PM to ask the King's permission to award Bowen a VC and his boat a George Cross. He eventually agreed to both suggestions. I was able to confirm to the Cabinet that my team and I had conducted a review of our aircraft fleet and concluded that all the Victors and Lightnings would be retired. 18 Hunters were to be kept on strength for training and currency. I had 68 combat capable TSR2s and they would remain in service until a replacement was found, which meant a very long time indeed, because there was nothing on the horizon. Four of the remaining VC10s would be converted to troop carrying and cargo roles, and six British Airways L1011s that we had stolen from maintenance hangars at Cardiff airport would be turned into our new tanker fleet. The Vulcans would also remain on strength, for the time being. The Hawk jet was still an ongoing project and the manufacturer claimed they could restart production at both Newquay and Exeter and that it would be adapted as a multirole platform for both training and fighter/ground attack. I also announced that I was setting up my new Headquarters at RAF St Mawgan at Newquay. The PM said that was all well and good, but that he actually wanted me to operate on a day to day basis from Dartmouth. I had ordered that our 48 remaining White Shadows were to be kept in fully operational condition, and that to ensure maximum attack coverage, twelve aircraft were to kept ready for take off at all times. The combat ready fleet was dispersed at all three operational airfields, St. Mawgan, Chivenor and Exeter, and the available types were rotated as serviceability dictated. During my last visit to each squadron, there had been five TSR2s at St. Mawgan, three Vulcans at Chivenor and four VC10s at Exeter. There were only just sufficient fully qualified crew for each, but training was ongoing and was, by all accounts, being relentlessly pursued.

Bowen reported to me that his review of the Navy had determined that with the significant reduction in the threat from enemy forces, only two Vanguard class submarines would now be completed to patrol standard. Vanguard and Victorious would each be equipped with 16 launch tubes from the new Trident Ballistic Missile system. HMS Vigilant, which was being constructed by Harland and Wolf, required significant decontamination before she could be completed and was no longer a viable proposition. The Royal Navy, therefore, would now consist of two destroyers, two frigates, one SSN, two SSBNs, two RFAs, six minesweepers and four fast patrol/torpedo boats.

I also finally received a report on the state of the Army, and it was truly miserable reading. In the years before the war, Regular strength had been round the 130,000 mark with 180,000 Territorial types. In the months and days leading up to hostilities, and with all volunteers and draftees taken into account, the British army totalled 1.2 million men and women. In the inventory of equipment were at least 900 Chieftain tanks. Fifty thousand soldiers remained on UK soil to repel any invasion planned by the enemy, and two divisions were deployed to both Singapore and Hong Kong. We had also sent three divisions to bolster the Indian army's effort at its borders with both Russia and China. However, almost all of the remainder were stationed in West Germany and West Berlin.

Nothing was ever heard from those British troops posted to either India, Singapore or Hong Kong and of the 650,000 in Germany, less than four thousand survived. Some made it to France and Portugal and less than five hundred had returned to the UK, almost all of them on a single ferry that they nicked from Zeebrugge harbour and sailed back to Plymouth. Not one single tank, self-propelled gun, AFV or piece of artillery came home.

The same day, I received a second file which reported that globally, the contamination seemed to be receding but was still lethal in many parts. There was now no question that Chile and New Zealand remained mankind's best hopes for a radiation free future. Northern France and west Cornwall had fared much better than those of us 'up North,' as we now called Devon and Somerset, but we weren't inclined to head down south. There simply wasn't room and there weren't sufficient naval or airfield facilities. In essence, we had all realised that life would be shorter than we might have hoped. By how much, of course, only time would tell.

I spent the odd night at the college, but most evenings, I would walk down to town to our new 'home' at the Angel hotel to be with Anna. We felt like a relatively normal married couple actually. We breakfasted together, then I would go to work and at around seven or eight I would be back for dinner.

Then, on March 10th 1984, what we thought then was the only remaining enemy nuclear threat, manifested itself when the Soviet SSBN Verdlosk surrendered to HMS Defiant in the Atlantic off the east of Argentina. At the same time, the other operational Soviet SSBN,

Admiral Gorky, was being escorted into what was left of San Francisco by the US Navy. As she passed under the Golden Gate bridge she blew up. Her twenty four missile tubes each carried three five megaton warheads and the combined three hundred and sixty megaton detonation laid waste to swathes of the western United States. The fallout covered an area bordered in the north by Calgary, to the east by Denver and in the south as far as Mexico City. The entire US Trident manufacturing facility had been destroyed. Despite an immediate request to sink the Verdlosk, we ordered HMS Defiant to stand by as the majority of Verdlosk's crew transferred to HMS Gloucester. Twelve crew members refused to leave, at which point the captain of Defiant got his wish, sinking the submarine with a single torpedo. It was impossible to comprehend what the crew of Admiral Gorky were thinking. What it was that made them blow up their boat, knowing that they would kill so many millions of people. We supposed that there had probably been a take over by the political nut cases, that the decent ones, maybe the captain, had been silenced or killed. What doctrine, what belief, makes you do such a thing? Anyway, that new radiation cloud now threatened all of us and we were watching the Jetstream very carefully.

On June 17 1984 the US Secretary of State confirmed that, following the west coast nuclear detonation, and the loss of most of the Pacific Fleet, the US Navy now comprised only three SSBN, two SSN, seven frigates, nine destroyers and one aircraft carrier. All were moored in east coast naval yards. However, most of their crews were dispersed away from their bases and many had perished. The intention was that all USN assets would relocate to Pearl Harbor as soon as practicable. Every surviving U. S. citizen, who was so inclined, was to be put aboard either commercial airliners, Fleet Auxiliaries or cruise ships and taken across to Hawaii as well. The American mainland was to be abandoned. In November 1984, US intelligence reporting confirmed that the entirety of the Soviet and PRC war machines and the combined surviving populations of Eastern Bloc, Chinese and North Korean nations had fled to Sakhalin Island on the east coast of Russia. The population of Sakhalin was estimated at 20 million and very probably significantly more. It was reported that there was widespread starvation amongst ordinary people and that civil disturbance was commonplace. The place sounded like a hellhole.

Maurice Bowen and I became very good friends over the following months, and as things in the south west started to take on a degree of normality, I think everyone was beginning to consider a future of some sort. We knew that we had all received a dose of radiation and that this meant we were all going die sooner than might be expected but I, for one, was happy with my life and a couple years knocked off, as long as I was with Anna, wasn't going to make much difference.

Bowen came to see me during my last day at St Mawgan before my permanent relocation to Dartmouth. It was just before Christmas, and he told me that as Admiral of the Fleet he had ordered himself to take Valiant out to sea to enable him to sail for Sakhalin should the need arise. If I agreed, he would reluctantly obey. I supposed that without much of the US Navy left, no recent contact with the French SSBN, and bugger all from anywhere else, Valiant and Defiant were all that the free world had left. I told him to go. When he left that day, we hugged. I never, ever do that with a man.

A couple of days after Valiant had sailed, I discovered from my new Adjutant, Squadron Leader Paul Maybury, that Bowen had spent quite some time recently seeking out his wife and three children who he had sent to St Davids in Pembrokeshire for safety's sake before the war started. When he had got there, he discovered that they had never arrived, but had instead travelled to Hampstead to be with his sister. He never said a thing about it to me. Not then, and not really since. On February 13 1985, I received a report from Pearl Harbor to the effect that a USAF U2 carrying out an overflight of Sakhalin had been fired on by a salvo of SAMs. The aircraft wasn't damaged and returned to Hawaii. Aerial photographs clearly showed a missile launch facility was being constructed. There were four gantries, each supporting what appeared to be a Soyuz type launcher. There were also numerous images of Soviet and Chinese fighter and bomber aircraft and warships. Our photographic analysts confirmed that enemy aviation assets were in excess of 170 Bear, Bison, Blinder and Backfire strategic bombers. Naval capability was one aircraft carrier, three cruisers, fourteen destroyers and six frigates. It was also believed that two SSBNs could be seen undergoing deep maintenance. With this sort of enemy task force, we would all be finished.

Within a month, the new US President contacted the British and French Prime Ministers and confirmed that it was estimated that the enemy would be launch ready within four to six weeks. The President asked for British and allied assistance to eradicate the threat, stating that whilst his forces were still relatively strong, they lacked the guaranteed capability to destroy all of the enemy. The PMs assured the President that our navies and air forces were ready to assist and that the submarines Valiant and Defiant would soon be on station. The French Prime Minister confirmed that his Command and Control had still not heard from their SSBN, and it was now presumed to be lost.

The US President proposed a pre-emptive strike. He stated that if the enemy was to attack Hawaii, there would be no America left and no American forces able to respond. The population on the Hawaiian Islands was now 9 million, and the infrastructure simply couldn't cope with the huge influx of refugees. Discussions were held to establish how the world's remaining maritime assets could be best used to begin transporting civilians away from Hawaii and on to France, England, Morocco, New Zealand and Chile.

The President stated that the US Air Force still had 66 B52s, 16 TSR2s, 103 F111s, 207 F4s and 72 KC135s operational. The serviceable Navy now comprised one aircraft carrier, one battleship, two SSBN, one of which was at sea and within missile reach of Sakhalin, two cruisers, nine destroyers and seven frigates. All the other surviving warships were too badly damaged to be reasonably repaired.

I was privileged to be in the Cabinet War Room at Dartmouth College when a pre-emptive strike was agreed, with the allied launch to take place on April 23rd at 1800. The US President and the Prime Minister's of Britain and France prayed together during this telephone conversation. I didn't.

CHAPTER SEVEN

On the morning of April 21st, I rang the duty officer at St Mawgan and asked him what we had ready for combat. He came back to me within twenty minutes confirming that there were six TSR2s with him in a serviceable condition There were two Vulcans at Chivenor that were combat capable, and we had four VC10s at Exeter. I told him to get them all bombed up and ready for action within two hours. He had hesitated at that point, and I had asked what was wrong. He said that we were short of qualified captains for one of the Vulcans and two of the VC10s.

Obviously, I had made contingency plans for this sort of episode but never really believed it would necessary. I also knew that we would be short of experienced aircrew. I called my driver and got him to prepare the car to take me to Exeter Airport within the hour. I then called my Adjutant on the intercom and gave him full responsibility in my absence.

He rather burst into the office. 'What absence?' he asked.

'I'm off to Exeter to finish a war. I should be back by tomorrow. Can you tell Anna?' I said rather melodramatically. I think he may have rolled his eyes as I flounced out of the office.

By the time I got to the airport, my two base commanders from St. Mawgan and Chivenor had already flown in aboard Gazelles. I told them to crew up and fuel up. Their aeroplanes, and the VC10s were off at 2300 that night. Both these chaps had flown in the war and both were brilliant pilots. I told them that they were to fly to Hawaii, where they would join up with the Americans in preparation for a joint launch against Sakhalin on the 23rd.

I asked if they were good to go, at which point they admitted that a Vulcan would have to fly either with two senior copilots or be scrubbed. I authorised the flight straight away, and signed the paperwork. They then stated that we had a VC10 copilot who had almost completed the conversion course to captain, and a Victor captain called Colin Edgecombe who had been recommended for VC10 command, but who hadn't yet attended the Operational Conversion Unit ground school, let alone started any flying.

'But he is currently a Victor captain?' I asked.

'Yes, sir,' said my St. Mawgan chap.

I had to think quickly. Could I risk a nearly competent trainee captain with a bombed up VC10. 'What shall we do, sir?' asked the Chivenor man.

'Send the VC10 chap who's almost done,' I said

'And the Victor man?' Too risky, if he hasn't even started the conversion,' I said, and they both nodded in agreement. I looked over at the aircraft sitting patiently on the apron awaiting their crews. Then I looked back at the chaps.

'You're not thinking of coming along are you sir?' asked one. I winked at them and told them to get going. We would rendezvous over the North Sea at 2345.

'Sir, this is not on. We'll just scrub a VC10. It'll be alright,' said one, but I was already making my way to flight dispatch.

I had phoned ahead to my engineering chief Rollo Geary, and despite his protestations that I was no longer fit to fly, he had caved in when I said that I would bust him to lance corporal if he even mentioned my name as being one of the pilots. Anyway, who was he going to report me to; the Head of the Royal Air Force?

'Rollo, I've told Maybury to tell my wife sort of what I'm doing, but he's such a fairy, he'll probably put it off. Please, please call my wife, or even go and see her. She thinks I'm coordinating the attack, not actually flying. Tell her there weren't enough pilots. Tell her I had to go,' which I know made him even more uncomfortable.

'And what if Maybury does tell her?' he asked, quite reasonably.

'He only thinks I've come here to see the chaps off; you have to tell her I'm flying,' I replied as I hobbled off towards my crew.

The Vulcan and TSR2 teams went off to their briefing room whilst I gathered all the VC10 crews in the hangar. I explained that we were going to join the USAF and the Armée de L'air and our fellows in the various navies to bomb the Soviet-Chinese missile base on Sakhalin, and finally finish off their air forces and remaining ground troops. We would route via the eastern fringes of the enemy site, in case of any intention by them to launch their Soyuz missiles early, and then we would continue across the Pacific to Hawaii. We would have a day to finally prepare and then we would finish off the enemy.

The French were supplying their four remaining Mirage IVs and were going to be our flying petrol station as well. They still had half a dozen serviceable KC10s and they would be our lifeline, both out and back, with additional fuel available from the Americans once we were in Hawaii, and again when on station before and after the attack. All intelligence now pointed towards an uninhabited and uninhabitable Russia. Therefore, we would fly outbound over northern Denmark, through the middle of Finland, up over the top of Russia and then down past the target and on to Hawaii.

After the flurry of excitement leading up to launch, the ninety minutes between me barking out my last set of orders and actually taking off were incredibly dull and longwinded. Stephen Thorpe was in the mess when I went in for a last coffee and to pick up some fags. He begged me to let him to come along but I refused point blank, saying that I needed him back here, not least to help with any returning aircraft. Then it struck me for the first time. Yet again, I was setting off on a mission that was almost inevitably going to kill all of us. This time, though, it would all be my fault. I had decided to launch our bombers, knowing full well that the yanks and our subs were probably perfectly capable. Despite that, what if the enemy clobbered our boats or shot down the Americans. What then? Four bloody great Soyuz rockets heading our way and 20 million plus Chinese and Russians with 150 bombers and their ballistic submarines storming into the last vestiges of civilisation left on the planet. No; I had convinced myself that I was right.

I said goodbye to Steve and walked out to the Land Rover that would take us to the aeroplane where I smoked a cigarette while I waited for the boys. When they arrived, I saw that whilst two of them were obviously in their later thirties or perhaps older, the other two were very fresh-faced. Rather than say a thing, I shook their hands in turn. They each told me their names and I instantly forget them.

Just as I was about to board the vehicle, a man in whites ran up to me. He introduced himself as the head chef in the officers' mess and asked what special meal I thought he should prepare for our homecoming. I had absolutely no idea, but I did ask him if each of the messes, Sergeants, Corporals and Other Ranks, all had head chefs too. He said that they did, so I told him to extend it to all messes. After I had climbed into the Land Rover, and as we headed off to the aeroplane, he yelled after me.

'What then, sir. What do you want?'

'I'll tell the tower and they can tell you,' I shouted back. My aircraft for this mission, like all the rest of the VC10 fleet, no longer had the facility for a White Shadow rotary launcher. We just had the six missiles under the wings and incredibly full fuel tanks. The aeroplane was painted differently to my war mount in that she had received a coat of primer and then a top coat of dull dark grey. I think the second coat went on before the first had dried properly. She didn't look too clever from the outside, but inside, she was very clean and tidy. I joined the Flight Engineer as he checked our inventory of kit for the mission. Apart from full tanks and six missiles, we had a pistol, each with two magazines, and a box of ammunition; food for forty eight hours; fifteen NBC suits and a respirator for each of us. We carried Geiger counters inside the aircraft to warn of radiation in flight, and each aircraft was also equipped with a portable unit with half a dozen spare receptor tubes. There were flares and water purifying kits, lots of cigarettes, six rolls of toilet paper, a portable shortwave radio and, of course, a broom.

Each aircraft also carried a list of airports and military airfields along the routes both out and back that could be used in the event of a forced landing. Naturally, nobody ever expected to have to use them, because it was almost certain that they would have either been destroyed in our first attack, or, if they were still intact, would be extremely hostile to incoming NATO bombers. It is very much worth explaining who my crew were on this mission. I have already said that when we were on the ground, I had instantly forgotten their names. Later, of course, I went out of my way to ensure that they weren't forgotten. The Flight Engineer was called Geoff, and he was thirty and originally from Spalding in Lincolnshire. My Comms officer was called Spike (I doubted this) and he was twenty-six, from Kent. The Weapons Systems Operator was originally from Malta but had settled in Cornwall years ago. His name was Chris and he was a mere forty-four. My copilot was the Victor captain Colin Edgecombe, and he had flown during the war. His was the only aircraft from his squadron to make it back in one piece, and after that, he had requested a transfer to VC10 tankers as he apparently, 'fancied a change.' I don't know if he knew then that I was probably grounded or if he found out later, but he never said a word. Not then, and not since.

As I was now the man in charge, I called the tower on behalf of the whole flight and requested start and taxi clearance. This was duly given, and at 2258, we started off towards the runway. I had briefed the other pilots that, on this occasion, I would take off last, primarily because I wanted to make sure the others got off safely. I taxied out as number four in line, breathing in other's burnt kerosene fumes and giving me a last chance to think about the good things in life. Clearance was given for take off and the first aircraft began her long and ponderous trundle down the runway. Because it was so dark, I couldn't see how long her run had been but it looked to be an age before her navigation lights appeared above the trees at the far end of the airfield. Soon enough, it was our turn and as soon as the aircraft in front had got to half way through her take off run, I opened the throttles to full power and held her on the brakes for a moment. When I released, acceleration was better than an expected and the rudder was effective much sooner too. We rotated with at least five hundred feet to spare and once the undercarriage was up, I got into line astern the others.

I contacted the tower and asked them to pass a message to all the head chefs. 'Please tell them it's roast pork. I don't care about the trimmings. Roast pork with apple sauce,' I said.

There was a moment's silence. 'Roger that. We'll pass it on,' they then replied.

'And tons of crackling,' I added.

'Crackling. Roger.'

I looked across at my copilot who quite obviously thought I was utterly insane.

We crossed the coast at Withernsea, and once established in the cruise at thirty six thousand feet, all twelve of my aircraft joined up into loose formation. I then handed over control to my copilot and headed back to check the others. We had now lost comms with Britain and were entirely on our own, at least until we met up with other allied aircraft.

We hadn't even made it to the Danish coast when one of the Vulcans called up to state that they appeared to be losing all hydraulics. I told them to get their undercarriage down and locked and then to turn back to home. I could probably get away with a few less missiles at Sakhalin, but I couldn't do without the intact White Shadows and the crew. I wished them good luck, and reminded the captain that if a landing looked unlikely, they were to launch the missiles out into the Atlantic and then eject and bale out (the pilots had ejector seats, the remainder didn't), but only once they were within the safe zone. We watched as he dropped his gear and then, when we had told them it looked to be properly down, the big delta wheeled away. The rest of us refuelled from three French KC10s at the nine hour point and then made course corrections that would ensure we passed at least five hundred miles to the east of Sakhalin. It was at this point that we were finally able to pick up some radio transmissions from the NATO forces on the ground in eastern Russia, and they were able to confirm that, according to a USAF AWACS aircraft, there was nothing currently airborne except us. That communication was logged at 0932 GMT.

My navigator/comms came on the intercom to tell me that one of our TSR2s was reporting difficulties and that everything was pointing to a failure of their White Shadow launch system. I told them to stay put with us and that we would sort it out on the ground in Hawaii.

The AWACS was now circling at 40,000 feet, about eight hundred miles off the east coast of the island and it was now our eyes and ears. They would ensure that if the enemy launched, we would be safely covered by the F4s that were now below him at thirty six thousand.

Each of our aircraft had now received a set of target parameters from the AWACS. The TSR2s and the Vulcan were to bomb the centre of the island, whilst the targets for my VC10s were at the top. We were six hundred miles off the east coast and roughly half way down Sakhalin when my copilot yelled out.

'Christ! Launch below!'

Before I could even respond, the AWACS commander was telling us that the enemy had launched. My heart sank. We had come all this way and now we were too late, and at least one of those giant missiles was going to finish off what was left of home.

'All aircraft, turn on target!' shouted the AWACS.

Unknown to those of us in the air, at 1119 GMT, all four of the Soyuz missiles were launched. Their initial target was uncertain but predictable, and after two minutes of flight, it became clear that they would all impact Hawaii. The complete destruction of the remnants of the USA was intended. Within two and half minutes of the enemy launch, the SSBN USS Monterey launched her 24 missiles and HMS Valiant her 16 SLBMs against Sakhalin Island. Defiant was not in the immediate vicinity but was well within range and she too launched her full compliment of missiles.

In response to the AWACS, the TSR2s and the Vulcan had immediately turned towards their targets and were already getting down low. I ordered my VC10 flight to follow suit and we set course for the six principal towns and the surrounding airfields and naval facilities. I could just make out the TSR2s as they disappeared into the clouds way below.

'Down to five hundred now!' I exclaimed, and we hurtled towards the ocean. My Weapons Systems Operator confirmed that the missiles were armed and ready, and as soon as we were at launch height, I called for line abreast and as soon as that was established, we went into echelon. The enemy ICBMs impacted, one over each of the principal inhabited islands of Hawaii, at 1202 GMT. Detonation was at 22,000 feet and the blasts were unrecordably large. All contact with the US was instantly lost. It soon became apparent that very few US combat aircraft had been airborne at the point of the enemy launch.

The French, Chilean and UK authorities began broadcasting shortwave radio messages advising any and all allied forces to reassemble in either north west France, southern New Zealand, any point within southern Chile or the south west England at their earliest opportunity. Even we were able to pick up some of that traffic. The US and Royal Navy submarine missiles had air burst over the complete southerly land mass of Sakhalin Island, with a total of 92 MIRVs fired by all three boats. It was splendid work. Just too bloody late for Hawaii and the Americans.

We were down low now, and I kept creeping down in increments until we were around two hundred and fifty feet above the sea. The buffet was moderate, but still disconcerting. We were almost at the point where we could climb and launch when there was a call from the AWACS.

'Multiple SAM launches. Stand by…SAMs, heading towards you now!'

'All aircraft. Break, break, break. Launch at one thousand. Good luck,' I shouted over the radio.

I immediately hauled the aeroplane up to five hundred, broke left and then dived down, jinking to the right to try and put the missiles off. 'There!' screamed Colin and I saw out of the right window as one of our VC10s exploded and trickled down to the surface in a million pieces.

'No more coming your way now,' was the cry from the AWACS.

I pulled up to a thousand feet and shouted for launch. Within a fraction of a second, the number one was on its way. Six followed, with two, five, three and four. We were done.

At the instant that Chris yelled, 'All missiles gone, skip!' I threw the yoke forward and dived towards the sea.

We weren't getting anything specific to our flight from the AWACS but we could hear his radio traffic, and whilst the impact of our missiles were being reported by some aircraft, others were calling out for cover. I heard at least three chaps call out that they had been hit.

Our missiles and the majority of the French Air Force ones had impacted across the northern and central areas. A total of thirty nine allied warheads had been launched; each of ours at 1.2MT yield and the six French at 1.5MT.

One of the Mirage IVs had been vectored towards what the AWACS had concluded were large surface vessels breaking for the deep ocean. They were, in fact, a serviceable SSBN of the Typhoon/Kursk class which was towing a smaller ballistic missile boat. The Mirage destroyed both with one missile. The USAF AWACS confirmed to us, to NATO and UN Command and Control that Sakhalin appeared to be ablaze across its entire six hundred mile by one hundred mile geography. From a conflict perspective, I couldn't have been happier. However, we were still hurtling towards the island and I had no idea whether it was neutralised or not. I had already lost one aircraft and I wasn't about to lose any more. I called the AWACS and asked if there was a KC10 or KC135 available to refuel us as we needed to turn out towards Hawaii. His response was chilling.

'Victor Charlie One. Hawaii is no longer viable. Your course is two niner five. Climb to your maximum altitude at your earliest opportunity'

I had worked with an American AWACS on one previous occasion, during an exercise, and you soon come to realise that they are people of few words. What does flow from them though, is always the right choice.

I ordered our flight to set course as instructed and we began a full power climb up to 41,000 feet. We never heard from that AWACS again and it didn't make it back to any allied country. I felt very sorry, and totally indebted to them for our survival. I was pondering quite how I was going to sensibly explain my absence to Anna, when the Master Warning light illuminated on the panel in front of me at the same time as its low pitched alarm.

'Fuel state!' exclaimed Colin.

I looked at the gauges, and sure enough, we were registering low pressure and low fuel in all the tanks. 'Christ, we're down to almost empty!' I said.

'We should have seen that coming,' said Colin.

Geoff was frantically scanning his panel behind us. 'There's fuck all registering here, skipper. We must have copped something!' he shouted.

'Comms, tell the rest of the flight that we're going down, and log our position,' I said over the intercom.

'Roger, skip,' he replied.

'Find somewhere to put it down,' I said to the copilot.

I called the whole crew up to the flight deck, and once they were there, I explained that at the rate we were losing fuel, we would be landing, one way or another, and including the glide, within about thirty minutes. I then sent them back to their respective stations having told them to strap in tightly.

My copilot was holding up a sheet of paper but I couldn't read what was on it.

'Chita airport skip. About twenty minutes away on two seven one,' he said matter of factly.

'That'll be us then,' I said. 'There's a military field to the north of the city but I'm guessing that's gone,' Colin added.

'Let's hope the civvy airport wasn't considered important enough,' I said. 'Chita is apparently an administrative centre for the region of Zabaykalsky Krai,' said Colin approvingly.

'Great. I've always wanted to go there,' I said.

'We're going to lose the engines in a minute skipper!' said the Flight Engineer with only a hint of concern in his voice.

'Okay, thanks,' I replied.

'This is going to be shit,' the Flight Engineer then said thoughtfully, and added, 'And I promised my wife I'd be home for breakfast.'

'Me too,' said Colin.

'I didn't even tell mine I was coming,' I said.

Colin looked across at me and said, 'You're a dead man, skipper.'

'Yeah, one way or another, I think you're right.' At which point, an engine began winding down.

'Number four gone, skipper!' said Geoff.

'Dropping the RAT,' said Colin, as he pulled a lever which deployed the Ram Air Turbine out into the slipstream. This clever little device would ensure that, even without engine power, we could still operate the flaps and the undercarriage.

'They're all going now, skip,' said Geoff.

The engine condition panel now had four pulsating reddish orange lights and the flight deck was significantly quieter.

I began the shallowest of descents and felt pretty certain that I could make the airport with our current speed and altitude.

It sort of hit me then. The rest were going home, and we were going down to land in what I presumed was Siberia. I wasn't sure, but I reckoned home must be five thousand miles away. From what we already knew, everything now in front of us, right up to the eastern reaches of France, was heavily contaminated. I very much doubted that our NBC suits would last. 'Guys, everyone get your suits on and be prepared to don your respirators no lower than ten thousand. Don't forget your pistols either. Divvy up the other survival kit and look after the radio,' I said over the intercom as calmly as I could.

We had lost the first engine at thirty nine thousand feet, so we were in very good condition for a decent glide down to the runway. The VC10 should be able to manage somewhere in the region of 120 miles without power, and we now only needed another thirty before we touched down.

'Do you want to take her in, skip?' asked Colin. So I thought about it. Should I say yes, carry on flying as a captain should, and risk killing everyone because I was a silly old sod who really should have been at the Royal Naval College biting my fingernails. Or, do I let a competent wartime V Bomber pilot land.

'You have control,' I said. He looked across at me with an expression that said 'really?'

'Are you sure?' he replied.

'It'll count towards your conversion hours,' I said, nodding my approval.

'Thanks. I have control,' replied Colin.

Comms brought the gear for the three of us flight deck crew, and then shot off to get his own on. I told Colin to suit up while I took back control for a while, and as soon as he was done, he carried on the descent, and I fought my way into the NBC outfit. At ten thousand feet, I called for respirators to be put on. From now on, we couldn't afford to remove them unless the Geiger counters registered low levels of radiation. Considering where we were, this was unlikely. As we broke through the overcast, Colin made a sharp intake of breath. 'Fuck me. Look!' he said, and pointed out to his three o'clock. I slightly loosened my harness and sat up so I could see out of the side window. There was a huge hole to the north east of the city and it seems to have swallowed up an entire district.

'They got one then,' said Geoff, leaning froward.

None of us had seen the effects of a nuclear blast other than in film of early tests. It was impossible to gauge the size of the crater or the yield of the warhead, but there weren't any buildings standing within a mile of the hole.

We could now see the military airport off on the right. It didn't look damaged, but it was a fair way away, so it was difficult to tell. Our runway was now right on the nose, and it looked plenty long enough for us and undamaged. I dropped the flaps in increments as Colin requested them, and at about three miles out, pulled down the undercarriage lever. Amazingly, all three legs seemed to lock down, and aside from the eerie silence, the approach was as normal as any I had ever experienced. On touchdown, the main wheels screeched slightly and Colin kept the nose high to assist with braking. When we were down to about sixty knots, he let the nose down and we both stood on the brakes. We rolled to a halt with plenty of tarmac left and I applied the parking brake.

'Well bugger me,' said the Flight Engineer, sounding very muffled and rather amusing through his respirator.

'Everybody out!' I yelled.

CHAPTER EIGHT

We all began scrambling out and all of us banged our heads at least once on various parts of the aircraft as we left due to the respirator's useless vision panels. The rubbery smell was horrible and a nasty film of sweat quickly accumulated around the inflatable seal. Once on the ground, we quickly looked around to get our bearings. I didn't really expect to see a platoon of Red Army soldiers sprinting towards us, but I was sure that we would have been seen by some survivor or other, and that we needed to get going very quickly. We could then hear the Flight Engineer shouting in a completely incomprehensible way from within his respirator. He was pointing up under the wing of the aeroplane. As we all walked over, I tried to make myself understood in my clearest respirator voice.

'We're going to have to get very good at hand signals,' I said by pursing my lips and sort of sucking in as I spoke.

'Eh?' said Comms.

'Look!' shouted Geoff, continuing to point upwards.

And so, the reason for our downing became clear. The underside of the right wing, just outboard of the undercarriage leg, had a bloody great hole in it. At least two feet across, it was a jagged mess of metal and wiring. The fuel in the tank above it would have vented immediately and then all the remainder would have automatically transferred itself to the empty tank, thus causing total starvation. There were quite a lot of smaller holes running from the wing towards the nose, which might have explained why Geoff's panel and mine were showing completely different readings. 'Must have been the other VC10 going up,' is what Colin actually said, although, in reality it sounded like a cow with its head in a bucket. He eventually explained what he was saying by gesticulating at our aircraft and miming an explosion and pointing at the wing. I don't think some of the chaps really got it.

We then hurried off the runway and headed towards a hangar. When I say hurried, I mean that all the rest hurried while I limped and winced my way across. I made up my mind there and then that I was the crew liability, and if anything did befall us in the form of approaching hordes, I had to be the one who stayed behind to hold off the baddies. The WSO, like all his compatriots, had been schooled in rudimentary Russian, and the use of the Geiger counter as part of their training. I guess Spike was the only one who had ever had to put this particular skill into practise. He already knew that it was pointless trying to make himself understood in the mask, so he just showed us the reading once we were in the hangar. It wasn't off the scale, but it was a fatal dose alright.

We went further inside the building, and parked in one corner was a Yak 42 airliner. Whilst Colin climbed on board, the WSO checked its radiation readings. He shook his head and shouted, 'High!' Colin reappeared shortly afterwards and came over to me. 'It's wrecked,' he shouted. I just nodded.

So, we weren't going to be saved that easily.

'Skipper, there's a train!' is what Geoff actually shouted. It didn't sound like that at the time, and some of the chaps were squinting towards the horizon for ages before they realised what he meant. Sure enough though, there were the roofs of engines and coaches and trucks, and they were only a couple of hundred yards away. This was no provincial station. There were four platforms and a big marshalling yard with dozens of trucks sitting in sidings. I called over Chris, the WSO, and asked him to find out where we were in relation to rest of Russia, and to work out how we could either get to the coast, or to somewhere that might offer us a better chance of survival. Spike and Geoff had gone over to look at one of the trains, and pretty soon, they were clambering up into the driving cab. At this point, Chris came back over and he was waggling a brochure about.

'Trans Siberian Railway, skip,' he announced, and proceeded to show me the map inside the booklet. Chita, it seemed was towards the eastern end of the line and is the junction where trains from Moscow either continue on to Vladivostok or turn south to head into China.

'That's a long walk,' I said.

At which point, we were interrupted by a whining sound as the engine of the railway locomotive started up. Geoff was hanging out of the cab window and was waving wildly at us to come over. As we got closer to the diesel engine, the cylinders must have started clearing themselves of accumulated oil and gunk, because huge plumes of filthy black smoke started swirling all around. The smell was penetrating the respirator which didn't exactly fill me with confidence for our long term survival from radiation contamination.

'The tanks are only totally full!' shouted down Geoff with great enthusiasm.

'That's brilliant,' said Chris, and then he added, 'What are we meant to do now?'

'Drive it down to the sea and find a boat,' replied Geoff.

'It's thousands of miles and the line will be buggered.'

'They're not stupid, you know. I don't think the Russians would have dynamited the track just in case a British bomber crew want to use it,' said Geoff as Chris and I climbed into the cab.

Colin joined us on board having finished his recce of the area surrounding the hangar. 'There are a couple of light aircraft but they're all either sabotaged or just not airworthy,' he said despondently.

'Don't need a plane, we've got train!' mumbled Geoff.

'There's also what looks like a husband and wife in the hangar office,' added Colin.

'Dead?' asked Spike.

'No, they were playing Scrabble,' replied Colin. 'Yes of course fucking dead. Poison or something, by the look of it.'

'Thank you!' I said.

'Skip, I can drive this bastard,' said Spike enthusiastically.

'Where?' I asked.

'My dad was a train driver, so I know what to do,' replied Spike.

'Where can we go?' I said.

'If we can work out how to uncouple this from the wagons and then also work out which track leads where, we can go anywhere you like, skip,' said Chris.

The weight of command. They were all looking at me, at the same time as talking to each other in an animated and stupidly muffled way. I could barely make out a single word they were saying. 'Chris, go and find some maps from somewhere and work out where's where, will you,' I said.

'Right ho, skip,' he replied and jumped down off the train and headed back to the station building.

'Spike, unhook the engine then and try and figure out which points are which,' I added.

'Now you're talking, skip,' he said and disappeared out of the other door.

Colin and I disembarked and set about divvying up the rations. There were biscuits, tins of beans with little sausages and 'apple flakes with custard,' which I doubted. 'How are we going to eat anyway. We can't take these bastards off,' he said stabbing at his respirator.

'During training they said that even in a hostile environment, you can lift the bottom momentarily to shovel food into your mouth,' I replied.

'I don't believe that,' said Colin.

'No. Neither do I. I'll leave it up to the chaps,' I said, placing my food back in its box.

'Skipper!' was yelled across at us, but it was unclear who from. Nevertheless, something good was obviously happening because the diesel engine was inching forward and it was no longer attached to its train. As Chris jogged back from the station, the others were whooping with joy at the success of their efforts.

'Can't do a thing with the points skip. They're all operated from a signal box that I can't find, and it's done electrically. And there's no electricity,' he said despondently.

I went over to the engine and shouted up at Spike, 'Go and work out if we can get out on to the main line safely will you Spike. We can't change the points.'

'Okay, skip,' he replied and leapt off the engine.

Chris then came over and he was motioning for us to follow him. He climbed up into the rear cab of the locomotive, and once we were inside, he shut the door. He then switched on the Geiger counter which immediately showed a fatal dose. He turned, and opened a door at the rear of the cab and as we followed, we saw that we were entering the engine compartment. The throb of the motor was deafening. He switched on the counter again but this time it showed only a moderate dosage. With that, he waved us back to the cab.

'As long as we keep the door shut skip, we can eat and sleep in there,' he said. I nodded my approval. Spike now appeared in the rear driving cab and was breathlessly trying to tell us about the points. But we couldn't understand a word he was saying. I got everyone down onto the ground and we walked away from the thrumming loco.

'Right Spike. Try again,' I said 'We can go straight onto the main line skipper. It'll be wrong road…'

He was interrupted. 'What's that?' It was Chris.

'Wrong road is not the track you should use for going in a particular direction,' explained Spike.

'We're hardly going to meet the ten o'clock to Cleethorpes coming the other way are we,' said Colin sarcastically.

'So which way are we going Spike?' I asked.

'We can only go east, skip,' he said.

'Well, Moscow is about five thousand miles the other way and the whole lot is lethal. And we wouldn't want to head to China anyway…' At that point I looked at them all. They were hanging on my every word. I thought this was rather sweet so I prepared to give them a shock. 'We're going to Vladivostok,' I said, expecting groans and complaints.

'Hooray!' said Geoff.

The remainder seemed equally satisfied.

'It is the wrong direction though, skipper,' added Chris.

'There's no right direction in this sort of environment Chris. Besides, if we can only go east, then east it is,' I said.

'Fair enough,' he replied.

We climbed back aboard our train and Spike gave us a lesson in train driving techniques. He released the brake, moved the direction of travel lever to the forward position and then pulled back one notch on the power handle. The engine note increased and we began creeping forward. 'Really slow over the points, you see. Then, once we're out on the main line, I can open her up a bit,' he said, like a child with a new, very big toy.

During the next half an hour or so, we each got a turn at operating the locomotive and, I must say, it was both very easy and unbelievably satisfying. I suppose we were about forty miles east of Chita when we trundled over a set of points that marked the divergence to the north, and then, by means of a great big loop around to the south, which ultimately led to Peking. Thankfully, the points were in our favour, and we seemed to be on the right track for Vladivostok.

Colin grabbed my elbow and led me into the engine compartment where he shut the door. He slightly lifted his respirator.

'Ollie, we need to put on new suits within the next hour or so,' he said.

'I know chum. But what happens when we've used up all three. We can't hide in for here long?' I replied.

'Once we get to a straight bit, I think we should just go as fast as we can,' he said and winked.

Back in the cab, I told the chaps to take it in turns going into the engine bay, having some food, getting some rest and changing into a fresh NBC suit. When Spike went back for his rest, I took control of the engine. Shortly after this, we seemed to hit what looked like a lovely long straight bit of track. I opened up the regulator to the sixth notch and we accelerated to a purposeful 120 kph, which I am reliably informed is 75 miles per hour. It didn't feel like it, because the engine was so big and we were so high up. After only about ten minutes at that speed, I had to ease off the power as we were approaching another ridiculous bendy bit which seemed to have been built for no other reason than to annoy train drivers. Once we were through, I handed over control to Colin and went back to eat a biscuit or two and change into my nice new suit. I sat down for a while and pondered our chances of surviving all the way to the coast. I rested my head on my equipment pack for just a second. When I woke, Spike was fast asleep on the floor next to me with his feet up against mine. I craned my head back and saw that Geoff was also asleep, but further along the compartment. I got up and walked back into the driving cab.

'Hello, skipper,' said Colin.

'Hello chaps. Was I out long?' I asked.

Chris pretended to look at his watch, 'About five hours sir,' he replied.

'You chaps go back now. I'll be fine,' I said with a hint of authority.
'I'm good to stay sir. You go back Chris,' said Colin

'Right ho,' said Chris and sloped off.

We settled into our turn at driving quite well. I did half an hour, at which point Colin took over. We got quite adept at braking gently whenever we approached a tighter than usual bend or if we were approaching a set of points. Whoever wasn't driving would peer out the front as we neared, to check that the points were in our favour. 'It's around a thousand miles in total isn't it sir?' asked Colin as we breezed along at 60 miles an hour on a nice bit of straight track.

'Near enough chum,' I replied. 'So, at this speed, or at least at this average, we'll be in Vladivostok by tea time tomorrow. ,' and he nodded appreciatively at his mathematical skills. 'If you say so. But we're not going into the city. Far too dangerous. We'll dump the train and get to the port on foot,' I said.

'Dangerous in Vladivostok?' asked Colin.

'Well, it will have got at least one bomb, probably more, and there could be loads of people still alive,' which I instantly regretted saying.

'It's been eighteen months, Ollie. There won't even be a woodlouse alive, let alone a battalion of Soviet Marines,' he said.

'Yeah, you're right,' I conceded.

Spike then appeared from the engine compartment and told us that as we'd been driving for six hours between us, it was his turn. We didn't argue. As Colin and I went inside, Geoff came out as well. Whilst Colin got his head down, I ate a few more biscuits and stared out of the tiny slit of a window in the side of the loco at the never ending desolation of the Russian steppes. It truly was grim. Shortly after, I too lay down, and despite the thrumming of the engine, was asleep in moments. When I woke, all I could see was darkness through the window slit and I wondered how long I had been asleep. There was no one else in the compartment, so I went to the front and the chaps were all there.

'New suit time again, skip,' said Geoff.

So, I about turned, and put on my third and last NBC suit. They supposedly had a useful lifespan of twenty-four hours, but most of us doubted that they actually did anything except make you sweat. Once I was dressed, I returned to the cab.

'We've been on the move for forty-eight hours now; shouldn't we be near Bloodyvostok soon?' asked Chris.

'No chance mate, we've been averaging about twenty the whole way,' advised Spike.

'But we were bombing along back there,' said Chris despondently.

'Yeah, and when we go over a point or through some shitty town?' and he raised his eyes.

'Bollocks,' was Chris's response.

'We're going to run out of NBC suits then,' said Geoff.

'Yep,' I said.

We were entering the outskirts of a city called Khabarovsk which had many heavily ruined buildings, and one had to assume it had taken a bomb hit, but from the train, there was no obvious sign of a crater. To get into the centre of the city, the line crossed a huge bridge which it shared with a multi lane road. Once we passed through the centre, it was clear this was a very big place and we saw lorries, trams, buses and cars on the streets, but they all looked as if they had been parked rather than abandoned. There were some bodies as well, but again, they seemed to be very orderly dead people. There was a man sitting on a bench beside a park. Another was propped against a low wall. There were certainly no piles of townsfolk spoiling the municipal tidiness.

Spike was back in control of the engine, and he was being particularly cautious as we threaded our way through the city's massive station, and then back out into the seemingly never ending suburbs which seemed to lead out again onto the plains of Siberia. When we were almost out of the town, we slowly passed by a small convoy of armour. There was tank and two BRDMs, and at the head of the line was a BMP, a light tracked tank and personnel carrier. But this last vehicle was pointing in the opposite direction, back towards the town and almost looked as if it was guarding the road.

'That's not right!' shouted Colin, as we continued at a snail's pace out of the eastern end of the built up area.

'Bollocks!' Spike exclaimed, at the same time as the engine lurched alarmingly over a set of points, and he slammed on the brakes. Even though we were slowing quickly, the engine began rising up and then shuddered to a halt. 'Fuck it!' screamed Spike, leaping down from the cab to inspect the damage.

'We're off. We're only fucking off!' screamed Geoff. We all climbed down, and sure enough, the front set of bogies were off the track. Spike was looking at the locomotive with an expression that suggested that he could hope to fix it.

'Well?' asked Colin.

'The points were set against us,' he replied.

'This isn't the main line anyway,' added Geoff.

'I thought it looked a bit funny,' said Chris, helpfully.

'Did you,' said Colin, sarcastically. 'So, we're off the main line, in Christ knows where.

Spike was still examining the front bogies.

'Spike?' I asked

'Oh yeah, skip. We're fucked,' he said and clambered back into the cab to switch off the motor.

'Well, I'd just like to say I'm really enjoying my holiday. Could anything else go wrong?' said Chris as he stomped off towards the town.

'Where's he going?' said Spike.

'We can't stay here boys,' I said, and began walking into town after him. As we silently trudged our way towards the main road I had seen from the train, I stopped, but I let the boys walk past the armoured vehicles. When they were a good distance away, I cleared my throat very loudly. Admittedly, through the respirator, it sounded like an elephant giving birth, but they all stopped. I made a sweeping gesture with my right arm towards the BMP, but they all just looked at me as though I was insane.

'What, skip?' said Geoff, as they all began slowly walking back.

'It's a BMP,' I said.

'Yes it is,' said Spike.

'And what is a BMP very good at?, I asked with a hint of sarcasm.

'Snorkelling. They're amphibious,' suggested Chris.

'And?' I asked.

There was general shaking of heads and respirator murmurs.

'Oh, for God's sake! They're radiation proof aren't they!' I bellowed.

'Oh fuck yeah. They are,' said Spike with a new enthusiasm.

'What, we're going to drive to England now are we?' said Chris.

'Shut up, you cock,' said Colin and shoved Chris aside as he walked towards the rear of the BMP.

Spike came over to and whispered in my ear, 'I can probably drive that skip.'

'What, your dad drove those as well,' I said.

'Nah,' he said excitedly, 'But my dad did take me to Bovington tank museum a couple of years ago and we both got to drive one. It's a piece of piss.'

At that point, Colin called us over to the armoured vehicle. He now had the doors open, and even though it was quite dark inside, there was clearly a figure sitting in it. I peered in, and caught my breath at the sight. It was a young looking man who was clearly a soldier from the tattered bits of uniform that hung from his mummified frame. On the floor was a heavy duty radiation suit and helmet and all around him were food containers and wrappers.

'The ignition is on skipper. I reckon he ran the engine to keep the bad air out until it ran out of juice, then put on the suit. I suppose eventually, he ran out of food and just decided to die,' said Colin.

'What a way to go,' said Chris as he turned away. 'He had about six whole chickens to eat by the looks of it,' exclaimed Geoff, flicking a bone with his finger.

'So, there's no fuel in this one. Can you check the others please chaps,' I said. I grabbed Colin's arm as he turned to leave, 'Do you know where we are in relation to the rest of Russia?' I asked.

'Yes, Ollie, I do,' he replied.

'And?'

'I didn't think you'd want to know really,' at which he pulled a piece of coloured paper from his trouser pocket. It was a two page map of eastern Europe and the Far East and it had been taken from a Times atlas.

'We really must get proper maps loaded on our aircraft from now on,' I said.

Colin pointed to Chita and then to Khabarovsk.

'Bloody hell Colin, we're almost back at Sakhalin!' I exclaimed.

He nodded, at which point he produced the Geiger counter from his rucksack and showed it to me. The needle was hard over to its maximum deflection. 'I should think we're getting fried to buggery through these suits,' he said, folding the map. 'What are we going to do now, Ollie?'

But I didn't really hear him. I hobbled back to the BMP and climbed inside.

Colin joined me and said, 'What?'

'Suits Colin!' I said frantically.

'What do you mean?' he asked.

I began hauling open all the little compartments inside the back of the vehicle. After about five minutes, we had discovered one NBC suit that was out of its protective packaging, but there were two more that were intact, and appeared useable. We then went on to the nearest BRDM and found another three pristine suits. I shouted over to the others to search the other BRDM and the tank for more. Ten minutes later, we were in proud, and relieved possession of seven of the dark green rubbery radiation suits with matching helmet and masks.

'Let's get back to the train and put these on inside the engine bit,' I said.

We traipsed back to the railway track, and got dressed on board our train. The suits were cumbersome, but they seemed a hundred times more substantial than our thin little NBC ponchos and trousers. And it was heavenly to finally get rid of the horrible respirator. Standing outside in front of our saviour locomotive, we all looked utterly ridiculous, but at least we could now see each others faces, and understanding what people were saying was no longer a problem.

'I'd forgotten how ugly you were,' Chris said to Spike.

'This train did us proud. I'm going to miss it,' said Geoff, patting the side of our locomotive.

'Yeah, well done train,' echoed Spike.

'Come on chaps, let's go into town and see what's what,' I said.

Spike then cleared his throat very loudly, so we all stopped. 'I just thought you'd all like to know that the engine probably derailed at just the right time,' he said.

'You're right Spike. If it hadn't come off when it did, we would still be wearing our issue NBC suits that were useless and we would be heading back towards a nuclear hell,' I said.

That night, we slept in the station waiting room. It was full of dust and discarded food and bottles and there was a handbag lying on the floor. Geoff and Spike had ventured into town for a few hundred yards, and come across a school building where they had found a group of what they took to be teachers lying dead in their chairs in the staff room. There was nothing to be said.

In the morning, we all had a few biscuits, and then prepared to search for a new means of moving away from this catastrophically irradiated spot. I thought we might find a bus or a lorry. Anything would do, just as long as we could get as far away from the east as possible. As we were walking away from the station Geoff said, 'I know what we should have done.'

'When?' said Colin

'Instead of bombing each other, we all should have got together and just bombed all the fucking politicians,' and then he was quiet.

Whilst Colin and Geoff went off to look for suitable vehicles, Spike and Chris went into the yard to try and locate a train that we could uncouple and drive to London. But when the latter two returned after about forty minutes, it was bad news. A few trains had been deliberately derailed, but whilst most of the remainder were in good order, none of them were on a track that appeared to be set to the main line. There was a signal box, but everything was again operated electrically. The three of us then sat despondently, and waited for the others to return. It was at least two more hours before we heard the sound of a car engine. Coming down the road towards us was what was patently a taxi. Green, rubber clad arms were waving from both front windows. Colin was driving and he was grinning as he braked hard next to us. Geoff was motioning at us to get in.

'Quickly everyone, there's hardly any fuel left in this bugger,' said Colin.

We all crammed in and headed back the way they had come from.

'Have we got a surprise for you,' Colin said as we accelerated along a side street.

Seconds later, off to our right, I saw our surprise. 'It's an airport!' I shouted

'Fraid not, skip. We had a look there, it's just for light aircraft and there aren't any,' said Geoff.

'Bollocks,' said Spike, echoing my thoughts exactly.

CHAPTER NINE

We drove on past row upon row of awful looking blocks of flats, and not one single window seemed to be unbroken. After another two or three minutes Colin announced, 'This is an airport!'

And it was indeed an airport. A real civilian airport with taxis outside, and Aeroflot signs adorning the big, cracked windows. There were only two bodies that I could see. One of them looked like a policeman.

'Fucking hell!' yelled Spike.

'Bloody hell boys, well done!' I said.

We drew to a halt outside the terminal building, and because it looked as though the roof of the terminal had collapsed, we walked through the broken security fence onto the apron. Off to our left was a burnt out Tupolev Tu154, but in front of us were two Tu134s and a great big Ilyushin IL86.

'Oh my God! Manna from heaven!' I cried.

'Yes indeed, skipper. Do you want to check out the big girl, whilst we do the little ones?' suggested Colin.

Without even bothering to answer, I went over to the huge airliner, but as soon as got within fifty feet of it, I could see there were no steps for it.

'Does it have airstairs Colin?' I yelled back.

'Christ knows skipper. Spike!' he shouted over his shoulder.

'Yes sir!' he shouted back.

'Let the others do the planes. You go and find some stairs for the big one!' bellowed Colin, pointing at the Ilyushin.

'Righty ho,' he replied and ran off towards the hangar.

Whilst I awaited my steps, I had a look at the airport from my vantage point. It was decent size, a bit like Bristol in overall dimensions, and it had two big hangars. The terminal itself was fairly normal, but in the middle of it was a building that looked like a block of flats, set at ninety degrees to the rest of it , and with the control tower stuck on the end nearest to the apron. It rather looked as if it had been dropped in as an afterthought. I saw that between the cracks in the concrete slaps of the apron, weeds were growing profusely. I grabbed one, but it wouldn't budge. It seems that humans, animals and insects are done in by radiation whereas some plants seem to positively thrive.

I inspected the outside of the aircraft and it was in remarkable condition considering it must have been on the ground for at least eighteen months. However, the tyres were inflated and there were no weeds growing up around the wheels like there were on the two smaller airliners. I turned as a heard commotion, to see Spike and Geoff lugging a set of steps towards me. Chris soon joined them and ten Colin came over. He had a grave expression. 'Both flight decks have been machine-gunned. Or at least, that's what it looks like,' he said breathlessly.

'Never mind,' I said.

'This one looks okay though,' he said.

'Yeah. Look at the other two all covered in weeds and mould and crap. This one looks like it landed yesterday,' I said.

Colin walked the length of her and came back nodding. 'You're right. She's only just in.'

'Here you go, skip. Steps,' said Spike as he struggled with the others to get the brake engaged.

They manoeuvred it up to the front door and there was a general air of resigned amusement when we realised that the steps were at least two feet too short for the door.

'Oh, for fuck's sake!' said Spike. 'Don't worry. We'll manage,' I said.

And manage we did. The door opened easily, and while the others climbed aboard, Colin told me to wait until last. They then all hauled me up into the aeroplane. The exertion on my knee of being pulled on board caused a searing pain to shoot down my leg. I was still rubbing it when I saw that the chaps had all gone to the left, towards the flight deck. As I turned to enter, Chris pushed past me and walked towards the back. He sat himself down in the first seat in the cabin and put his head between his knees. I then saw what had made him react in such a way. On the floor by the cockpit door was a little girl. Her face looked like a porcelain doll. Her dress was grubby and streaked with dirt, but otherwise she looked like a little girl who had just fallen down. Geoff was kneeling next to a boy of perhaps ten or eleven who was sitting on the floor in front of the jump seat. His eyes were wide open and he had flecks of vomit running from his mouth, and the floor around him was covered in dried liquid patches. The other two chaps were standing next to the occupants of the flight crew seats. In the captain's seat was a man. He was wearing a white shirt and his head had lolled to the right. In the copilot's seat was a woman who wore a pale blue blouse. She was slumped forward. Both of them had their oxygen masks on. Colin had his finger up against the man's neck. 'I can't feel anything through these poxy gloves,' he said.

'I don't think it's worth it Colin,' I said.

'Shall I check her?' said Spike, looking at me and with his hand on the woman's mask. I just nodded. As he lifted the mask, a collection of dark blood and vomit poured out through the gap. He recoiled, and pushed past me to get off the flight deck, leaving the woman's mask sitting on her lap. Colin then took off the man's mask and a similar thing happened. His eyes were partially open and were red. There was congealed blood in his ear and thick dark blood was trickling very slowly from his mouth.

'We've got to get them out and try and get this thing going,' I said to Colin.

He was staring at the woman's face, and I could see tears in his eyes as he left the flight deck.

I stood there for a moment, trying to work out what it was I was seeing. The aeroplane wasn't like the others at the airport. It was clean; only recently arrived. The man had to be a commercial pilot, because no novice could fly this type of aircraft. And I supposed the woman was his wife, and they had brought their children along. They were killed by the radiation which was already lethal, and had now been added to by the fallout from our bombs on Sakhalin. Had they flown in because this was their home town or had he somehow managed to get the aeroplane out of one of the hangars here, planning to fly elsewhere? Whatever the reason, that's why it wasn't covered in weeds and grime. I picked up the girl's body and I was amazed at how light she was as I began walking with her to the back of the cabin. Colin and Geoff were sitting in the front row of seats. Both were staring out of the windows. As I passed the passenger door, I saw that Spike and Chris were now back on the ground, and were walking away, back towards the terminal. Colin briefly looked up as I walked past. I put the little body in the aisle seat in the middle of the very back row and then returned to the chaps at the front. I pulled down the crew jump seat in front of them and sat down. They looked up. 'Boys. We've got to get on,' I said. Colin nodded. 'I know it's awful, but we've got to think of ourselves now. There's nothing we can do for them.'

'This isn't right skip,' said Geoff in a weak voice.

'I know.'

'Where are the other two?' asked Colin.

'They went back to the terminal. Let's leave them a while, eh?' I suggested.

I returned to the flight deck with Geoff, and together we got the boy onto his shoulders, and he was carried to the back where we sat him next to the girl.

'Brother and sister? asked Geoff.

'I suppose,' I said. Then, with Colin's help, the three of us managed to drag the woman out of her seat. It was covered in blood and sticky substances and I tried to imagine how foul that sort of death must have been. With a fair bit of effort on my part, we pulled the woman along the floor to the back to be with her children.

Colin retrieved the bag with the Geiger counter, and put the last fresh sample tube on it, and then he switched it on. The needle shot hard over to the right. We just looked at each other, and he threw the device onto a seat. As we headed back to the front, Colin called out and Geoff and I joined him at the door. A tanker lorry was trundling towards us, and from the frantic waving coming from the left hand window, it was obvious that Spike and Chris had found us a fuel truck. They pulled up under the right wing and began unravelling the hoses.

'Can you fill this thing up?' Colin shouted down.

'Week two of training. Rudimentary stuff. It might all be in gibberish, but it's the same principle,' replied Spike as he connected the earthing strap.

'Guys, before you do that, can you come up here and help us move the pilot please,' I said.

Spike and Chris looked at each other briefly, and then clambered up the steps and lifted themselves in.

Colin shooed me away as I was about the enter the flight deck. 'You did the girl. They haven't done anything yet,' he said.

I watched as they struggled to get him out of the seat, and try as hard as they might, there was nothing they could do to make the man's exit graceful. Eventually, they dragged him, feet first, down the back to be with the rest.

'Can you cover them with blankets lads,' I shouted down.

When it was done, Spike started rummaging around in the overhead bins.

'What are you looking for?' I asked.

'Plastic sheets or something for the seats. They shit themselves, and there's blood all over the place,' he said as he pulled the protective sheets from around some blankets and headed forward.

During the next half an hour or so, the chaps went about cleaning up the flight deck. They tore out the crew oxygen masks and pipes, and then used a fine water spray on the yokes and the panel. They then put plastic on the seats, and covered that with folded blankets. Once they were finished, it actually looked almost presentable.

'It'll be funny if we can't get it started after all this eh skip?' said Spike.

'Hilarious,' said Colin. And then he came over and sat down with me. He had a folder.

'What have you got?' I asked.

'These were the approach plates he was using. He did fly in here, and from his map, it looks like they took off from Sakhalin,' he said, showing me the paperwork.

'So, they escaped from one hell, straight into another,' I said.

'Yep,' replied Colin.

'How did he ever land it in his condition?' I said.

'I don't know. I suppose you do anything for your family, don't you,' he said.

Over the next hour, Spike and Geoff filled the tanks to the brim, and then we tested the electrics. Colin's basic Russian language skills didn't stretch to complicated flight deck instruments, but the whole thing was fairly well laid out, and most of it was obvious anyway. The primary instruments were identical to ours, and appeared to be working.

Colin's escape and evasion pack didn't include this airport or, indeed the region, but we did know roughly the direction we wanted to go.

'So, up to find NATO then, Ollie?' he said.

'I reckon so, don't you?' I replied. 'We'll fly due north then,' he said.

Whilst Colin and I went through what we thought were the correct preflight checks, and Geoff did the same with his Engineers panel, the others had tied a rope to the stairs and had rocked them back and forth until they toppled to the ground. Spike said he would stay at the open door to make sure they didn't snag as we taxied.

Colin opened the high pressure cocks, turned the starter to 'Start,' and then, as the number four hummed into life, he began pushing the fuel lever slowly forward. When the engine sounded as though it was established, he turned the starter to what we hoped was 'Run,' and then we waited. Everything was powering up nicely, and we then set about checking that the control surfaces and the flaps were functioning correctly. Once we were satisfied that we'd got it right, we started the remaining three engines.

Even though there were only the five of us living crew on board, the aircraft needed a lot of throttle to get moving, and I was very careful to cut back to idle power as we moved off, so as not to have the stairs flying up into the tail from the jetwash. Spike yelled back that we were clear, and I advanced the thrust levers to taxi out onto the runway. There was a good sized turning area, so I lined her up with the wind and we ran the engines up to full power. There was an enormous roar, much louder than the VC10, and more akin to a Vulcan, but everything seemed to be okay. Colin then took over, and we did a fast taxi run to the end of the runway to get into the wind. I set the flaps, and told Colin that I had control.

'It'll be tight, Ollie,' said Colin reassuringly.

'I know,' I said, as he pushed the thrust levers to the stops. We really weren't making very good progress for the first quarter of the runway but then she began gaining speed quite well. V1, the point where I was committed to fly, was way beyond where I had hoped, but now there was nothing else I could do.

'Faster!' yelled Geoff from behind.

I could feel that the rudder was now effective, and she finally felt as though she wanted to fly. Just before the point where the nose wheel was about to run onto the gravel at the end of the runway, I hauled the yoke back into my lap and we rotated. The moment that I knew we were airborne; I pushed the yoke forward so that we climbed at as shallow a rate as possible but eventually, we actually achieved a positive rate climb.

'Gear up,' I said, and Colin retracted the undercarriage. I looked across at him and even through his helmet mask, I could see that he was quite grey. I was sweating like a pig and desperately wanted to wipe my forehead.

'Christ, Ollie. Don't ever do that again,' he said and patted my leg. I winced because he had managed to smack my rotten new knee.

Geoff lent across and patted my shoulder.

Spike entered the flight deck and said, 'I think we may have collected some runway lights back there skip.'

'Who cares,' I said. 'If we did, we'll just have to land wheels up.'

'Righty ho,' he said, and slunk off into the cabin.

As we climbed out, we could see that the allied bomb had hit to the south of the city. Where once the river had obviously run as a single channel, now there were dozens of little tributaries spinning off from a huge lake which had formed in the crater. The impact seemed to have all but obliterated the whole area. I presumed that this had contained military or industrial sites. 'Have you still got your Boys Own map of the world?' I asked Colin.

'Yep,' he replied, handing it to me.

I examined the crumpled pages almost immediately hatching a plan. 'You have control,' I said.

'I have control,' he replied.

As we climbed up to our cruise altitude, with the altimeter disconcertingly showing metres instead of feet, I calculated our options for landing in the NATO held area to the north east.

'Colin, if they haven't got enough fuel, or any fuel, we're going to be stuck in Russia for the rest of our lives,' I said.

'What do you suggest?, he replied. 'Well, it's not only in the wrong direction for home, but it's going to be terrible up there, isn't it,' I added.

'Yep, full of soldiers and sick Russians,' said Colin.

'Exactly. So we've got four thousand miles of fuel for certain, and maybe, if we're lucky, four and a half,' I told Colin.

'That's no use for home though is it,' he replied.

'No. Not for home. Norway,' and with this, he perked up.

'I went to Tromso once on an exercise. Nice big runway,' he said.

'What do you think?' I asked.

'You're in charge, Ollie,' he said, unhelpfully. I saw that the pilot's public address microphone hadn't suffered the fate of most of the rest of the flight deck, in that it appeared to be blood free and clean. I picked it up and made my first ever airline pilot announcement. 'Ladies and gentlemen. After considerable thought, we have decided to refuel in Norway instead of the arse end of Russia,' I said feeling very pleased with myself. There were 'hoorays' from the cabin.

'Seven and a half hours, Ollie,' said Colin.

'Splendid,' I replied.

During the cruise, we tried our shortwave radio and the aircraft's equipment, but there was nothing but static on all channels. After that, we settled into an almost normal flight routine. Colin and I took it in turns as pilot, whilst Geoff kept an eagle eye on his engine and pressurisation instruments. Spike and Chris remained in the cabin and got some well deserved sleep. When it was my turn to take control again, about three hours into the flight, I sent Colin back to get some rest, and Chris took his place.

The next thing I remember, was waking up with a jump. I looked across at Chris and he was fast asleep as well. I turned and saw that Geoff too, was out for the count. I had slept for an absolute age, as we were now only an hour out from Tromso, which meant that below us we were almost in friendly territory. As the autopilot was doing its job perfectly well, I slid the seat back and stretched my legs in the cabin for a while. I walked past the deeply sleeping Colin and Spike, and went back to look at our family. The blankets had all slipped down and their poor faces looked back at me through their bloodshot eyes. I covered each of them up again, and made sure that the blankets came up over their heads and then I tucked them in behind.

With that done, I returned to the flight deck and settled back in. When we were sixty miles out from Tromso, I reduced the throttles to idle, and set the autopilot into a gentle descent. I could see the little island that the airport sat on even from this distance, and its shape reminded me of a slipper. I could see the airport from twenty miles out, so I started the turn to line us up for an approach. It then occurred to me that a Russian or Chinese bomb could have taken out the airport or the Norwegians could have made the tarmac unusable or blocked it somehow. I supposed that I would find that once we were down low enough, although it looked okay from where we were.

Soon we were at ten miles, and stabilised at five thousand feet, which I knew was too high, but I could see that it was a decent sized runway, so I wasn't bothered. I had dropped the flaps to twenty degrees, and as we passed the five mile point, I lowered the undercarriage. Despite Spike's suggestion that I might have torn the wheels off, I got three green lights and then I put in full flap. The runway appeared to be clear of obstructions, and as we passed over the threshold, I could see a couple of refuelling trucks parked near the terminal building. I closed the throttles and we touched down very nicely, followed by a bit of reverse thrust and some moderate braking and I yelled out. 'Welcome to Tromso!'

Chris snapped awake and hit himself in the face with his hand as he struggled to work out where the hell he was.

'Bloody hell!' exclaimed Geoff, at which point Colin and Spike re-entered the flight deck.

'I'm so sorry, Ollie. I never meant to fall asleep,' said Colin.

'Don't worry boys. I enjoyed it,' I said, genuinely meaning it. I taxied towards the fuel trucks and shut down. 'How do we get down?' asked Colin.

'Ah, I've worked that out,' said Spike. 'Whilst you were all sleeping,' and he continued, ignoring the scoffs, 'I looked at the crew instructions booklet and found a diagram that tells me that we've got airstairs on the cargo deck.'

'Well done Spike,' I said.

'Well get them open then,' said Colin tersely. Once the stairs were deployed, we all left the aircraft, and whilst Spike and Geoff went to get fuel, the rest of us walked to the terminal building.

'I suppose it's possible there are people actually alive up here,' said Colin.

'I don't think so,' said Chris pointing at signboard propped up by the airside entry door. It was written in Norwegian and English. 'Contaminated area' was all it said, but that was enough.

'Shame that, skip; I thought we might be able to lose these stupid suits once we got here,' said Chris.

'Not if we're getting back on that heavily contaminated aeroplane chum,' I said, and he looked crestfallen.

The terminal was deserted, but appeared to be very clean and tidy. I don't really know what we were looking for. There were plenty of chocolate bars and crisps and things in the shop, but we couldn't touch any of it. We went upstairs to where all the airline and security offices were and they all had reams of paper lying around on the floor. But there were no bodies and no sign that anyone had been near the place for ages.

'Let's go,' I said and we headed back to the aeroplane.

The chaps had refuelled within forty minutes and driven the truck back to the front of the terminal building. Once we were all back on board, we closed up the doors and retracted the stairs and then Colin got the engines started.

'I'm happy to do this one, skipper,' he said.

'All yours, old boy,' I said.

Once we were airborne I made sure that Spike was broadcasting nonstop on the distress frequency and listening in on the shortwave channels. Satisfied that my crew were all doing what they were meant to, I let Chris take my seat and I got my head down in the cabin. I knew I had about two and a half hours before we reached Scotland, so I shouted forward to be woken before we started our descent. When I woke, I realised that Colin had got his revenge. We were clearly at no more than twenty thousand feet and we were descending very gently and were in a left bank. I walked to the flight deck and was about to give him a giant bollocking, but stopped in my tracks. In front of our aircraft, and just slightly off to our left was a Hawker Hunter from my Royal Air Force.

'Oh, hello skipper. Good snooze,' said Colin with a stupid grin on his face.

'How?' I asked.

Colin turned and said, 'They said they heard us on 121.5, and scrambled to see who we were. They didn't believe we were RAF until I recognised that Hunter's markings.' At that he pointed to an aircraft off to our right that I hadn't seen. 'He's Baz Cummins and he was my CFO on the Victor OCU.'

'Yes, and...?' I said.

'I just said 'hello Baz' over the radio and eventually he recognised me,' Colin said, and he leaned back and squeezed my arm.

'Yeah, but we've got to go to fucking Wales first though skip,' said Spike.

'Oh yeah,' said Colin, 'That's right. They said they don't want a filthy contaminated Ruskie jet polluting their clean countryside, so we're putting down at Valley, and then we've got to go for a shower,' he added.

Colin asked if I wanted to land it, but I let him do the honours. As we set up for the approach, we saw the unmistakeable profile of two Soviet bombers parked on the apron in front of the operations building.

'What the fuck?' was Spike's helpful comment.

CHAPTER TEN

After we had taxied in and shut down, I discovered that we had actually been intercepted by four Hunters and six Hawks. I learned later, that we were approximately two minutes from being shot down. Which proves, once and for all, that it's not what you know.

We were given a frequency to dial into the short wave radio, and were told that as we were in a zone of moderate contamination, we were to find the railway line and walk along it until we got to a station that was called Rossniger, or something like that, and then ditch everything except our dog tags, underclothes and boots. We were told not to take our footwear off but to cut away our flying suits around them. Once that was done, we had to walk to the next station which was named Ty Croes, go over the level crossing and walk north along the road until we reached a pub called the Queens Head.

We did as we were told and took off our life saving suits, making a special point of not letting any part of the outside material touch our skin. We very quickly regretted it, as the weather was terrible, and wandering around north Wales in our underpants was not only an unedifying experience, it was also bad for our health. Worse still, the stupid pub was locked, so we just sat in the garden like lemons for an hour getting soaked. With the relentless drizzle and penetrating cold making me wish that I was dead, I wondered how we were finally going to be delivered from our little bit of hell. And at that very moment, a wonderful sight appeared over the horizon from the south east. The unmistakeable shape and sound of an RAF Chinook swooping low over the trees and coming in to land in the field opposite the pub.

A crewman climbed out, and stood to the side of and just in front of the aircraft with his hand raised as if to say 'stop.' After the engines had shut down, he came towards us and told us to wait as he had special clothing for us to wear for the trip back home. He went to the rear of the helicopter, and retrieved some boxes which he brought over to us.

'Gentlemen, please come forward, one at a time, take off your underpants and throw them in here,' he said indicating a yellow box.

'Next, take off your identity tag and place it in here.' An orange box.

'Then, please remove one boot, throw it to the left and place your foot in this trough. I will then pour liquid over your foot. You will then repeat the process with your other foot.'

So that's what we did. The pants got chucked away, the boots got chucked away, our dog tags were washed and we each had our feet decontaminated. We then had to stand on a soggy blue pad on the ground and put our clean feet straight into the new protective suit. These were great big yellow rubber all in one things that made us look like bananas. The helmet section dangled over the backs of our necks and had to be hauled up and over and then secured with velcro and a collection of heavy material strips. The helmet was very good and the clear visor meant we could see out very well.

Once we were all dressed, and it took an awfully long time, the crewman walked over to me, halted and snapped to attention. 'Sir, it's a pleasure to have you back. If you and your crew would be kind enough to follow me please,' he said, shaking each of the guy's rubber hands as they boarded. We entered the helicopter via the rear loading ramp and were shown to our seats and strapped in by the crewman. As soon as that was completed, he gave us back our now cleansed dog tags, closed the ramp door and we lifted off.

The flight lasted well over an hour, and after we had landed, the crewman waited until the engines had run down before he opened the rear door. Waiting outside were a group of men and women who looked very purposeful indeed. We followed them into a single storey building where we were each shown to a large cubicle. It was like something you might expect to find in a family changing area at a public swimming pool and there was a fine mist of some liquid spraying from the walls, ceiling and floor. A loud man's voice told me to remove my suit and deposit it into the chute at the side of the cubicle. 'This is a decontamination shower gentlemen. It's a little cold but you can have a hot one straight after. Please remain in here until you are told to leave,' said a voice from behind. The fine mist now turned into a rushing, gushing avalanche of what smelled like disinfectant and it bloody well was cold. I reckon I was in it for about ten minutes before the water flow stopped.

'Please now leave your cubicle by the rear door'

I left the decontamination chamber and entered a little anteroom. The voice then told me to put on the towelling robe which hung on a peg by the door of the room and then exit.

We all emerged at the same time and entered a very large block and were shown to what appeared to be more conventional showers. This was much, much nicer. Lovely and warm, and with plenty of soap and shampoo in handy dispensers. When those went off after ten or so minutes, we were each handed a razor and some shaving foam, and when we had all finally scrapped off our week old beards, we were given a big white towel and another dressing gown and told to follow one of the staff.

We entered a long corridor and were each shown into a room, and the door was closed to enable us to dry ourselves in privacy. I put on the dressing gown and looked around. The room contained a sort of doctors examination couch, a table and a chair. A woman's voice from outside asked, 'Are you decent sir?' To which I replied that I was. She then entered the room, 'Mr Marsden, I need to examine you. Is that alright with you sir,' she asked.

'Of course,' I said, expecting it all to be over in minutes.

Two hours later, after I had been measured by what I presumed was a Geiger counter, and had given samples of blood, urine, stools and saliva, I was finally released back into the corridor and shown to another area where a variety of civilian type clothes were laid out on a table. A military looking chap invited me to try on whatever I liked, to see what fitted best. I tried on a number of things, but finally opted for M&S boxers and socks, some lightweight cotton trousers, a rugby shirt and a pair of slightly used, but serviceable deck shoes. As soon as I had finished dressing, I was released into a canteen area. In here was a chap of advanced years who told us that as we had probably eaten very little during our journey, he recommended that we sample the high protein rice based goo that sat on a table in front of us. To be honest, it tasted alright, and it did fill me up quite well, and even the others agreed that whilst it wasn't fish and chips, it would do.

We were then led to another building and each presented with a cup that was filled, almost to the brim, with pills of various shapes, colours and sizes. These were washed down with a disgusting orange-coloured, vomit-flavoured drink.

Three hours after our arrival, the chief medic, a Doctor Banks, joined us at our dining table and sat down. 'Welcome to the Predannack military medical facility gentlemen. Each of your contamination test results is almost identical, so I thought I would let you know them, as a group. You are all showing moderate levels of radiation penetration. This is astonishing low, considering where you have been recently. I would have expected you to be registering much higher readings. However, the level of absorption is higher than most survivors in the UK, but is not a matter for immediate concern. I have to tell you, though, that the long-term effects will lead to a shortened lifespan,' he explained, leaving us to take that on board for a few moments.

I was expecting one of the boys to ask a question or two. But nobody spoke.

'Thank you doctor.' I said on behalf of the crew.

He continued, 'You will be staying here tonight and leaving tomorrow after lunch. I expect that you are all very tired, so please feel free to get as much rest as you like.'

We all went to our little bedrooms straight after our meal of pills and I don't even remember lying down. I was asleep in seconds. When I woke, I had no idea what the time was so I wandered back to the canteen and found that I was the only one there and that it was getting dark. At that moment, my medical examiner from earlier walked in and I suddenly realised that she was utterly beautiful. How I hadn't noticed that before I immediately put down to fatigue.

'May I join you sir?' she asked.

'Of course. Please do,' I replied with a dry mouth.

She knew who I was, so I asked about her. She was Doctor Helen Flint, thirty nine years old, single, originally from Cambridge and beautiful. I added the last bit, not her.

She told me about the facility we were in. The hospital was much bigger than it seemed, stretching to two hundred rooms spread over a site of thirty acres. 'Most of our patients are long-term. Trauma from the war and other psychological injuries are our main concern. We also carry out research projects. You are our first returnees in three months and I think we'll probably be shutting down this reception area and incorporating it into the main unit once you are gone,' she explained in detail.

'I see,' I said stupidly, staring at her lovely blue eyes far too obviously. She laughed. 'What did I say?' I enquired.

'You were staring at me,' she replied not even slightly embarrassed.

'Sorry. It's just so bloody nice to see something beautiful for a change,' I said, also without a hint of embarrassment.

'You're very sweet, sir,' she said getting up.

'Do you have to go?' I asked like a simpering schoolboy.

'Work to do, I'm afraid. I'll see you at dinner though.' And she left so I went outside into the cool early evening and sat on the patio overlooking the very large outside space. It was very calming and naturally, I was asleep again very quickly. I was woken by a clattering and banging of what was obviously cutlery being put on tables, so I walked back in and found my crew already seated, ready for their tea. We were served a chicken stew in a light sauce with mashed potatoes and peas, and then presented with another cup full of pills, although this was washed down with a choice of traditional hot or cold drinks. The crew were all very quiet during the meal.

Dr Flint didn't appear, so at what I was informed was ten o'clock, I returned to my little room and tried to fall asleep. In a disturbing turn of events, I found myself bursting into tears and sobbing uncontrollably for a good many minutes before I decided to get up and have another shower. Having dried off and after putting on the dressing gown, I lay back down and this time I drifted off successfully. When I woke, I felt properly refreshed but also deeply miserable. I have no idea why really. We had survived our landing, travelled across vast swathes of enemy territory and then made it back home. All of us too. I hadn't lost a single man. Sure, we were all going to die sooner than we might have hoped, but then, so was everybody else. I guessed I was just feeling sorry for myself.

I showered again, got dressed and went back to the canteen. Half my crew were scoffing bacon sandwiches out on the patio with the remainder still in bed. It was eight-thirty. We were all up and about by ten and actually getting quite bored. We cheered up no end when we heard, 'Gentlemen, your transport awaits,' from an elderly medic who then guided us outdoors to where a minibus was parked. Before we boarded, Spike went around and spoke to the driver. He returned seconds later with a cigarette for each of us and a lighter. I have never enjoyed a fag so much in my entire life. Needless to say, within minutes of the journey starting, I was fast asleep again, and when I woke this time, I was rather delighted to see that the other four were also lolling around in their seats. We finally stopped in a little place called Bickleigh, which is just south of Tiverton. I had heard of it, but had never visited. It had a lovely looking pub, but unfortunately, our destination was a school which had been requisitioned by the army. Firstly, we were shown into a room with dining tables and chairs and we were given another cup of pills and another cup of orange vomit. Once we had finished, a very young Captain entered the canteen area and asked me to follow him into a small office where I was asked to wait briefly and was offered tea or coffee. Shortly after my drink had been brought to me, an army Colonel entered. He snapped smarty to attention and asked if he could shake my hand. I suddenly remembered that I outranked every single person I was ever going to meet, so I didn't mind his enthusiasm. 'Sir, if I might say, this is a privilege and a pleasure,' he said breathlessly.

'Thank you,' was all I could think to say.

'Now, if I might be so bold, I just need a bit of info on where you went down, how you managed to escape, and to survive, and then we'll get you briefed up on what's what,' said the Colonel.

I wasn't clear what he meant by 'what's what,' but I told him how we had been struck by debris from an exploding aircraft, all about our train ride, and our theft of an aircraft. He was most impressed, and thought that perhaps our escapades would make a 'splendid film.'

I added, that as far as I was concerned, the greatest success of our entire escape had been that our British NBC and Russian rubber suits had seemingly worked so effectively. He agreed with me saying that he had always thought ours were just issued to make the chaps feel safe, but were actually of no use at all. He made a note of it.

There was one very important thing I needed him to do for me.

'There are people on board that aeroplane that deserve a proper burial. Can that be arranged please,' I said.

'I presume they are hugely contaminated, sir?' he replied.

'Yes, hugely.'

The Colonel then debriefed me on the result of our mission. He confirmed that Hawaii had been destroyed, but that we had done an equally good job on Sakhalin. I wasn't convinced the trade offs matched up. America was effectively gone and we had only managed to knock off some soldiers, tanks and submarines. The Royal Navy and USN SSBNs had done most of the work.

He went on to explain that our interception by the Hunters and Hawks wasn't the only time in recent days that our fighter aircraft had been scrambled. Whilst my crew and I were stealing our train in Chita, the two Soviet aircraft we had seen at Valley, a Bison and a Blinder, had flown low into UK airspace, but had allowed themselves to be intercepted by the Hunters that had been scrambled to meet them. Both aircraft were guided to Valley, where they landed successfully. I was then delighted to then hear that the Vulcan that I had sent home did make it back safely. Astonishingly, my remaining two VC10s had also got back in one piece.

'The downside sir, is that none of your TSR2 s or the other Vulcan made it back.' And even though he was still talking, all I could actually think about was those poor bastards in the other aircraft.

'The array of SAMs that the Ruskies had deployed on the island was astonishing. According to the U2 that made it back, there were around sixty launch sites. It's a miracle anyone got back at all. '

The Colonel told me that the only two remaining U2s flying anywhere in the world had been able to confirm that the Royal Navy and USN SSBNs had totally destroyed the Soyuz sites. They had also laid waste to significant parts of the remaining Russian, North Korean and Chinese navies that had congregated around Sakhalin. My chaps and the American and French bombers had destroyed all the remaining naval vessels, tracked vehicles and hundreds of thousands of enemy ground troops. He added that no enemy submarine, warship or landing craft was visible on any of the U2's displays. Our destruction of the enemy was complete. The mission had been a total success.

'You are bloody heroes sir!' and he pushed a report towards me. It contained a list of all the allied aircraft that had survived the mission, where they'd landed, and a précis of the enemy's capabilities.

The French had received three USAF F4 Phantoms, three B52s and a single KC135. Five B52s and an F111 landed in Chile. Britain got two F4s, two B52s, one U2, six F111s and a KC10. All the French Mirage IVs safely recovered to their base with their crew's unharmed. The pilots of the two Soviet aircraft that had landed at Valley had been taken into custody and interrogated, and it transpired that the Bison was a tanker variant, and that the Blinder bomber had not been armed. The Soviet crews confirmed that their forces on Sakhalin had consisted of twenty four Bear bombers, thirty two Bisons (a mixture of bombers and tankers), sixty eight Blinders and seventy three Backfires. All the aircraft had been scheduled to take off from Sakhalin within ten minutes of the missile launch on Hawaii and had clearly not been expecting such a swift response from us. Indeed, their intelligence apparatus had suggested that the NATO allies had no functioning ballistic missile launch capability, let alone submarines. The targets for the Soviet bombers had been the remaining populated areas of France, the UK, Norway, Iceland, Chile and Morocco. Each aircraft had two 2 or 5 Megaton weapons loaded.

It seems that the enemy commanders' vision was that the Soviet-Chinese Empire would find its new home in New Zealand. They had dozens of warships docked in the northern ports of Sakhalin, along with many hundreds of civilian ships for the planned invasion of New Zealand. The majority of all remaining Russian, Chinese and North Korean soldiers, and many of their families, were located in the north of the island. The pilots stated that there had been between eight and twelve million soldiers and civilians on the island. They had been told that only about one million of those were fit enough or likely to survive the radiation doses they had already received, and that they were to start a new life in New Zealand. Around fifty thousand of the most important people wore protective suits day and night, and only removed them for food and visits to the toilet. The sick majority would be left to a miserable death on Sakhalin.

It was about four hours after we had arrived in Bickleigh that we were shown outside to our vehicles. The chaps had got a big seven seat taxi, and I had been given a black staff car. Spike, Geoff, Chris and Colin lined up in front of their vehicle and when I turned to them, they all came to attention.

'Stand easy, you arses,' I commanded.

Colin extended his hand, but I hugged him instead, and then proceeded to do the same with the others. I then stood back, came to attention myself and said, 'Gentlemen, it has been a complete pain in the bottom,' at which, they mercifully, laughed. I was about to let their car go when it suddenly occurred to me that I would very probably never see these guys again. I quickly got out of the car and told the driver to wait before limping over to the seven seater. I got both the drivers together and asked them about their respective local pub knowledge. The rest of my crew watched this from their vehicle with increasing interest.

It turns out that my driver had a brother who knew the landlord of a pub about ten miles away from where we were. Since this particular publican was also a Special Constable, he was, according to my driver, almost certain to open for us.

Our little convoy took less than twenty minutes to reach the Bell and Dragon and the landlord was seemingly overwhelmed not to just have customers, but customers who were to his mind anyway, 'complete heroes.' We shuffled in, slightly embarrassed to be honest, but after the second pint, all the tiredness, worry about our contamination and my fears of being murdered by my wife all simply disappeared.

In the end, we had four pints each, plus a big Cornish pasty and some bloody fabulous pickled herring, cockles and mussels. We sat out in the garden and to be honest, I think all our cares just slipped away in a bit of an alcoholic haze. After three hours at the pub, I finally said my goodbyes to the boys and slipped into my car for the journey back to reality and a damn good thrashing from Anna and a fair few others, I didn't doubt.

CHAPTER ELEVEN

I was feeling extremely nervous as we came down the hill into Dartmouth, and at the point where my driver indicated left to turn into the College, I told him to stop the car. He did, and then he climbed out and opened my door for me. I thanked him very much for his time and told him he could be on his way. He replied that as he was based here, he was actually home, so I told him to go off and do a circuit of town before he came back. I then walked very slowly towards the entrance and as I turned the corner, there was Squadron Leader Paul Maybury pacing around outside the guardroom. He didn't see me, but one of the Royal Marine guards did, so I motioned for him to come over. Even though his SMG was down at his side, I could see that he was ready to level it at me in a second. As he drew closer, he must have recognised me, because he stopped dead in his tracks, stamped to a halt, went through an elaborate transfer of his weapon into his right hip and then slapped his left hand across his body. He then very unhelpfully yelled, 'Sir!'

Before I could say a word, Maybury was on me. He first saluted, then stuck his hand out, but then thought better of it and gave me a big hug.

'God Almighty, Oliver, how are you still alive? You gave us all a fright,' he said in a quite emotional voice.

'What's going on Paul? Why are you lurking about?' I asked.

'To save you embarrassment, old boy. There's a big welcome committee for you at the main house, so I came out to forewarn you,' he said.

As we walked towards the guardhouse, I asked, 'Why is there a welcoming committee?'

He looked confused, 'Because you bombed the buggery out of the Russians, got shot down and then made it all the way back in a nicked aeroplane.'

I stopped and grabbed his arm. I think my voice was a bit panicky at this point, 'I mean, how did you know I was coming back at this precise moment? 'Oh, the army told us you were on your way,' he said. If I ever drew up a Christmas present list, that Colonel was definitely not going to be on it.

Maybury wanted to walk on, but I kept my hand on his arm, 'Who the hell is up there then?' I asked.

'Well, that would be the Prime Minister, the Secretary of State, every high ranking officer from the Army, Navy, Marines and Air Force, all the staff of the College and, of course, your wife,' he replied smiling at me absurdly.

I put my hand up, indicating for him to stay put and then called over the Corporal Guard Commander. I couldn't stop him stamping about and saluting frantically, but after he had calmed down, I asked him if there was a way that the Squadron Leader and I could sneak around the side of the guardroom, and get to the side or back of the main building without being seen from the steps. He said that not only were there a number of paths that were out of view, but that he would personally show us the best way. So, the Corporal, Maybury and I sneaked through the trees, catching glimpses of the assembled masses on the steps at the front of the College. After about five minutes, we had successfully made it to the western edge of the building and our Marine slinked back off to his duties.

'Ready?' said Maybury, as he looked me up and down.

'No,' I replied, and turned towards the back of the building where I knew there were other ways in.

'You can't leave them waiting sir,' said Maybury. 'I'm not Paul,' I replied as we entered the library through the French doors. 'You're going to find Anna and bring her here.'

'But...' was all I allowed him to say.

'And then I'll go straight out. Promise,' at which, he turned on his heels and left the room. It was only a matter of a minute or so before I heard

Maybury's voice in the corridor say '…I had to think of something, and a phone call seemed like a good excuse.' At which point he and Anna entered the library. I smiled and nodded my thanks to Paul as he left.

I looked at my beautiful wife, who I had left seven days ago without saying a word, and she put her hands up to her face and sobbed. She didn't move from the doorway, but simply stood there crying. I went over, put my arms around her and held her tight, and I could feel that she was shivering. She pulled away. 'I am so sorry my darling. I should have told you,' I said feeling even more hopeless and awful than I thought I would.

'I found out from Paul!' she shouted. 'Bloody Paul,' and she punched me on the left shoulder.

'I'm so sorry. I don't know what to say,' I said pathetically. 'And then that bloody Rollo came down to the hotel and told me again,' and it sounded almost as if she wanted to laugh. I chose not to make light of it in case she really decided to really hit me. There was nothing I could say. I looked at her like an idiot and I just mouthed the words 'I'm sorry.' I put my arms around her again, and this time she didn't pull away. After a moment, she put her arms round my neck, and without looking at me said, 'Bastard,' which was absolutely fair enough.

'I've got to go and see all those idiots out the front,' I said. She stepped back, looked at me properly for the first and nodded, 'Okay,' she said, 'I'll wait in the office.'

I went out and found Maybury. He had a jacket which he said I really should put on. 'You look like you've just arrived from Twickenham,' he said. I put it on, and together, Paul and I went out through the library doors and walked to the corner of the building.

'Ready now?' he asked.

'I suppose so,' I replied.

A couple of heads turned towards us as we emerged from around the side of the College but, then turned back. However, after a moment or two, everyone was looking in our direction, and a couple of people started clapping, which was followed by a rising tide of cheers and whistles. The PM strode forward and grasped my right hand and patted my shoulder. I was surrounded by well-wishers who all wanted to say 'welcome back' and 'well done,' but all I wanted to do was run away. There was no getting away from these people, and eventually I had to accept that I was stuck with them. After fifteen or twenty minutes of relentless handshaking, backslapping and a few hugs and kisses, we all went inside to the mess bar. The stewards were awkwardly clapping whilst standing to attention, and then they began pouring glasses of champagne. The PM shouted for quiet, and then spoke to the assembled masses about how our deliverance was a blessing from God, and that we had saved the free world from tyranny. In the finest traditions of great British homecomings, after about an hour of drinking and chatting and congratulations, people started splitting off into their little groups, and the main reason for the celebration was forgotten. It was round about this point that Anna came into the mess. If it had been earlier, doubtless, everyone would have gone quiet, expecting her to come over and kick me in the nuts, but no one even seemed to notice except Maybury, who made one of his tactical withdrawals. She came over to me, grabbed my hand, kissed me on the cheek and said, 'Bastard,' again. Which was still fair enough.

We were then approached by a flustered, but surprisingly chipper looking Maybury. 'Oliver, sir, there are some people on the steps who would like to see you,' he said.

'Who now!' I asked feeling that I couldn't take much more of this.

'No, you'll like this. Really,' he said.

'Oh come on,' said Anna, grabbing my arm and hauling me out of the mess.

When we got outside, the College steps were crowded with my engineering team and the Hunter and Hawk pilots who had guided us into Valley. There was an awful lot of noise and I couldn't avoid walking straight into it. As they sang 'For he's a jolly good fellow,' I grinned like an idiot. I knew there were tears in my eyes, but I didn't care. These were my real heroes; the chaps who saved my neck, either by keeping

153

the aircraft safe for us to fly, or who were with me at the end of my most ridiculous ever adventure. I loved them all dearly, and I couldn't help but get caught up in the emotion of the moment.

I called Maybury over and told him to inform the chief mess steward that the drinks were on me. A couple of chaps overheard this and once their cheering has subsided, and as I was about to go back into the building, a figure approached. 'Twenty one hundred hours sir. Roast pork, apple sauce and more cracking than you can shake a stick at.'

Of course, it was the chef from the mess. 'Great,' I replied, and then added, 'Really great, thanks.' He seemed very pleased, and so was I.

Whilst everyone else went into the mess to get sozzled, Anna and I went into my office where we talked for ages, or rather, she talked at me for ages, principally about what an utter shit I was, and how if I ever, ever did anything like that again, she would cut my dangly bits off and then kill me. I admitted that I was an utter shit, and agreed that my testicles were hers to dissect, if I ever did do anything like it again. Which I then added, I wouldn't. Ever. She then told me that I looked ridiculous in my 'borrowed' clothes and went and got me some more suitable attire from my limited selection of civilian clobber in the office bedroom. Once I had dressed again, she finally gave me a hug and kiss that implied that she wasn't in any immediate rush to murder me, and we went to the mess to join the others.

The roast dinner, as it turned out was utterly and totally fabulous. I had never tasted meat so tender or crackling so crackly. I looked around the mess at all my colleagues, from the senior ranks right down to my mechanics, and it struck me that it didn't matter whether you bombed the enemy, cooked the food for the base personnel, guarded the gate, fixed the aeroplanes or sorted the post; everyone was important. Everyone was as important as the next. I called Paul Maybury over, and asked him to get the communications cell to send a telex of congratulation on my behalf to the French Mirage IV crews for their superb efforts.

It was late in the evening when Anna said that she thought we should stay overnight at the College, which is when I looked at my watch. It was gone eleven, and I realised that I was shattered. By then, some people had left, but the mess was still very lively, and I could see that for some, it was going to be an extremely long night.

Anna and I left at that point and were quickly snuggled up in the little double bed in the office bedroom and I fell into a delicious deep sleep within minutes.

In the morning I woke at seven, shaved and showered and, after breakfast in the still very untidy mess, I saw Anna off when she walked back down into town. I then went back to the office, and I had barely sat down when Paul Maybury entered with piles of documents, reports and telex messages. He then told me that both the King and the Cabinet wanted to see me at a joint gathering the next day. Then his expression changed dramatically, and I wondered what on earth was wrong.

'What. What is it?' I asked.

He cleared his throat. 'There is somebody here who is very keen to see you sir,' he replied sombrely.

'Who?'

'A Doctor Macmillan,' he answered.

'I don't think I know him,' I replied, trying desperately to work out who he could be.

'He's your Chief Aviation Medical Officer and the man that grounded you.'

'Shit,' I said

'He's in the library waiting for you.'

'Why for God's sake? I said.

'Because when he called, he ordered me to tell him the minute you got back,' said my Adjutant, slightly sheepishly.

'And you did!' I shouted.

'He outranks me'

Before I could reply, a man who I took to be the doctor walked into my office.

'I chose not to knock, sir. I thought you might try and hide under the desk,' and he wasn't smiling.

The Adjutant fled the scene and I asked Dr Macmillan to sit. I then offered him a cigarette at which he blanched. 'I am a doctor and you think I smoke?' he said in a slightly raised voice.

'Sorry,' I replied, putting the box back on the desk.

'As it happens, I do,' and he leant forward and took two, putting one in his mouth and the other in his top pocket. He then proceeded to wave my medical file in front of me and asked me if I could read the word in red letters that adorned the front cover.

'Grounded,' I responded.

'Grounded. Bloody well grounded,' he said wagging the file about. 'Do you appreciate what that means?' he then asked slightly sarcastically.

'It means no more flying.'

'Yes. Precisely. No more flying and that is effective from your original grounding on the 5th of August 1983'

'In my defence, you did only ever say that you were considering it. It wasn't actually official…'

But he went on, 'I know why you did it. But, you could have jeopardised your crew and your aircraft. In effect, the whole mission,' his tone was slightly more conciliatory now. Only slightly though.

'I was going to say I won't do it again,' and I smiled weakly.

'Indeed not. You won't. I do accept that my original instruction wasn't clear, and that I may have said that I was only considering it it, but you must have known you couldn't complete a successful operation with your knee as it is? And you're half bloody deaf man!'

'You're right. I'm sorry,' I said.

He looked at my file and said, 'But since you make the very good point that at the time, I didn't make myself clear, we shall assume that your grounding is effective from today,' at which point he smiled and lit the cigarette.

'Thank you very much, and I'm sorry I've been such a nuisance.'

'Oh, it's not just you. There are at least two others who made it back that have grounding notices as well,' and he got up to leave.

'Who for God's sake,' I asked, genuinely shocked.

'You think I'd tell you that,' he said, and before I could respond, he got up, came to attention, and left the room.

At lunchtime, I decided to walk down to the hotel. The streets were relatively busy, and not a soul recognised me, which was just how I wanted it.

I walked along South Embankment and was almost at the Angel when I came to the corner of the Station Cafe. Locked inside a glass case attached to the side wall of the building was a copy of the English Times as the new national was now called. *HEROES!* it read and immediately under that, a picture of me and, as it turns out, my crew from the original War mission. The sub headline was of more interest to me. *Reds Finished Off By Stunning Allied Raids' 'Amazing Escape by our Boys.* I walked into the hotel foyer, at which point the duty manager elbowed the receptionist and they both began clapping. I nodded my appreciation and then looked up to the staircase to see Anna descending. She walked purposefully towards me and stopped very, very close. She put her mouth to my ear and said, 'Bastard.' At which point I kissed her.

I decided that I wasn't going anywhere near the College again for the rest of the day, so I rang Maybury to tell him, and then Anna and I went out into the rear courtyard of the hotel and had some drinks. During the afternoon, we walked around the town and returned to the Angel for an early supper. After a few more drinks, we agreed that our best course of action, because we were both very, very tired, was to go to bed extremely early.

After an excellent night and a splendid breakfast, with perhaps just a little bit too much hovering by the staff, I set off for the office. Three files took centre stage that morning.

The first was from the office of the Prime Minister. It told me that the Cabinet had unanimously agreed my recommendation that we introduce martial law.

The second folder contained the personal files of the aircrew from the Vulcan and TSR2 flights that flew with me to Sakhalin. I already had the details of my downed VC10 chaps. I would write to all their families that very evening.

The last folder was an embossed invite to an audience with the King for later that day, where the principal guests would be the entire bloody Cabinet and almost everyone who still wore a uniform in the whole of Britain.

At lunchtime, I was collected by car from the hotel and taken straight to the Prime Minister's new residence at Prideaux Place near Padstow. It was a beautiful building with manicured gardens and a wonderful array of Autumn flowers. It was also hugely well protected. Long before you got near the property, you came across a guard house and further along the drive were a number of soldiers and vehicles.

I was greeted by a Brigadier at the entrance and he showed me into the hall which immediately struck me as one of the most magnificent rooms I had ever seen. The Prime Minister was there and he was beaming. He shook my hand rather furiously.

'I am sorry to drag all the way down here Oliver, and to pretend that it's some sort of grand welcome back affair, but His Majesty has ordered that you should receive a Knighthood, and knowing how busy you are, I thought I would just take a risk and call you down on the pretence of some war-related banquet and reception or other. I hope you don't mind?' He said that as if it was a fairly common occurrence.

I was utterly speechless, and had barely gathered my thoughts when the far doors swung open and the King entered the room. The ennoblement took a matter of seconds, followed by a ten minute discussion on how terrible the destruction of Hawaii had been, how marvellously our bombers had performed, how brilliantly my crew and I had made our escape, how was the rebuilding of the Services going, and finally, how lovely the flowers were in the garden. We then all sipped champagne and the King left.

In the car back to Dartmouth I just sat quietly pondering the unbelievable sequence of events that had led me from a test pilot's job in Weybridge to being head of the armed forces and a knight. As we swung into the entrance to the college, I began laughing, and I believe my driver thought I might have gone mad. My main regret that day was that I hadn't been given the opportunity to telephone Anna or dad to invite them along.

When I got to the hotel late that afternoon and told Anna, she simply didn't believe me. It was only when I showed her the Polaroid photograph, the little medal and the citation, signed by the King that she believed me. She was completely and utterly thrown when I pointed out to her that she was now Lady Anna Marsden.

Later, when we were in bed, she said that now that I had been knighted, received the Victoria Cross and had saved the civilised world, it was probably time to retire. I laughed, but I knew she was right.

The next day, I called the Prime Minister's office and asked his permission to award my crew from the Russian escapade with the Distinguished Service Order. He told me that if I could find out how to get hold of the medals, they were mine for the giving, and with his blessing. He added, that the King was currently indisposed due to illness, but that he could make the presentation, if I thought it was appropriate. I then phoned the station commander at Exeter and asked him if he could tell me where the chaps were during the next few days and to keep my plan a secret. He said that he would find out where they were and get back to me within the hour, but added that as the DSO is only awarded to officers, Spike wouldn't be eligible. I told him that I intended promoting Spike just prior to the ceremony. I then asked Paul Maybury to use all his skills to find me my medals.

By the end of the day, I had four DSOs being brought over by courier within 48 hours, and a list of my crew's activities for the next two weeks. It transpired, that in ten days time, two squadrons were disbanding and immediately reforming as a new, single entity. It's not uncommon, but it is a very RAF thing. There weren't enough VC10s left to make up two units, so they were merging into one, and relocating to St. Mawgan. The good news was that the chaps would all be wearing their dress uniforms and would be perfectly attired for a medal ceremony and an audience with the Prime Minister. The following day, I called the station commander again and told him that the PM and I would be down to watch the lowering and raising of the colours ceremony. He was immensely flattered, and said that he would make all necessary arrangements. I had decided that I would tell him the real reason on the day. I asked Paul Maybury to track down the chef who had cooked my memorable roast pork welcome home dinner, and I was surprised when the chap telephoned me less than thirty minutes later. I asked if he would be kind enough to liaise with the kitchen team at the base and prepare a special meal for me and my boys for late on the evening of the medal ceremony. He said he would delighted, and would call me back as soon as he had everything arranged. On the appointed day, and having told Anna precisely what my plans were, and having received her complete blessing, the Prime Minister, Paul Maybury, myself and four Distinguished Service Orders set off for the relatively short drive to Exeter Airport. When we arrived, there was a beautifully choreographed 'present arms' for the PM at the guard house and then we swept up to the parade ground, which was actually just a part of the airport, and took our places on a nicely constructed podium. The parade was very well done and even my chaps were marching in time. At the conclusion, the two squadron flags were lowered for the last time and the new flag was raised. The small band then played an awful tune rather well, and then it was my turn.

'Prime Minister, ladies and gentlemen, it gives me great pleasure to be here today to witness the disbanding of two glorious squadrons and their merging into one. I am here to witness the merging of two very fine Squadrons, but I have to confess at this point, that the principal reason for the presence here today of our Prime Minister, is to award gallantry medals to four heroic and magnificent airmen,' and as I looked out into the assembled airmen's faces, I caught a glimpse of Colin Edgecombe as his shoulders very slightly slumped at the realisation. Each of the officers would be promoted, and Spike was to be commissioned into the rank of Flight Lieutenant. 'Can Group Captain Edgecombe, Squadron Leaders Staples and Griffith and Flight Lieutenant Finch take two paces forward.' At the mention of his name, and of his new rank, I am pretty certain I heard Spike say 'Oh fucking hell.' The Warrant Officer running the show did a marvellous job of shouting and stamping about, and eventually the four of them managed to take those two paces forward pretty much together. The Prime Minister and I went down the steps of the podium and waited as Colin managed to get the four of them into coming to attention, marching forward and halting at roughly the same time. I gave the PM the medals and he pinned them on the chap's tunics. He had a brief word with each and then shook their hands. There was then a rousing 'hip hip hooray' from the other airmen. Colin then saluted the PM, ordered about turn, and 'my' boys returned to the squad. The whole parade concluded with a very well executed Present Arms and was then dismissed. I thanked the PM very much for his time, and walked with him to his car. I joined the chaps in the mess at 6 pm, where Spike was being teased mercilessly about his Flight Sergeant's stripes being inappropriate for the officers' mess. I shut them up, shook their hands again and I ordered a round of drinks.

CHAPTER TWELVE

The next two weeks were very quiet. No enemy left to worry about and hopefully, no more sneak attacks. I got word from the Signals Group at the Naval College that HMS Valiant was in contact and I was delighted to know that Maurice Bowen and his crew were safe. I had instructed Bowen that, as long as it didn't put his boat in significant danger, he was to reconnoitre for surviving pockets of Americans around the Hawaiian Islands. He had signalled back stating that they had found no obvious signs of survivors anywhere in or around the archipelago, but that they had made contact with the SSBN USS Monterey, but that her crew had decided to return home. In spite of Bowen's best efforts, they intended sailing to San Francisco and certain death.

In that previous week, whilst Valiant and Monterey had been sailing together, they had established that not a single Soviet, Chinese or North Korean surface or subsurface vessel or any aircraft, aside from those which had 'defected' to the UK, appear to have survived the bombing of Sakhalin Island. HMS Defiant finally made contact as well, and confirmed that she was ten day's out from port and in good condition. On the 22nd May, the United Nations, sitting in Reykjavik, and consisting of just seven member states, confirmed that, to all intents and purposes, the United States of America, the People's Republic of China, the Union of Soviet Socialist Republics, the Democratic People's Republic of Korea, South Korea and Japan had ceased to exist.

I don't think I can ever look a Russian or a Chinaman in the face again. In fact, I won't have to. I've had them all locked up.

It was the 16th August before HMS Valiant docked at Dartmouth, and I went down to meet her. She still looked massive and ugly but, by God she also looked rusty and completely knackered. I was the first to board her from a little ferry boat and Maurice Bowen laughed his head off when he saw me. He had already heard of my escapades in Russia. 'Bloody hell, Ollie; escape and evasion at your age,' he said.

'You look terrible,' I replied.

The Prime Minister was on the quayside waiting whilst the crew were brought across to dry land for the first time in months, and he thanked them for their extraordinary work and personal sacrifices during the war. It was heartfelt, and we all agreed they were absolute bloody heroes. After the PM and his entourage had left, I told Bowen that his whole crew were to get a five day leave pass, effective at noon the following day. He and I then joined the rest of his crew as they shuttled back to the boat, and gathered in the ratings' mess. I had brought over a couple of my chaps from the aerodrome and they had unloaded a half dozen boxes of booze I had made them go and buy from a cash and carry outside town. The crew were doubly happy when I announced that I had temporarily rescinded the standing instruction that kept Royal Navy vessels dry. I then debriefed them on the Sakhalin mission's success and the general state of our world.

Bowen and I then went to his cabin where I spent long, infuriating minutes adjusting my head so that I could hear what he was saying over the constant buzzing of the boat. Or maybe it was my ears.

'I bloody well knew you couldn't resist one last bash at the Soviets,' he had said.

He shut up when I produced a bottle of ten year old single malt which we consumed far too quickly as we discussed his latest patrol and he read the reporting on the Sakhalin and Hawaii attacks. Then we both fell fast asleep; there in our chairs, him, because he was almost certainly exhausted and me, because I was getting old and running out of steam. His cabin clock said 0715 when I woke and I was alone. Bowen re-entered the cabin a few minutes later as I was standing up, stretching my leg and trying to stop it hurting so damn much. Shortly afterwards, we headed to the packed officers mess and enjoyed a very good breakfast. The boat had been reprovisioned as soon as they had arrived back in port, and the fresh eggs, bacon, sausages and bread were in great demand. Baked beans, corned beef, tinned mushrooms and frozen potato cakes had been the normal fare, or at least it was normal within a week of leaving port on a patrol, once all the fresh food had been consumed.

'What's going to happen to my boat then Ollie?' Bowen asked me.

'Well, there's no sign of Vanguard or Victorious being ready this side of nineteen ninety,' I replied.

'Christ, we can't do much more of this, Ollie. We're shagged out and so is the boat.' He meant it. His eyes looked ghostly grey, and he looked completely done in.

'I know. But there doesn't seem to be much rush frankly. There isn't an enemy any more. There's no one left to fire our missiles at'

'Thank Christ. What are you going to do with us then?' He was relieved.

'I had a long discussion with your mate Tony Cooper off the Dauntless and he said it would be perfectly feasible for you and Defiant to be port-based. If there was new threat, which there won't ever be, but if there was, you would have plenty of time to put to sea, submerge and launch,' I suggested.

'That could work. Yes. Can I put in a request that we stay here and Defiant goes to Plymouth.'

As requests go, it made sense. 'Yes Maurice, that's what we'll do.'

After a tour of the reactor area, a look at the SLBM tube array and the torpedo rooms, Bowen took me around the sleeping quarters. My long held belief that submariners were insane was borne out. How anyone could even live, let alone fight a war in those bloody awful cramped conditions, I'll never know. And this was a big boat. I could only imagine what it must have been like during earlier wars.

'There's one last thing I want you to see Ollie. It's quite an eye opener.'

I imagined it was some ultra-secret part of the boat, but I was quite disappointed when we returned to his cabin. Once inside, he locked the door and retrieved a small, deep-red-coloured Top Secret file from his safe.

'I was going to shred this but I rather thought you should see it first and then maybe you can decide what to do with it.' He handed me the folder.

I opened it and inside were perhaps a dozen pages of photocopied paper stapled together at the top. It was a US Navy file and referred to an operation entitled 'Dark Matter.'

'The yanks are very good at operation names aren't they,' I said.

'They were. You'll like it,' said Bowen.

It started out as a bit of a story. Then there were some typed comments, signed by the Commanding Officer of 22 Special Air Service. I then got to the content labelled, *Top Secret. US Eyes Only. NSA Select List*

It showed a clear photo of two very large submarines on the surface probably being resupplied at a dockyard. *Comment: To the eye of a submarine enthusiast or even a US Navy submariner posted to and working on an Ohio Class Ballistic submarine, these appear to be two Ohio Class Ballistic submarines. However, it is clear that the one on the right is not an Ohio in the true sense. It is an adapted, modified version.*

There was a plan diagram of the two boats. *Comment: You will see that the Ohio has twenty four tubes. Each of these carries a ballistic missile with the capability to deliver either single or multiple warheads to their targets.*

There was a photograph. *Comment: This picture shows the other boat, the modified one. You will see that it has only eight missile hatches.*

A photograph. A launch tube and a warhead. *Comment: Each of the missiles is based on a shortened version of the Minuteman launch vehicle utilising only the first stage and each carried only one warhead. The yield of each of those single warheads was limited to forty megatons. Although, according to separate documentation, each device was capable of producing a yield of eighty megatons or up to one hundred. It is explained that anything above fifty is a waste of energy as it will principally go straight upwards and have no additional destructive power?*

A map of the world. *Comment: It would appear that these adapted submarines were designed by the Americans to be the ultimate weapon. In any global nuclear conflict in which the USA is confronting either the Soviet Union or China, these weapons were to be launched, without any consultation with allies and with the single aim of annihilating the enemy. This is confirmed by separate reporting and by contacts within US intelligence structures.*

A diagram. *Comment: The launch targets for Submarine One are shown as Hong Kong, Chengdu, Bangkok, Singapore, Sydney, Omsk and Tashkent.*

A diagram. *Comment: The launch targets for Submarine Two are shown as Leningrad, Kiev, Tehran, Khartoum, Addis Ababa and Ankara.*

A diagram. *Comment: The launch targets for Submarine Three are shown as Peking, Shanghai, Astana, Bombay, Madras, Perth, Tokyo and Delhi.*

A diagram. Comment: *The launch targets for Submarine Four are shown as Dakar, Lagos, Windhoek, Berlin, Rome, Madrid and London.*

A map with a piece of tracing paper taped at the top edge. When flipped over it had written on it *Likely fallout patterns. Comment: You will see that the fallout over China and Japan merged as do the ones in western and eastern Europe. They in turn link up with the Russian fallout. It seems that the American intentions are to destroy their enemies and all those supposed allies who pose a future economic risk to them. According to my contacts, they have long been aware that their global influence is waning and elements within the Administration now feel threatened. This is their response. Whilst no confirmation has been sought, sources state that prevailing winds had been studied in minute detail and targets chosen because of the almost complete certainty that every square inch of the planet, excepting north, central and the northern reaches of South America would either be destroyed by blast damage of would ultimately be infected with fatal radiation doses. US air and ground forces then intended to sweep southwards with the aim of subsuming the entire continent into the United States. Canada would be offered the opportunity to join the Union. If they did not agree, they were to be invaded.*

I was silent for a fair while; I can tell you. Dumbfounded would best describe it. The Yanks were going to kill us all. Or at least, some Yanks were planning to do it.

'So when you left port for war, you knew that we might actually be attacked by the Americans rather than the Soviets and Chinese. Or even as well as?' I exclaimed.

'Yep. Sworn to secrecy. Our top brass said there was nothing we could do. Four of our attack boats were actually off the States rather than anywhere near Russia or China. We were as likely to launch against Uncle Sam's poxy boats as we were against the Reds' explained Bowen.

'But there weren't enough bombs there to actually wipe everyone out. It would have been a long game, would it?' I said

'Yeah, definitely. A slow, creeping radioactive cloud spreading across the world. And then anywhere that wasn't properly done in; a secondary attack. They could take their time and surgically remove any country they wanted; when they wanted. ,' added Bowen

'But they didn't do it,' I said.

'No. Apparently, the FBI discovered the existence of the programme and arrested all those involved in its inception and half the high ups in the CIA. It was bloody mayhem by all accounts. Almost three thousand people from Admirals and Air Force Generals through to Senators and Congressmen were locked up' said Bowen.

'Then what?' I asked.

'The whole programme was going to be closed down and the ships decommissioned and broken up. But that hadn't happened by the time the war started'

'It's possible then, that the Yanks actually used those boats and those missiles on the Soviets and Chinese' I suggested.

'Almost without question. In the end they came good'

I left Valiant with the file inside my coat and once back in my office, I sat staring at it for long minutes. I then pressed the intercom button and told Maybury that I was about to burn some extremely sensitive papers, that he wasn't to come anywhere near the office, and then he was to get in here with one of his cigars lit as soon as I told him to. I took out the photocopied pages, tore then into pieces and placed them and the folder in my metal bin. I then lit it and got up and opened the window. I whizzed the embers around with my letter opener and finally called in Maybury who filled my office with cigar fumes.

'Very secret then, sir' he commented.

'Very,' I replied.

'Now, you know that I read all your correspondence?' said Maybury, out of the blue.

'Yes. Of course I do,' I replied, slightly concerned.

'Which includes the report of your levels of contamination from your Russia escapade,' he elaborated.

'Okay. So you know that my crew and I got a bit more than is advisable in times like these,' I replied, giving him a look that I hoped might convey my real feelings. There was definitely and awkward silence.

'We're leaving it at that then are we?' he asked.

'We are Paul. We are,' I added.

'Does Anna know?' he asked.

'No. And she mustn't. I could go on for years yet'

'Right.' Paul Maybury took a few more gargantuan sucks on his cigar and blew the smoke around the room. He gave me a weak smile and then left.

Bowen did later ask what I did with the SAS file but apart from telling him it was destroyed, we never discussed it again.

It occurred to me that I had been privy to two of the most extraordinary documents ever produced. A detailed plan for the cessation of Nazi hostilities in western Europe and now, a scheme by the Americans to wage war on the entire world not just the communist states.

Now back at the college, and I assumed for good, I made the final arrangements for the Care and Maintenance crew to board the Valiant, and was pleased to see that amongst the temporary replacements were two women volunteers. Very cheering.

I was just thinking of heading home one evening when the Adjutant knocked and entered. He presented me with what appeared to be a very hastily prepared report. At the same time that I had been aboard Valiant, there had been a civic reception for the crew of the recently returned Defiant in Plymouth. Now it was either terrible planning or just bad timing, but when the terrorist attack took place, the Deputy Prime Minister, the Mayor and most of the other dignitaries had already left the site. Four men and one woman opened fire with a variety of small arms and managed to kill six bystanders and a constable before all were shot dead by the army and police. Special Branch went into overdrive, and fearing that some sort of Soviet spy ring had infiltrated the country, they rounded up every single remaining foreigner from allied countries or otherwise and in the process managed to arrest fourteen people who were plotting further attacks. One was Russian, another was from Armenia, there was a Cuban and an Angolan. The remainder were British born.

A few days later, and with the approval of the Cabinet, I signed an order that required every person living in Britain to be registered and issued with an identity card. Anyone found without a card, or who had avoided registration, would be imprisoned. There were to be no exceptions.

On June 7th, the fourteen conspirators were hanged at Usk prison. There were no more terrorist incidents.

The Britannia Royal Naval College is an extraordinarily large and beautiful complex of buildings overlooking the River Dart. My office had been constructed in one of the day rooms off the central or main entrance. The enormous window allowed me an unobstructed view down to the water, and what a fantastic view it was. I had a large and very impressive desk with two telephones on it, a computer and printer, a table lamp and a pretty little sign block which informed anyone coming near the desk that I was Chief of the Defence Staff. I had been given a very powerful and noisy document shredding machine and a slightly quieter teleprinter. In the middle of the room there was a conference table with chairs for eight, and, against the far wall, a very large, deep and comfy settee and two high backed chairs. On a unit between these was an extremely large colour television set and a video player. The builders had done a very good job of partitioning off the main office to create a decent sized bedroom containing a smallish double bed with a bathroom off that. To be honest, I never really needed to leave the office, I had everything I could ever ask for. I even had the option of having all my food brought to me, but I couldn't bear that thought and took most of my meals in the mess with the combined commissioned remnants of our armed services. In the early days, whenever I entered the mess or the bar, everyone would stop doing whatever they were doing, and stand to attention, with the senior man present shouting 'Good morning/afternoon/evening Sir!' I put a stop to that very quickly and now they just go a bit quieter.

The bedroom was fine for the odd stopover and Anna and I had used it a fair few times for afternoon escapades or if she was staying at the college, but I don't think it was really suitable for long term occupancy or a great deal of comfort. I knew that there was still tons of work to do, but I had neglected one very important thing since the war and that was my dear old dad. I had no idea whether he was alive or dead or where he even was. I drove to St. Mawgan, and once there, I told the Ops Officer that I needed someone to fly me across to Colerne near Bath. After ten or so minutes sitting in the pilot's ready room, drinking tea and smoking their cigarettes, one of the Hunter chaps I recognised from the College reception came in, and told me he would be delighted to be my chauffeur. The flight to Colerne in the two-seater was a delight, and once we got there, the station commander leant me a car and I drove on to Kelston. There were a few people about, and one, who I recognised, came across the road when he saw me. He told me that it wasn't really his place to tell me what had happened, and that I should perhaps talk to the local bobby. Since I didn't know that we had a local bobby or where to find him, I told him to tell me. I knew at this point that my father was gone. The man told me that the day after my knighthood ceremony, my dad had climbed into the car in the garage and put a pipe from the exhaust in through the driver's window. He was ninety four.

I went into the house and found a letter from dad addressed to me. I decided to read it when I got back to Dartmouth. I then locked up the house and drove back to Colerne feeling wretched. I genuinely didn't hold him responsible for his actions, though. In peacetime, of course, it would have been a completely different matter. But this was so very different. I couldn't blame him. When I got back to my office, I told Maybury I was not to be disturbed and I locked the door. I was as nervous as hell as I opened dad's letter. I needn't have been.

My dear Oliver As I write this, I fervently hope that you are well and that when this is all over, you will return home to some sort of normality. For me, though, there is nothing left. As you know, since your mother's passing, I have found life rather difficult and I believe that now it is time for us to be together again. I am sure you will understand one day. I thank you for being the most wonderful son. I am so very, very proud of you. All my love, forever, Dad

I have never really been inclined to outbursts of emotion, and for a short while after reading the letter, I was holding myself together quite well. I rang Anna and told her what had happened. She was wonderful about it and said she would come up if I liked. I told her not to, and that I would stay at the college. That evening as I lay in my bed, I cried. I cried for my dad but also for my mum, for my lost crew members in all my bombers and then for the world. It was a truly, unimaginably miserable evening. I ordered that tomorrow's breakfast should be delivered to my office and left outside the door. I didn't emerge back into reality for another eight hours. When I did, I think Maybury had worked out what had happened, and very gamely deflected all callers and any questions for the rest of the day. I got through some depressingly bland paperwork during the next day and when that was dealt with, I went down to the Angel and hugged my wife. She said she understood; and I know that she did. At dinner that night, I told her that I was now coming 'home' every night.

CHAPTER THIRTEEN

Over the following days, I had to set my mind to one rather pressing task and also to one other that had been consuming most of my time for the last three months. The first was how to shape the air force for the future. The more important one was civil defence. But then I got sidetracked, and spent the next week completing and signing off orders for the re-arming of the submarines. We were going to load six Spearfish torpedoes and four, single 2 Megaton warhead SLBMs aboard both Valiant and Defiant. The principal reason for only loading a total of eight SLBMs was that that was all we now had left. Both submarines were to be maintained as launch platforms until such time as the Trident fleet was fully war capable. On that matter, the manufacturers and the seconded and borrowed engineers from throughout the west of England had worked tirelessly to get the new boats ready and had achieved staggering rates of progress. Both the subs would be ready on schedule and crewing was already under way. The Trident missiles were being kept at a facility near Bude and whilst we had only got around to receiving eighteen before the war started, it was enough to keep one boat fully armed whenever it was on patrol at sea. It had been established that all other remaining British nuclear assets had been relocated to storage in Wiltshire in the days before the war started. The bunkers were deep enough, and sufficiently hardened to survive a direct hit on the nearby airbase. If our missiles had remained in their prewar dispersed locations, we would have had nothing, because Greenham Common, Faslane and Aldergrove had all received direct hits. I despatched four C130 Hercules, packed with Royal Marines, across to Brize Norton and they collected every last nuclear device we had. Brize was quite badly contaminated but hadn't received a direct hit. The crews were fully suited up throughout the mission and they, their aircraft and the weapons were decontaminated at Valley before flying on to St Mawgan where the missiles were then transported to Dartmouth and Plymouth by road.

This was a huge logistical effort as we had needed to send a full decontamination unit to Valley for the C130s and a secondary one to St. Mawgan to clean the first unit when it finally arrived in Cornwall.

The Brize team had recovered the last eight White Shadows left anywhere in the world, and we now had enough of those to fully arm two TSR2s or partially arm half a squadron. The issue there was that the TSR2 was now becoming increasing complicated to maintain. They were old and getting very tired. I spent another few days completing my instructions for the reshaping of the RAF, which I cleverly entitled 'The Royal Air Force for the 90's.' I had concluded that my air force for the 1990s and beyond would consist of eight TSR2s, thirty eight Hawks, three 146s, eight passenger/freighter VC10s, five tanker Tristars, fourteen Hercules, eight Chinooks, eleven Pumas, fifteen Gazelles and fourteen Hunters. I know I go on about them but I must admit, I didn't like seeing my trusty VC10s being turned from nuclear bombers into little more than airliners, but needs must. They had proved themselves in every role we had demanded of them, and they were almost beyond compare. Now, converted into passenger carriers and freighters, they got a nice new lick of light grey paint, but still looked like they could carry out a bombing raid at a minute's notice. They still had the pointy nose with the radar in, and the only thing that really distinguished them from their forebears was that the missile hard points under the wings were now gone.

However, now I had to concentrate on what to do with Britain.

I spent the next three months consulting with every military and civilian adviser I could find, and eventually we drew up a plan for the best way to protect the remnants of Britain for the foreseeable future and way beyond. If you look at a map of Britain, the bits that we were told were going to survive were roughly bounded by a line between Stroud, Frome and Lyme Regis to the east and Stroud and Cardigan in the north. Everywhere above those lines had unacceptably high radiation readings, and the further north and east that you ventured, the more the dosage would have been. Certain places like London, Glasgow and around Faslane had received such large concentrations of weapons, they were going to be uninhabitable for decades. However, what was actually safe and what we told the public was safe were two different things. The published area was between Weston super Mare and Exmouth, broadly speaking where the M5 motorway was. We didn't want people straying into areas where there were potentially higher doses of radiation, and we also needed some zones where we could carry out military operations and treat survivors and refugees without prying eyes.

We had a prewar population of around a million in Devon and half a million in Cornwall. Quite a fair number had escaped down here after the outbreak of war. We had only accepted those that weren't contaminated, but could now count the population of the 'new' Great Britain as around 2.2 million. Obviously, we couldn't leave survivors out in the cold, as it were, and I had plans quickly put in place for large reception centres to be created to the east of the M5 motorway, but far enough west of the contaminated zone to make treatment of those that could survive worthwhile. All my personnel had maps which clearly showed the extent of the invisible safety zone, and that If you strayed too far north, you would receive a potentially fatal dose of radiation. The only ways to access Wales from the remainder of the south west of England, was either by the heavily guarded Seven bridge, the Severn railway tunnel or via military boats. Thus, my concern was how to secure the contaminated 'border' whilst permitting the controlled flow of refugees into a safe zone for medical examination and assessment.

We concluded that we should fence off the entire length of the west carriageway of the M5 whilst building entry points for refugees. These reception areas were considered to be most useful if located at Almondsbury, west of Bristol, Clevedon, RAF Locking, Highbridge, Bridgwater, Wellington, Hele, the A30 at Monkerton and Clyst St Mary. Patrolled barbed wire stretched the entire length of this line with funnel points at the reception areas. These had started life as tented camps, but soon we had more permanent structures built with co-located hospitals and decontamination areas. In their first full twelve months of use, all the entry points combined processed a total of two hundred thousand people. Each person was examined for their level of radiation contamination and, if they were considered to be treatable, were then

174

dealt with by a medical team accordingly. We allowed in seventy thousand people who showed little or few signs of radiation sickness, which is an incredible number really. Of the many tens of thousands that we couldn't accept, many were irradiated and dying on their feet, but an awful lot had typhus and it was rife outside the secure zone. In the end, out of the remaining people, we only managed to save another ten thousand or so. It was heartbreaking work for the teams, but they did brilliantly.

Once we had completed the collection, assessment and treatment of all our refugees, I received approval from the PM to close the remainder of the infected country off from our safe area. Royal Engineers, TA volunteers and civilian contractors, assisted by as many able bodied people as we could muster, eventually erected a barrier all the way from Stroud, through to the east of Bath and Frome to the west of Yeovil and down to the coast at Lyme. Essentially, the route followed the A46, the A36, A359 and the A303. Using a mixture of rigid metal fencing with razor or barbed wire on top or precast concrete panelling, all at least eight feet high, the job took a total of seven months to complete and was nearly a hundred miles in length. During construction, patrols were maintained by soldiers, Royal Marines and armed police. After completion, sentry posts, which were portacabins or shipping containers, were located every mile, and a constant watch was kept via closed circuit television and radiation monitors. When the refugee access points were sealed again on 24th September 1987, one hundred and twenty thousand survivors had been processed. The majority were British but there were many from western Europe and a total of nine hundred American nationals who had arrived in a variety of boats.

After giving it a lot of thought, and following glowing recommendations from Maurice Bowen, I appointed Richard Fitzjohn as the commander of HMS Vanguard. He had been the skipper of HMS Triumph, an SSN that was lost in the war. He had been taken ill with pneumonia a few days before the war started and despite this, he felt he should have died with his crew. We strongly disagreed, and I called Fitzjohn up to my office and persuaded him that he was the only man for the job. He grudgingly accepted. Bowen popped up to the College to congratulate Richard on his new command, but after Fitzjohn had left, he asked if he could have five minutes of my time, and he told me that his crew were going stir crazy. You would have thought that after all the months of misery at sea, they would never want to go out again. But it seems I had underestimated the mindset of the submariner. He said that all they needed was a short patrol, just to get a feeling of that pre-war exercise mentality going again. He assured me that they would only go as far as the Azores and then come back in for the last time. He promised me a public crash surfacing just off Dartmouth if I agreed. Valiant was conked out but still seaworthy, so I approved another patrol of a maximum duration of three weeks. I then informed Bowen that when he returned, his new suite of offices would be ready.

This came as great surprise to him. 'I don't need an office, Ollie; I've got my boat. '

'Ah, but you see, when you get back, your ugly boat is going into care and maintenance for good and will cease to require a captain,' I responded.

He looked perplexed and perhaps a little annoyed, but I think he knew what was coming. 'The Prime Minister, remember him, nice chap, has approved my recommendation that you should be promoted to Chief of the Defence Staff upon my retirement from service.' I think my eyes were twinkling.

'No no no. You can't bloody retire. What will I do. I haven't a clue how to run the military. I don't even know what a tank looks like' he pleaded.

'I will be staying on for six months after you start, and will help you in any way you need. Your offices will be just across the reception area from here. You can pop in any time,' I said

'Then what?'

'Then, dear chum, I'm off to my house to live out my retirement pressing apples.' I smiled at his discomfort.

'Pressing apples?' he exclaimed, miming an apple being prodded.

'We have an orchard and I am going to make my own cider and then drink it all.'

I took him to see the four bare walls that would soon become his office, and it was a huge area which I could see made him feel very uncomfortable.

'But I like small spaces,' he had yelled out.

'March next year Maurice I turn seventy and I've had enough. On the first day of October, you're it, on your own and I'm off pressing apples.'

'Bloody apples,' said Bowen.

'Yes,' I replied.

'Oh cobblers,' said Bowen.

Bowen took HMS Valiant out on its final patrol on 2nd November 1987. They sailed to the Azores and then began the return journey. At noon on 24th, in perfectly calm conditions, a flotilla of Royal Navy vessels, commercial ships, ferries, pleasure craft and small boats, joined by television news crews assembled two miles off Dartmouth. I was there as well, and my stomach knew it. I really didn't like the sea, especially anything more than a few yards from shore. And here I was with my beautiful wife, on board a fast patrol boat and barely able to see dry land. The great thing was that Maurice Bowen had postponed his arrival by 48 hours to allow for a superb, calm day. The Captain of our boat could hear Valiant's crew on the radio set and all eyes were told to look out for an orange flare that had been dropped into the sea. Anna was laughing her head off at my queasy condition and kept suggesting that perhaps I would be more comfortable with my head over the side. Exactly on time, HMS Valiant's bulbous bow burst from the sea and the whole submarine erupted from the deep. It looked to be at angle of around forty five degrees although it was probably less. Apart from the stern and the propellor, the whole thing was airborne. And then, just like a great breaching whale, it gently flopped back onto the surface with a huge plume of spray. It was utterly, brutally, fantastic.

This was the final display by the greatest vessel ever to sail the seven seas and a fitting end to its magnificent life.

All the vessels out on the water then followed Valiant back into the Dart. However, only our patrol boat was allowed to proceed to the mooring pontoon. Valiant tied up on the far side, and we did the same but on the side nearer to Dartmouth. As I disembarked, the vents and the missile tube doors were opening. Maurice Bowen emerged from the sail and we shook hands.

'That, my friend, was about as good as it gets,' I said.

'Pretty good trick isn't it,' he replied, beaming. 'And what's more, you get one very last trip'

'How?' he asked excitedly.

I explained that as the first of the Trident subs was now ready to take over the deterrent role, I had agreed with Richard Fitzjohn's request that HMS Vanguard should be escorted out on her first patrol from Plymouth on 14th February by Valiant and Defiant. I also told Maurice that his boat was going to get a thorough deep clean, an above the waterline repaint and a general buffing up. He was delighted.

On the 14th February 1988, the newly refurbished Valiant sailed to Plymouth where she met with Defiant. The two vessels then rendezvoused with Vanguard which had sailed from her temporary home at Avonmouth. The flotilla sailed across the top of north Somerset, Devon and Cornwall and then around the south Cornish and Devon coasts, keeping as close to shore as possible, with Valiant and Defiant leading. When they reached Exmouth, the three submarines turned out to sea and Vanguard was allowed to take the lead. Still within sight of land, she then dived onto her first patrol. Defiant then returned to Plymouth and Valiant to her new and now permanent home in Dartmouth.

When Valiant had tied up for the last time, I didn't go out on to the pontoon. I rather thought that Bowen needed time to be alone with his boat, and when he eventually joined Anna and I on the Dartmouth quayside, he was visibly emotional. I can fully understand why. 'You get attached to them Anna. I don't know why. Stupid isn't it'

'Not at all,' she replied.

He didn't look at me. In fact he looked away.

Anna kissed him on the cheek and then he cleared his throat and walked off.

Valiant and Defiant, like HMS Victory before them, would remain commissioned ships of the line, but would not sail on operations again. Both were to have their reactors removed, which would then be used, once suitably adapted, in domestic power stations. Defiant would be berthed at Plymouth as a training vessel with a skeleton crew formed from her wartime charges, whilst good old HMS Valiant would be moved from her midriver pontoon, and relocated upstream and secured on the Dartmouth side of the river adjacent to the Dart Marina, just up from the Upper Ferry slipway.

After all the excitement of the submarines arriving back, I decided it was about time I set about paying a few visits to our active airbases. St Mawgan was in very good condition and was working extremely well. It housed all the bombers, refuellers, half the transport fleet and half of the Hunters. Chivenor was also in good shape. It now housed the remainder of the transport and Hunter fleets, all the Hawks and most of the helicopters.

The American military aircraft that had made it to England were now all here too and some had been cleaned up and were available for public inspection as part of the recently opened 'Last War' museum. We had refurbished and returned the single U2 to service for any future high altitude reconnaissance that might be needed. I doubted that this would ever be necessary though. The F111s and F4s had not arrived in the best shape and they were both immensely complex types. The decision was made to ground them permanently and they were the first to go on display. The KC10 was surplus to requirements and ultimately we gave it to the French to bolster their air to air refuelling capability. I decided that RAF Valley would be decommissioned and that the two Soviet aircraft would be used, alongside 'our' Ilyushin as gunnery targets for our fighters.

I then turned my attention to Exeter. This was now the UK's principal civilian airport and I had decided quite early on that as our new main gateway, it would need a longer runway. It now measured 10,000 feet and was able to host visits from our friends in New Zealand, Chile, Iceland and Canada.

More importantly, for me anyway, it still held my war aeroplane on its inventory. Rollo Geary, had telephoned me weeks ago to ask if he could 'tinker' with the airframe to make it a little more presentable. I had agreed, expressing surprise that it hadn't already been scrapped, but I was in for a big surprise. When I got to the maintenance area, Rollo took me to the hangar where he and his team did their collective, out of hours, strictly off duty tinkering. He told me that all the condemned airframes, VC10s, Victors, the lot, had all been stored wingtip to wingtip on the hardstanding outside the hangar. Now this area was in pristine condition with just a recently repainted TriStar outside. He then handed me a life story of my aircraft which I still have to this day and it read as follows:

VC10 ZD243

17 July 1973 Rolls off production line

4 August 1973 First flight

11 January 1974 To 19 Squadron at Conningsby

3 November 1976 To 182 Squadron at Wittering

12 June 1979 To 617 Squadron Marham

13 May 1981 To BAC Warton for conversion of internal space to rotary bomb bay. One of fourteen mid-build variant VC10s converted. The dispenser located over the wing root to hold six 'White Shadow' missiles.

7 May 1983 Dispersed t o Wroughton

3 August 1983 Airborne for fourteen hours with one outbound inflight refuel. Armed with twelve 'White Shadow' of 1.2 MT yield each. This airframe holds the record for the longest airborne period of any RAF aircraft on that day and the most damage sustained whilst remaining airborne. The radio/radar operator, the copilot and the captain, who were the only surviving crew, received numerous wounds.

1983 October Deemed irreparable. Major subassemblies to be removed.

1984 August Because of the aircraft's provenance, the Chief Engineer of the RAF has determined that this aircraft is to be given a cosmetic repair.

1985 March After remaining outdoors for over 18 months, the airframe is placed under cover with a view to commencing minimal maintenance.

1988 February A phased 'return to taxi condition' regime is approved and all damaged external areas are to be replaced with non-airworthy, time-expired or spare parts from surplus examples. Internally, the aircraft will be made serviceable with all flight deck instrumentation functional. It is to be repainted into prewar camouflage colours. Non-airworthy but functioning engines are to be fitted.

When I got to this last bit, I turned and looked at Rollo. He was grinning at me inanely.

'I knew you would approve sir,' he said.

'Thanks Rollo. You're a bloody star,' I replied, and then added 'I don't recall approving the return to taxi condition, though?'

'Just my little treat sir,' he said, matter of factly.

After dinner that night, I was called to the hotel reception desk and was handed the telephone by the manager. It was Maybury, and he informed me that two of the six Soviet aircrew had died of radiation sickness and that the other four were all in critical conditions. They were being kept comfortable but they were not expected to last much longer. A footnote, handwritten by the consultant, said that just before he lapsed into unconsciousness, the pilot of the Bison had asked him to thank me for the kindness we had shown to him and his men.

Maybury then told me that there were two files awaiting my attention. The first, was a UN report and the second was a NATO assessment of allied military capabilities. The following day, Maybury brought me the files and then left, closing my office door.

I decided to start with the UN report. It was, to say the very least, difficult reading, but the opening paragraphs only really served to confirm what we already knew. The United States, including Alaska and Hawaii; Canada, excepting the north eastern seaboard; central America, and south America, to a point 500 miles south of Bueno Aires, were all still experiencing unacceptable radiation levels and were bereft of human life. Greenland was relatively free of contamination and significant numbers of refugees have made their way there. Iceland is now recording very low levels of contamination. Africa remains devastated by radiation, with only Morocco, the western regions of Mauritania, most of Western Sahara and the northern reaches of Algeria still habitable, and with each hosting significant local populations, swollen by millions of refugees from southern countries. However, there was a great danger of cross contamination of the healthy by those suffering radiation sickness and Morocco had closed its land and sea borders.

Europe and Asia were worse than previously reported and were uninhabited and uninhabitable from central Germany and northwards through central Sweden in the west, to the Indian Ocean, the Tasman Sea and north Pacific Ocean in the south and east. There are, however, areas in the very far East of Russia where the contamination remained low to moderate and NATO forces there were still receiving refugees from Canada, Alaska and as far afield as India. The southern regions of the South Island of New Zealand were recording very low levels of radiation and with very few refugee arrivals. The very good news contained in an otherwise miserable and depressing report was that whilst eastern areas of Norway remain toxic, the western areas encompassing Bergen, Stavanger and Trondheim were recording minimal concentrations of radiation. In a gesture of almost unimaginable kindness, the Norwegian government had offered vast swathes of land to the north of Sogne Fjord, which is itself around forty miles north of Bergen, as a new and permanent home to the displaced people of Canada, America and Europe, a safe return to any of the world's the less contaminated areas being deemed unlikely for at least five to ten years. The United States, the Soviet bloc, China, and much of the far East would remain lethal to any form of human habitation for at least fifty to a hundred years.

The UN now estimated that with the prewar global population of almost 5 billion, and taking into account those still suffering the effects of either radiation, typhus or cholera, they would only expect to see a hundred million disease free survivors worldwide by the year 2000. The report then went on to deal with the effect of lower levels of radiation on the populations in the, so called 'safe' areas. It stated that there was growing evidence that all survivors would have received some level of radiation poisoning, and it was concluded that lifespans were likely to be reduced by as much as 50 percent in some areas. Eventually though, babies would be born in the low and medium risk areas of the world who would be free of any form of inherited radiation poisoning. These people would form the basis of our future generations.

The NATO file was essentially a list of military equipment figures. It started with the current strengths of the surviving nation's armed forces, many of which I was already familiar with. The French were relatively well equipped and whilst they had now finally conceded that all their SSBNs were gone, they had a total of six serviceable Mirage IVs and their associated nuclear weapons. The French Navy consisted of three destroyers and two frigates plus an assortment of patrol and mine clearance vessels. Because the French had not had time to commit their armour to the East German theatre, they were in the fortunate position of having two entire tank regiments at their disposal. The Norwegians had a number of capable ships and aircraft left and had also received up to two dozen escaping bomber aircraft and six warships from Finland and Sweden as well. I flicked through the entries for Morocco, Iceland, Chile et al, and then I stopped and closed the file. What difference did it now make if we had eight air launch nuclear bombs and the French had twelve of their own. Now, surely, we had to get rid of the bloody things and learn to live with each other. I called Maybury on the intercom, and when he entered, I gave him the reports to read. I told him that he could invite suitably cleared staff into his office to see them as well. After another half hour or so I decided to go back to the hotel. It transpires that those were last files I received that were specifically addressed to me as Chief of the Defence Staff.

I chose to make Maurice's handover as painless as possible. My original plan had been for an office swap. Mine was rather a lot bigger than his and the move of furniture and equipment would only have taken a couple of hours. But he persuaded me that things were fine as they were. Since it was a Sunday, my plan was that we would hold a little reception in my office, followed by a big roast lunch. Then it would be off to the bar until it got dark one way or another. The meal was excellent and was attended by the Prime Minister, Secretary of State for War and the Mayor. Numerous top brass, other officers, senior NCOs and Other Ranks from the Navy, Air Force, Army and Marines and a cross section of representatives from the Police, Fire Brigade, the Health Service and the press made up the numbers. There were a little over three hundred for lunch. Anna sat with me throughout, and Maurice made a splendid speech in which he praised everyone present for their sterling efforts during and after the war, before announcing that his first policy review, which would be published the following day, would see female service personnel being given access to all front line roles including Infantry officers and soldiers and fighter pilot and navigator positions. It went down rather well, and Anna was very, very impressed. By around nine that evening, things had thinned out a lot and there were only about a dozen of us left. I could tell that the booze was having an effect on poor old Bowen because he was very quiet. Even Anna was nodding off.

'Is there any chance you could stay beyond October?' he asked with a bit of a slur.

'I am going on the 30th of September old boy, and that's that,' I replied.

'Well bollocks to you then,' he helpfully added.

CHAPTER FOURTEEN

Over the weeks that followed his appointment to the top, Bowen took to it like the proverbial duck to water. Some of his initiatives were clever, others quite irritating. All made sense, though, and I knew that our armed forces were in very good hands.

My final job as Bowen's mentor was to join him at Exeter Airport on May the 14th to form part of the high level party that greeted the Heads of State and senior military personnel from all the allied countries who were arriving for the first and up to the date of this book's publication, only global post war summit. They represented Canada, Iceland, France, Morocco, Western Sahara, Norway and the Italian people who now resided in Sicily. The representatives from New Zealand and the South Seas Islands of the Pacific were coming by sea because they didn't have any commercial aircraft capable of in flight refuelling and they only had the one KC135 tanker left and that was grounded for repairs. We and the French had offered one of our TriStars and one of their KC10s to do the job but they said they would prefer the sea journey. The airborne delegates were all shuttled to Dartmouth by helicopter. Every machine we had available was pressed into service and it was amusing to see Heads of State, ministers and top military and civil servant types being herded into the backs of Chinooks and Pumas. It took three or four round trips to get them all off the airport.

Once the last helicopters had departed the College, there was a champagne reception on the front lawn and when everyone was suitably relaxed and refreshed we moved inside where a lavish banquet had been laid on. Considering some shops that I had been to recently were still experiencing difficulties in obtaining everyday basic items, I was amazed at the variety of dishes that were available at the College that evening.

After dinner, the delegates retired to their rooms which were the bedrooms of the officers usually stationed at the College who had, naturally, all been turfed out for the duration.

I stayed at the college overnight, and when I woke, I was greeted by the sight of a Royal New Zealand Navy destroyer at anchor in the middle of the river. They had arrived at dawn, and had been driven up to the College in time for the start of the morning's fun.

By nine, and with breakfast out of the way, His Majesty welcomed all present and then it was down to our Prime Minister to start the summit. Each representative was introduced, and by the time we had got through that and the agenda for the coming days, it was lunchtime. At two o'clock, I took my place with the PM and his Deputy, the Head of the Army, Maurice Bowen, the Commissioner of UK Police and a whole bevy of civil servants. We had twenty two people present; the Kiwis had forty! The remainder of the delegations numbered somewhere in between. The United Nations and NATO were separately represented and the former opened with confirmation of existing and projected global population for the next one, two, five, ten and twenty years. We then listened intently as a UN meteorologist described the expected movement of winds and jet streams and how their effects were still spreading and dumping the remaining radioactivity across the planet. Parts of western Europe, central South America and north western Canada were only a matter of months away from being able to report low contamination. The rest of the previously uninhabitable world would remain that way for the foreseeable future.

The Heads of State of each of the countries then proceeded to outline their current and projected future populations and also the numbers of refugees that they were hosting. Norway had welcomed over thirty five thousand people from thirty different countries, but had added that whilst they were having few difficulties finding these people homes, it was another matter to keep them gainfully employed or sufficiently well fed. The UN delegation then sought reassurances from all those present that assistance would be given in respect of food distribution to all member states.

We then closed for the day, and at eight that evening, we all filed into the main hall where we were presented with four banqueting tables laid out for two hundred and eighty people. The King made a speech and welcomed all our friends, and then, after a few others had said their piece, we got down to the business of demolishing half the farm animals of England. The King left at nine thirty and shortly after that we all repaired to the mess bar.

The next day started at ten, and this was the big one for us military types. It was agreed, in writing and with respective Heads of Sates signatures as confirmation, that each delegate was to be entirely open. No secrets were to be held in reserve. There were to be no sleights of hand and no claims that couldn't be challenged. It was also agreed, following a motion from the Chilean Prime Minister that every country must have permission to inspect the others' armouries at short notice and in perpetuity. This was approved without dissent and we then each went through our own country's capabilities.

The upshot was, that whilst the British, the French and the New Zealanders could probably conduct a small war outside the boundaries of their own country, and that in the case of the French and us, nuke the enemy as well, the remainder only had sufficient military projection for localised conflict. There was widespread agreement that none of us ever intended to use our weapons again. The voices of concern were those of Morocco and Chile. They asked whether the British and French nuclear arsenals were necessary in the 'new world' that we now, so fragilely, inhabited. It was eloquently put and was a persuasive argument. The Canadians agreed and, soon the only topic of discussion, was that of a bomb-free world.

The moderator saw that Maurice Bowen had raised his hand, and gave him the floor. 'There can't be a soul alive today who wouldn't want to see an end to nuclear weapons.'

Nods and murmurs of approval.

'But until there is verifiable proof that the Soviets and the Chinese are as destroyed and as emasculated as we believe they are, no such decommissioning can take place'

A few nods. far less murmurs.

'So let's find out,' Bowen suggested.

At the end of this protracted get together, the decision was that the best intelligence people in the world or at least, those that were left would put their heads together and come up with a definitive answer to the question; 'Do the enemy still exist, and if they do, do they pose a credible threat, nuclear or conventional?' It could already be said that based on everything we knew before the war, that the only countries that had nukes pre-war were the U. S., the Soviets, China, India, Pakistan, Israel, France and Britain. The latter two would decommission their remaining weapons if the experts could prove beyond doubt that the remainder had either used all of theirs up during the war or that they were beyond use. If there was doubt, the allied deterrent would have to remain.

Just before the break for lunch I left the room, having decided that the detail of our response to this mammoth exercise was up to Maurice. I returned to my office and dealt with the very few bits of correspondence that crossed my desk these days.

Maurice knocked and entered at twelve thirty. 'You buggered off,' he exclaimed.

'You're the main man now, not me,' I replied

'Oh bloody hell,' he said, and trounced out of the room.

I called Maybury on the intercom and told him I was not to be disturbed until the summit broke at the end of the day. I then went into the bedroom and lay down.

Maybury woke me at five forty. 'They're done sir.'

After a quick freshen up, I joined Maurice at the mess bar.

'We're going to send out a global task force with ships from each country. Some will be naval, most will be merchant vessels, and we're going to take loads of soldiers and scientists with us to Israel, Pakistan, India, Russia and China,' he explained.

'Bloody hell. That's good stuff,' I replied, genuinely impressed.

'The Brits are doing China.' He raised his eyes heavenwards.

'That'll take for ever,' I said, helpfully.

'Yep, it sure will. We're giving the whole programme at least a year. '

'Bloody hell,' I repeated.

The plan was that the Canadians and the Italians would enter Israel, the French, Chileans and the Western Saharans would go to India and Pakistan, whist the Icelanders and Norwegians would cover all of Russia and the eastern Bloc countries up to the NATO controlled areas in the east. Prewar intelligence on the location and likely dispersal points of all nuclear silos, bombs and missiles was very good indeed. The plan was to start at the places where the weapons would have been launched then establish how many actually had been, what their targets had been and if any were outstanding. I didn't envy any of those teams their task.

'Are you having anything to do with it?' I asked Maurice.

'Without a submarine to play with? You must be joking. No, the Army and Marines are running this, although Richard Fitzjohn said he would go along, if I asked him to,' he replied.

'And will you ask him?'

'No,' said Maurice.

On Friday the 20th May, the New Zealand and South Pacific delegates were whisked down to the river to rejoin their ship, whist the remainder boarded a variety of helicopters for the flights back to Exeter. The first of these shuttle aircraft had taken off at nine. By the time the last one had left, it was gone twelve.

Once the clatter of rotor blades had finally subsided, Maurice and I took tea on the front lawn and watched in silent amazement as the College staff began the clear up operation. We then went for a walk in the grounds and when we eventually went back inside at two thirty, we peered into the banqueting hall and were stunned to see that the furniture had already been put back into storage and that the cleaners were finishing up the hoovering. The mess bar was back to usual with a few lunchtime tipplers propping it up.

By three o'clock, the officers who lived in the mess accommodation were beginning to trickle back to the College. It was very gratifying to see. Everything was getting back to normal.

As we were returning to our respective offices, I stopped and said to Maurice, for no particular reason, 'In sixteen weeks I'm done you know.'

'Bastard,' he said.

During that time, Maurice and I helped prepare the schedule for our ships' China expedition, and on the first day of August, we saw them all off from Plymouth.

We then spent the rest of the month working hard, laying the foundations to try and get all the old closed or dismantled railways from the Beeching cuts re-laid or reopened. Petrol for cars was a precious commodity but diesel oil for railway locomotives was relatively abundant.

On the 28th and 29th September, I toured the bases at St. Mawgan and Chivenor, saying goodbye to some wonderful friends and colleagues, and on that second evening, Maurice and I joined a few others for drinks at the College mess bar. I left at eight and a car took me down to the Angel.

Back in our room at the hotel, I took off my uniform for the last time, and as I closed the door of the wardrobe and turned, Anna kissed me and said, 'Well done sir.'

On the 30th September, at my farewell do in the mess, Bowen made a gushing speech about how I was the single greatest inspiration in his life and that without me, he would not be where he was today. He added that I was the luckiest man alive having Anna as my wife, and that he would miss us both terribly. I was certain he had been secretly drinking from quite early on. He added that he didn't know what he would now do without us. I shouted out that he didn't need me any more, which got a cheer and rather steered him onto just simply saying goodbye and letting the drinking get started.

The next day at noon, Anna and I checked out of the Angel for the last time. A team of strong chaps had packed up all our gear, both from my office suite and the hotel, and had it placed in the car that would take us down to the lower ferry for the very short hop to Kingswear railway station. Maurice had offered us a car all the way to Kelston, but I had decided that as I was now a civilian, I should travel like one. Anna had agreed that this was the sensible, nonmilitary, approach to things that we should now be taking.

When it was time to go, Maurice Bowen and Paul Maybury, were waiting on the College steps, and we all embraced before Anna and I set off. Both of those splendid chaps promised that they would keep in touch regularly, and Maurice said he would be down to see us within weeks, if not days. It was a sad moment, and I was tremendously touched by all the messages of goodwill. But most of all, I knew I would miss Maurice and Paul. And the RAF.

In reality, I knew I would miss it all.

CHAPTER FIFTEEN

On our first full day of retirement, we hired a car and went over to the house at Chew Valley. It was so pretty, and had so many lovely memories, that we agreed that we couldn't bring ourselves to sell it. We decided there and then, that we would keep renting it out until we had decided if we wanted it back as our main home. The next day, a chap came to look at dad's old car, and even though he knew of its history, he bought it on the spot. During the following weeks, we got some decorators in and bought a lot of new furniture from Colmers in Bath. By springtime, we had the garden tidied up properly, and when it was finished, it looked a picture. By then, Maurice Bowen had not called or written once.

In June, our first batch of early harvested apples had fermented successfully enough to begin drinking. Whilst a little on the sharp side, what they lacked in flavour, they certainly made up for in alcoholic kick. I had two bottles on the first afternoon and didn't wake up for three hours. Mind you, they were very big bottles. Frankly, I was in heaven.

One early afternoon in August I was dozing on the terrace when I was disturbed by a voice at the side gate. It was Maurice. I was so pleased to see him after so long. It seemed he had given himself forty-eight hours leave and had thought of no better place to spend it than with us. He had been brought up by official car, and his driver was using the time visiting relatives in Weston. Anna was delighted to see Maurice, and we three spent the evening in the pub and had an excellent dinner. Once the food was finished, we went outside with our drinks and Maurice gave us an update on the bomb finding expeditions. 'I get the odd report from the other groups, but I receive something from our own team almost every day. In a nutshell, it's been a bloody nightmare for them,' and he handed me a report. Even though the China expedition had been there for very nearly a year, they had only managed to visit ten potential launch sites so far, although they had travelled vast distances already. Our soldiers and Marines came under fire from occasional bands of roving refugees. They had come across numerous groups of people; all of whom had somehow survived the radiation, but who were now desperately ill from either typhus or cholera or were simply starving. The team had found no evidence of a structured Chinese military presence. They had visited every major city and a great many of the smaller ones. Most were merely ghosts towns, liberally populated by mummified corpses. Every airport and airfield with a runway capable of launching a MiG15 or larger had been surveyed and every seaport and naval base had been declared safe. The greatest find of the expedition was in May, near the port city of Hangzhou, where they uncovered a vast intelligence centre, hidden in an otherwise innocuous looking government building. The Chinese had made great strides in the years leading up to the war in the production of nuclear weapons, but they were nowhere near as well equipped as the Russians. Despite this, material retrieved from Chinese army intelligence facilities showed that on the day of the launch, three thousand four hundred warheads were available. A further eleven thousand had been planned for production over the next five years. The information gathered had almost certainly saved our team another year or more of searching. Armed with that intelligence, they were able to go to each site where they now knew for sure that there was a launch facility, and confirm if all the missiles had successfully launched. It seems so far that they had been.

The team were now travelling inland to an area to the south of Peking called Daxing where they hoped to locate the factory where the new build missiles and warheads were being produced. Their intention was to destroy the facility and then regroup at Hong Kong. Their major concern was that they were running very low on fresh food and protective clothing.

'God almighty Maurice!' I had exclaimed.

'I am just so pleased I was too old to go,' he said.

When we returned to the house, we proceeded to demolish most of my remaining cider, and Maurice was extremely impressed with Anna's ability to keep up with the boys. We spoke a little of the war but mostly, we talked about the post war period. When it was really very late, Anna went to bed and Maurice and I sat drinking. He then told me about the successes of the other expeditions.

'It's not that I don't want Anna to hear it, it's just that a lot of the intelligence coming out of the other countries isn't really mine to spread about,' explained Maurice.

'I understand. You don't have to tell me either if it's that sensitive,' I replied.

'Yeah, right,' he scoffed.

The Canadians and the Italians had wrapped things up in Israel after seven months, and all of the expedition members were now back in their respective countries. The Israelis had only had a few weapons, but had used them to good effect against the Soviets; not, as everyone with a liberal mind might have thought, against the Arab states. The country was ruined and the pathetically small number of survivors that the team had come across were heavily contaminated. There were categorically no outstanding nuclear weapons in Israel.

The French, Chileans and the Western Saharans who were tasked with establishing the military capabilities of India and Pakistan during and after the war, were now all on their way home after eleven months of horror. The teams had very quickly established that the Indians had lobbed their weapons exclusively at China whilst the Pakistanis had fired theirs only at India. Throughout their entire expedition, they barely saw a living soul. The last signal received from the French led team had confirmed that there were no viable nuclear weapons left in either India or Pakistan.

The Russia taskforce had begun their enormous task in central Ukraine and had then started the long trek eastwards. The fact that their expedition comprised over three thousand soldiers, sailors, scientists and engineers had helped, but the task was still too big for them. To date, after almost a year, they had only just reached the eastern outskirts of Moscow. The NATO troops in the occupied east of Russia had been in regular communication, and were doing their bit up there whilst slowly moving westward. 'I don't honestly think they'll be finished for another couple of years,' added Maurice.

'Why the hell don't they divert those who have already finished over to Russia then?' I enquired.

Maurice looked at me as though I had just had the best idea in the world. 'And to think, we let you retire,' he said

The following morning, after breakfast, Anna left for a shopping spree in Bath, so I took the opportunity to show Maurice our orchard and explained our plans for the future. I then took him for a stroll around the village. We returned home for lunch, at which point he and went over to look at my collection of photographs of my parents.

'Lovely people,' he said. I just nodded.

Maurice then took his wallet out from inside his jacket and produced a small colour photo. He handed it to me.

'My lot,' he said.

His family were standing on a quayside in front of what was obviously a huge ocean liner. His wife was bent forwards slightly and, with a radiant smile was encircling their three children with her arms. She was blonde and truly beautiful. The children, two girls and boy, clearly didn't have a care in the world and were grinning at the camera.

'They're beautiful Maurice,' I said.

'Shut up,' he replied.

'Southampton?' I asked.

'Yep. Queen Elizabeth.' At which he retrieved the photo and put it back in the wallet. Then he added, 'They went to bloody London, Ollie. I told them to go to St. David's and they went to London.' His voice trailed off.

'Cider?' I rather over-enthusiastically suggested.

'Yes please.'

Anna returned shortly after that and we then had a nice lunch in the garden. Maurice's car arrived in the late afternoon and as he left, he promised to return within four weeks.

A few days later, I was sitting out on the terrace and had arranged all my photos of mum and dad on the table when it struck me that I couldn't really remember how they sounded and that if I turned away and closed my eyes, I couldn't even remember their faces that well. Believing that this was some form of senility, rather than precisely what everyone experiences after a while, I decided I should start documenting my recollections of them. After a few hours of rather frantic scribbling, I determined to keep a record of everything I remembered from my teenage years right through to my last meeting with Maurice.

During the late morning of the next day, when Anna had gone to the Chew Valley house to prepare for new tenants, it was raining hard when there was a knock on the door. It was Squadron Leader Paul Maybury. I was absolutely delighted to see him. He was standing there in a soggy raincoat, so I ushered him and we sat in front of the fire with a small whiskey each. He explained that he wasn't just passing, he had come here specially.

'Well that's lovely Paul. You're always welcome. You should have told us you were coming, we haven't got much in,' I said.

'It's fine Ollie, I won't be staying. I just want to let you know something,' he replied.

'Tell me, are you retired or promoted?' I asked.

'I retired six months after you. It was getting a bit much, and besides, Mr Bowen had his man from the Navy brought over.'

'Oh yes. I see. Well here's to happy retirements,' and I raised my glass.

Maybury put his glass down on the table. 'Ollie, Maurice Bowen is very ill,' he said gravely.

'How. What with?' I asked.

'He was exposed to radioactivity,' he explained.

'I know. We all were,' I responded rather surprised.

'No, his was deliberate,' said Maybury

'How?' I enquired.

'When he realised his wife and children had died, and when he was sailing off Sakhalin, he deliberately went up onto the top on his conning tower and stayed there for over an hour,' he replied.

'And he knew how dangerous that was?' I asked.

'Oh yes. The readings were off the scale,' he answered.

'But surely in doing that, once he went below, the crew would have become infected?'

'No, not at all. He said that he called down to clear the area and he went straight to the decontamination showers and washed himself and then incinerated his uniform. The medic on board checked him over but as they were all displaying symptoms of radiation exposure, at low levels, nothing much was thought of it. But I think he knew that eventually it would get him. Obviously hoped it would.'

'But instead of quickly, years later…'

Yes,' he said.

What an absolute bloody idiot. What state of mind could you ever be in that would make you go out into lethal radiation, or anything else lethal for that matter, knowing that you could wait years to die.

Paul wouldn't accept my offer of a bed for the night, but he did stay for about an hour and we chatted happily about the war years. After he had gone, I didn't honestly know what to do with myself, so I went up to the pub and had a few pints.

Later that evening over dinner, I told Anna about Paul Maybury's visit, and it was obvious that she was sorry that had she missed him. I didn't mention Maurice's illness.

Over the next couple of months, when we had had filthy weather almost every day, we set to work on the apple harvest. There were literally tens of thousands of the little buggers, and on one day, I was in the outhouse squeezing juice from the press from eight in the morning until gone six in the evening. I reckoned it was my first full day's work since I had retired. We used to go over to the pub pretty much every other evening for our dinner. They did excellent meals and all the staff were charming.

One evening, as we contemplated heading back to the house, one of 'my' Hawks flew overhead at about five thousand feet and it suddenly struck me that I hadn't flown in any sort of aeroplane since my trip to Colerne in the Hunter.

It was May before I heard from Maurice again, and he asked if we fancied coming down to Dartmouth. Since we hadn't been there in ages, it seemed a great idea. He said that we both had to come, and that the first day would include a trip to Plymouth to welcome back the British contingent that he had diverted to Russia.

'They're done then are they?' I enquired

'Yep, all done. They've been off the coast of Milford Haven for a couple of days getting hosed down by decontamination ships, but they're ready to sail home properly now. We'll get a briefing too. Dead exciting'

'Looking forward to it, chum,' I said.

'I'll get you two a nice room in the mess, and we'll have a lovely big dinner or two. I'll send a car'

We accepted. 'What a delightful idea.'

Two days later, the military vehicle arrived outside the house. I have no idea what time the poor driver had got up, but if he'd come from Devon, it must have been around four. The drive down was mostly down the A36 and the A303 and less than twenty feet off to our left, for the entirety of the journey, was my Berlin Wall.

I asked if we could motor through the town when we got there, and I'm pleased to say that Dartmouth was still beautiful. HMS Valiant loomed on the quayside to our right before we drove up College Way. The Royal Naval College looked a picture as we swept through the gates and up to the main entrance. We thanked the driver profusely, entered the building and headed straight to Maurice's office. His Adjutant, a rather elderly looking fellow, didn't know me and was mightily confused by the presence of Anna, but was seemingly impressed when I told him who we were. Before the Adjutant could call Maurice on the phone, he burst out of his office and we all shook hands, hugged, kissed and slapped backs. He looked remarkably well and seemingly in very good spirits.

'Fantastic to see you both. This is going to be a trip to remember,' he gushed enthusiastically.

We headed straight to the mess where there was an awful lot of snapping to attention and 'afternoon sirs,' all of which he acknowledged with a cheery wave. We sat in what had always been 'our' corner and settled in to a very pleasant early evening drink.

I was desperate to bring up the subject of his radiation poisoning but, I needed Anna to be out of earshot. On the odd occasion when she popped out, each time I thought I might get the chance, someone would come over to either talk to him or me. A number of fellows, including the Head of the Army, a Police Assistant Chief Constable and a couple of pilots I vaguely recognised had eventually planted themselves at our table, so I knew that now was not the time. All thoughts of talking about illness evaporated as we all got more and more pickled and more and more tired. By eleven, Anna and I had had quite enough and we went to bed in what turned out to be the largest bedroom in the whole college. When I woke, it was well past nine, which was extraordinary because I rarely slept beyond six when I was a home. My head was a little fragile but I was ready for food nonetheless. Anna was, as ever, fresh as a flipping daisy and completely lacking in headaches.

Anna and I breakfasted alone and there no sign of Maurice until we went back to his office at around eleven. The door from the Adjutant's office to his suite was open and we walked straight in.

'Ready for a trip to Plymouth?' he asked, beaming from behind his desk.

We left at noon and even though we had a couple of motorcycles clearing the way, it still took an hour and a half to get there, but it was worth it. The main bulk of our remaining Navy were either tied up or at anchor and they all looked splendid. The second Trident submarine, Victorious were there as well and she was vast. It would have dwarfed Valiant.

We had time for a really good nose around before there was an amazing display of ships horns that announced the arrival in the Sound of our expedition vessels. We had sent a frigate, two RFAs and three cruise ships, all packed to the rafters with troops and scientific types and they had bolstered our effort in Russia. 'Altogether, we had seven thousand people out there. With the other allied teams, Russia finally ended up with over twenty thousand soldiers and scientists,' said Maurice.

It took an absolute age for the ships to dock, and then for the ferries and lighters to get all the personnel on to shore. But it didn't matter, it was totally worth it. These people now getting off the ferries and small boats, had gone into hugely contaminated enemy countries, surrounded by all manner of hidden dangers, and a fair few murderous locals, and had searched for hidden nuclear weapons. Most of the gathered masses were from the British contingent, but we were also hosting elements from Norway, France, Chile, Iceland and Morocco. The remainder were returning to their home countries to equally lavish receptions. It was six o'clock before everyone was off the ships, and sort of lined up on the dockside. It was quite a sight though, I can tell you. Maurice made his way to the raised platform and was then joined by the Prime Minister who made a good speech about how our people had gone into a dangerous environment and done their work without complaint (which got a cheer) and with little thought for their own safety (which got another one).

Then it was Maurice's turn.

'Standing here this evening are the bravest people it has ever been my privilege to meet. Many of you sacrificed so much during and after the war, but when you were called upon to travel to Russia, even though you had already surveyed other counties, you didn't hesitate. To do what you did, to go where you went and to see what you saw, is an act of the utmost bravery. And for that, we, the people of the free world, will be forever in your debt'

He was very good.

By seven, it was all over, and the gathered masses were able to disperse, and could either make their way back to their ships, head for their bases or homes, or head into the enormous workshop which had been hastily, but cleverly, converted into a huge catering facility for the day. The amount of food and drink available was incredible, and all of it good.

At eight, Maurice guided me and two dozen or so worthies into a very large office complex adjacent to the workshop for a briefing on the expedition's findings.

Anna was invited, but chose not to stay, 'Don't worry, I'll be fine. There are lots of lovely people to talk to,' she said.

We took our seats in a conference area hidden away in the middle of the second floor. The Secretary of State for Defence was there, as were a number of other senior civil servants, and government representatives from Norway, Morocco, Iceland and France. The briefing was given by Maurice's recently appointed Admiral of the Surface Fleet.

We were told that the joint international expedition had worked tirelessly for over twelve months, at which point, a very large British task force had set sail to reinforce our allies' efforts in Russia. Two weeks after that, the French Navy also transported over a thousand of their service and scientific personnel to the region. They were then followed by all the other countries' soldiers, engineers and scientists, until the total number in theatre had been nineteen thousand nine hundred. The British and French had relieved the others in western Russia and continued the push eastwards. Norwegian, Moroccan and Icelandic teams relocated to the central region and worked eastward as well, with the intention of eventually meeting up with the NATO forces from the occupied areas. A number of intelligence facilities were located and accessed and when the groups finally met up at the end of March, they were able to compare the information they had gathered, and to categorically state that during the war, the Soviet Bloc had expended over nine thousand nuclear warheads. There were a further seventy two aboard the submarine Admiral Gorky when she blew up, and it was established that, aside from the fifty megaton bombs on the Soyuz launch vehicles on Sakhalin, there had been in excess of four hundred, 2 or 5 megaton warheads ready for deployment on the Soviet bombers on the island. It is certain, beyond any shadow of a doubt, that if we had failed to destroy Sakhalin when we did, Britain and all our allies would have been annihilated. Information obtained by the expedition showed that the Soviet and Chinese bombers would have been airborne no later than 10 p.m. on the day that we attacked. We had got them in the nick of time.

'Gentlemen' the Admiral continued, 'When our Air Forces and our Navies destroyed Sakhalin Island, not one single weapon would have remained viable because of the utter and complete devastation, and the contaminated nature of what remains. .'

I must say that the murmur level reached new heights at this very specific assertion. Maurice stood up and walked to the front on the conference room. The Admiral snapped to attention and moved quickly to one side.

'Admiral, thank you. Secretary of State, gentlemen, as you know, in the last few days, we have been speaking with our counterparts within the French government and with their military. We believe that we can achieve the eradication of nuclear weapons within four weeks, but it is now up to you to fully appreciate what our reporting will tell you, and then it is for you to decide if our proposal meets with your approval.'

I had no idea what proposal he was talking about, but then, I wasn't in charge any more. As I was considering leaving to find Anna, Maurice cleared his throat. 'Before we close and join our friends and colleagues downstairs, I would like to bring to your attention the details of a particularly interesting find at an airbase near the Chinese bomb manufacturing facility in Daxing. A party of Norwegian scientists were sifting through a huge collection of intelligence files, and came across one that was particularly interesting, which pointed towards the true intentions of the Chinese after they had sailed from Sakhalin. As we know, the Russians, the Chinese and the North Koreans were planning to live together in peace and harmony in the uncontaminated parts of New Zealand. '

This produced a ripple of laughter.

He continued, 'It is thought possible that this arrangement might have worked, with perhaps one nationality on the western side of the North Island and the other two on the South. But, in reality, the documents shed light on what the Chinese were actually planning to do. Whilst they were still sailing south towards the North Island, and in deep water, they were going to attack and sink the Russian and North Korean ships. The world of the future would, therefore, have comprised of fifty thousand or so relatively healthy and uncontaminated Chinese people living merrily on New Zealand's South Island. Their intentions towards the population of their new home were also less than honourable. They planned to enslave the people, having first eradicated all the elderly and the sick.'

One chap from the Norwegian contingent then asked what were the enemy's plans for their bombers if they had got airborne and once they had returned from killing all of us.

'That's very interesting. We know that there were around two hundred aircraft on the island at the time, and that they were to have taken off the same evening that we attacked. We also know that the aircraft, and probably most of their crews were already heavily contaminated. It is likely we would have shot down some of them, but what remained would have had to make their way to New Zealand after bombing us! Frankly, for most at least, that was impossible. They did have tankers, but not enough for every aircraft, specifically those that would have flown to bomb Chile. Thus, we had contaminated crews and planes with little or no fuel. I suspect that there was never any expectation of a return home. It was a suicide mission, and the crews would have known it'

After listening to a few more rounds of questions and answers, most of which revolved around a general feeling that we should have attacked the enemy years ago, I excused myself and went down to find Anna. It was now almost nine fifteen, and I had no idea where she was. As I was gazing around, a Naval Provost NCO marched smartly up to me, halted, saluted and informed me that Lady Marsden was in the main workshop building talking to the 'boys and girls.' I thanked him very much and sauntered over. As I got nearer, I could hear that there now appeared to be a bit of a party going on. Loud music was wafting about and there were raised voices and laughter. The nearer I got, the more people I could see were outside. Some were smoking, others chatting in small groups. Quite a lot were just sitting quietly. A couple were asleep.

When I got through the door, the heat that hit me was extraordinary. So was the smell; it was bodies, booze, fags and food. And there she was. My beautiful wife. Lady Anna Marsden. Plastered. She was half dancing, half talking with a man I could only describe as good looking. Very good looking. He was a navy type but not ours. Could have been Norwegian, I think. They were both laughing like drains and when he spotted me he sort of tried to stiffen up but I waved him away. Anna turned, and as soon as she saw me she turned and very cheekily kissed the sailor on the nose and hurtled towards me. She flung her arms around me and squeezed me tightly. Then she stepped back.

'Has Lady Marsden had a few?' I suggested.

'Slightly,' she replied, her eyes darting all over the place.

'Are you a tiny bit sloshed?' I enquired.

'Do you know,' she began 'I think I may be'

'Shall we go home?' I asked. She was nearing seventy and she was behaving like a twenty year old. I suppose that's why I loved her.

As we left the building, Maurice appeared out of the gloom and he pointed towards our car. 'Maurice!' yelled Anna, and flung her arms around his neck. he looked at me, but I just smiled.

'Had a few?' he asked.

'No he hasn't,' offered Anna.

'Yes,' I said.

With Anna holding on to both of us very tightly, we tottered over to our car. The driver didn't look totally happy as we decanted Anna inside. Maurice then opened the other door for me, and climbed into the front seat himself. It took an age to negotiate our way out of the dockyard, but once we got through all the gates and out into the city, progress was swift. Anna had gone very quiet really very quickly and was now slumped over me.

'You're a lucky bloke,' said Maurice. 'I know,' I replied. I think I must have fallen asleep at that point because, when I woke, we were back at the College and I was being nudged by Anna.

We made it to our room and quite literally conked out.

The following morning, and for the first time in years, Anna had a post drinkies headache. She took a couple of pills and said she would have a bit of a lie-in. I popped off for a bit of breakfast in the mess. After that, I took a stroll through the grounds and then returned to our room to find Anna up and dressed. She admitted that her head still felt a bit fragile but that she was otherwise okay. There was no sign of anyone else, least of all Maurice, so we decided to walk down to the town and have a look around.

When we got to the Angel, we were surprised to see that it appeared to be closed. A sign said it was for refurbishment, but the boards on the windows suggested otherwise.

We returned to the College for lunch, but before we could make it to the mess, a chipper looking Maurice diverted us into his office and retrieved a file from his desk drawer.

'Ollie, Anna, come and look at this,' he said enthusiastically. Spread out on his desk were engineering drawings and manufacturers photographs of an aircraft I did not recognise. He slapped his hand down on the desk and smiled broadly. 'What do you think then?' he asked.

'I think I'm going,' said Anna and left the room.

'Fair enough,' said Maurice and nudged one of the sheets towards me.

The joint *Future Global Aircraft' programme* was underway with Britain, France, Norway, New Zealand and Chile having all contributed amazing concepts and ideas. The new aeroplane was going to able to operate effectively at all altitudes and all weathers and was a twin-engined, two crew design. Current plans would apparently see the prototype rolled out at Nantes in eighteen to twenty four months.

'It isn't decided yet, but it will be called either Hurricane or Typhoon,' Maurice said.

Lunch was a spectacular affair, almost a banquet, and included a wonderful array of desserts and some very good wines. Obviously, as soon as the tables had been cleared, we all moved to the bar. So began another afternoon of requests for stories about 'our' war to both Maurice and I from a variety of guests from within the military and civilian worlds. By four o'clock, Anna said she couldn't take any more and went for another walk. By five o'clock I too had absolutely reached capacity, so I made my excuses, and went to see if I could find Anna. As I got to the main entrance, she was coming back in.

'Did you lot really go to war or did you just sit here and drink your way through it?' said asked, slightly sarcastically, but also with a bit of a slurred voice.

'I think I'd better put you to bed,' I replied, instantly regretting it.

'Oliver. Really!' she said in a very loud voice and grabbed my arm, steering me to our room.

By seven we were fast asleep. The following morning, I woke at the more customary six thirty, and after a shave and shower, and not wishing to wake Anna, I went into the mess for breakfast alone. I wasn't in the least bit surprised to see Maurice and two others still slumped in chairs and deeply asleep. The mess stewards had thoughtfully covered them with blankets. We decided to skip lunch, and spent almost the entire afternoon in the college library thumbing through some of the magnificent books there. A steward kept us refreshed with tea or coffee whenever we needed it. It was very pleasant indeed and a nice restful way to spend our last full day.

'Ah, there you two are. They said you'd be in here,' said Maurice when he eventually emerged at gone six.

'Just been reading some of these beautiful books,' I replied.

'You ducked out a bit early last night didn't you,' he whined.

'And you had a good time did you? You were ratted, with your mouth open and fast asleep in a chair. I think, on balance, we did the right thing,' Anna retorted.

'Fair dos,' he said. 'Now, you're not rushing off tomorrow are you?' he added.

'Not really. Why?' I asked. 'I've got a trip home for you arranged from St. Mawgan, if you're up for it?' he replied surprisingly.

'Oh thank you, that's brilliant. Thanks Maurice.'

The remainder of the day was a much more sensible affair. Dinner was served at eight and immediately after, we repaired to the bar for a very few drinks and were in bed by ten thirty. Which was much more like it.

On the last morning, we breakfasted early and then went back to the room and packed. I then walked through Maurice's Adjutant's office, and in to his suite. He was at his desk and appeared to be engrossed in a telephone conversation. Even though he waved me in, I went back out and sat in the entrance lobby.

Shortly afterwards, Maurice came out to join me. 'There are a few things I have to do today, so I can't join you, I'm afraid,' he said apologetically.

'Thanks though, chum, it's much appreciated. We'll see you down in Kelston soon?' I replied

'You will Ollie, you will. And please say goodbye to Anna for me.' We shook hands, and as he disappeared back into his office, I heard him coughing.

Rollo Geary then emerged from the accommodation wing. 'Would you like a hand with your bags sir?' he asked.

'No, we're fine, Rollo, and please don't call me sir. It's Ollie,' I said

'Righty ho sir,' he replied.

Anna was waiting on the steps as Rollo and I loaded up the car. We then drove towards the main gate but then veered off to the right and drove to the larger of the playing fields. Sitting in the middle was a Gazelle helicopter. I looked across at Rollo.

'Our carriage awaits sir, ma'am, Ollie,' he said without a hint of irony.

Our pilot, an army Staff Sergeant in his late thirties, flew fast and low most of the way to St. Mawgan. Rollo then took us into the hangar where he showed us the aircraft he had 'tinkered with' to prepare them for display as part of the *Last War Memorial Collection*, a celebration of those types which had flown in the war and which had been preserved for posterity. Rollo told us that the signed order to make it happen had come from Maurice Bowen. There was a Hunter, a TSR2 and my VC10 from the day of the war. She looked resplendent in her newly applied grey coat, and all the damage she had received had been carefully removed and replaced with parts from other airframes. I was immensely touched.

Rollo then took us over to the ready room where we were introduced to our pilot for our next flight. After we had said our goodbyes to Rollo, we climbed aboard a Puma which was going to take us almost all the way home. We started with a fairly short spin around Newquay, and then embarked on a fantastically low level flight almost until we reached Bristol Lulsgate. After landing, and after we had thanked the crew profusely, we were shown to an official car, sent from Avonmouth dockyard, which took us right to our front door.

CHAPTER SIXTEEN

There was an awful lot of mail on the mat once we got inside, but one in particular stood out. It was a large foolscap sized buff envelope with OHMS across the top. I put the kettle on the gas ring and opened it. There was a short note in Maurice's handwriting that said 'Give it some thought!!' and then a typed letter from his Adjutant inviting me to consider an offer to become the *Adviser (Military Aviation matters)* to the Chief of the Defence Staff. Bloody hell.

So, I gave the whole thing a quick read, but my eyes were glazing over even as I did so. I realised, all of a sudden, that I was no longer interested in how our Air Force looked, or how it might shape up in the coming months and years. I had my new life and that's the one I now wanted to live. I knew, almost for certain, that if I said yes to Maurice's request to be his future aircraft adviser, I would be spending time away from Anna and home and actually probably achieving nothing in the long run because the 'procurement' people would almost definitely mess it up. So, I gave Maurice one more evening of my time, and compiled a short report with recommendations for the future. I then added a letter to Maurice saying that my work for him was done, and that my only toil from now on was cider-making. And with that, I sealed it in an envelope, took it to the Post Office the next morning and, having paid for it to go 'special delivery,' I turned my back on the armed forces for good. Four weeks later I received a nice letter from Maurice thanking me for my suggestions, most of which he said were very sound and would probably be put into effect, and a cheque for £500 for my time. He closed, saying that he would try and come and see us soon, if we were available.

Anna and I decided that because the garden was looking so wonderful we would throw a party for the village. On the appointed Saturday afternoon, with tables laden with food and drink brought from near and, in a few cases, quite far, we opened proceedings. I thanked everyone for coming and reminded them that our cider was available both to taste and to buy. As the afternoon turned into evening, a youngish chap came over to speak to me. He was, he claimed, running a couple of very successful farm shop outlets in Somerset and north Devon and asked if I could produce enough of my drink to satisfy his customers. As I could now manage two hundred bottles a week, I said I thought I could.

And so started my second, and last career. Hobby cider production had suddenly become, for us at least, big business. Throughout the season, we were managing to exceed the quantities required and once we got to the late autumn, Anna and I talked at length and realised that if we bought some mature trees and planted many more, we could make the whole thing into a very lucrative venture.

Over the winter, we sold all the sheep and all but twelve of the chickens and, having ploughed both fields, we planted fifty young trees and three hundred saplings. I discovered that a few miles away in Bitton, a chap was selling two very large presses. One was manually operated, the other was powered by a small electric motor. After a bit of bartering, I got them both for what I thought was a bloody good price.

I had recently come to the indisputable conclusion that I was slowing down. In the beginning, I thought that maybe I had the sickness, but I was pretty sure it was simply that I was getting old. We decided that from the next apple season onward, we would employ some local people to do the hard work for us. Anna would do the accounts and I would, naturally, quality control the product. Christmas 1990 was a lovely affair. The pub in the village had invited everyone who was inclined to do so to have lunch there. There were forty or so of us, and the turkey and most of the vegetables had come from local producers. The wine was from a Devonshire vineyard and the cider was from me. Anna and I paid for everyone, and at around eight that evening, I offered to take over the bar so that the landlord and his wife and daughter could have a few drinks themselves. It was a bloody expensive day, but worth every penny.

Maurice rang me in early January and asked if he could come and visit us again. I replied that he didn't need to ask, just to let us know when he was coming.

He came down by train this time and then got a taxi from Bath. As soon as he dumped his bag in his room, he suggested we should go to the pub for a late lunch. It was there, in the slightly harsh winter sunlight that I saw that he looked rather grey around the gills and very much as if he had lost some weight. His appetite didn't seem to be adversely affected though nor, once we had got home, his ability to decimate my supply of domestic cider. All three of us were in bed by ten that evening.

The following morning, after breakfast, Maurice, Anna and I sat in front of the fire in the lounge with our cups of tea, and he told us about progress in getting rid of our remaining bombs. The allied governments have finally agreed that, aside from the stash of Chinese warheads and missiles at the factory near Daxing, there are no other nuclear weapons left in the world apart from those inside HMS Vanguard and hanging off our TSR2s and the French Mirage IVs. The British and French governments had offered to destroy the Chinese nuclear warhead manufacturing facility using all our remaining missiles. 'Trouble is,' added Maurice, 'the Kiwis have reservations.'

'Why?' I asked.

'Well because if the prevailing winds shifted, some of the contamination could be dumped on them.'

'And the South Sea islanders, surely?'

'Indeed yes. But actually, they think it's a good idea and they're happy with our contingency plans. That is, that we would only launch when we're sure the wind is blowing in the right direction.'

'Can't we just use a few to get rid of the factory and then disarm the rest?' asked Anna, sensibly.

'If only we could, my love. You see out of all the survivors in our new world, we haven't yet found anyone who could be reasonably described as a warhead dismantler.'

'Not one?' asked Anna.

Maurice shook his head. 'No one. Besides, we have absolutely no idea what to do with all the uranium, once we've got it out of the weapons' It was a fair point. There would be no point disarming, only to find the remnants of our weapons leaking into the ground in ten years' time. 'We're going to send the submarine and the aircraft to China all bombed up, but all but two of the weapons will be released without being armed. Once they've hit the general target area, one last missile each from a TSR2 and a Mirage will be armed and should vaporise everything that's left,' he explained.

'Not too much fallout,' I replied.

'No, although it's not that I'm fussed about contaminating them, it's just the long-term effects will be reduced if we do it that way,' he added. 'So, who wants to hear about my great successes in reversing the wanton destruction of Dr Beeching then?'

Anna put her hand up and nodded.

It seemed Maurice had instructed that the rail engineers try and reconnect all the previously abandoned lines. They had already managed to reopen the lines from Barnstaple to Ilfracombe and Bideford and were still working on some of the long closed lines in Devon and Cornwall. Padstow would be reopened before the end of the year, but some lines were beyond practical help. The good news was that thousands of people were now using the trains to get to and from work and for weekend leisure trips. Car usage was down and, as a country, we now almost had enough petrol reserves to allow drivers a day a week of unrestricted motoring.

Midmorning I took the car to Bitton to get some shopping in, and when I got back, I saw that Maurice and Anna were in the garden. I put the stuff away and then went to the French window to see if they wanted a drink. They were standing half way down the lawn, and Anna was holding Maurice's outstretched hand. I couldn't tell for certain, but she seemed to be crying. At that point, she looked over at me. She smiled and then gave Maurice a hug before they walked back towards the house.

'We were just talking about all the people we miss because of the war,' she said.

'Yes. Terrible,' said Maurice.

After lunch, we drove to the house in Chew Valley to show it to Maurice, and then we motored on to Cheddar and then to Weston before returning home. It had been a splendid day. The following two days were spent lazing around the house, visiting the pub and going for some short walks. On the third afternoon, we drove Maurice to Bristol Temple Meads station and waved him off. After the train had disappeared around the corner, I turned and saw that Anna was in floods of tears.

'I already know,' I said.

'He's dying, Ollie. Maurice is dying and it's all his own bloody stupid fault,' she said. She told me that in the garden that day, she had mentioned that he was looking a little peaky. He had replied that there was a very good reason for that and he told her the rest just as I heard ir from Paul Maybury. He had indeed ended up committing a slow suicide. No time scale could be confirmed, but he now had tumours spreading through his body, and he was passing blood in his urine.

The next week was very gloomy, and Anna spent rather a lot of time at the Chew Valley house on the pretext that she had found some new tenants and wanted it to be all ship-shape.

On the first day of February, I took a phone call from a hugely excited Maurice. 'You have both got to come down to Dartmouth,' he had insisted. 'I'm sending a car for you in the morning. Don't ask why. Ta ta.' And with that, he rang off.

We were both intrigued and also delighted that he sounded so very chipper. The car duly arrived and the young driver proved to us that you can easily do the trip as quickly as supersonic jet. Not only did he drive unbelievably fast, he was also terrible at it.

Maurice had arranged for us to be put up in the biggest bedroom at the College again, and after we had unpacked, we joined him in his office. He was positively bouncing around, and, all things considered, he looked incredibly well. 'There is now no opposition to the launch,' he said with great excitement.

'Oh that's marvellous,' said Anna.

'When do they go?' I asked.

'The wind is tracking east at the moment, which is okay, but the Met people say that in a day or so, there will be a period of forty-eight to seventy-two hours where it will be blowing north westwards. And that is perfect. It will head up towards Russia, and the even better news is that there are rain and snowstorms forecast, meaning that most of the fallout will settle all over the bastards.'

There really wasn't an answer to that.

'We're telling everybody as well. No secrets. No cloak and dagger. It will be in the papers and on the radio and TV. I'm sending two of our TriStars for tanking and two Hercules to dump the Polaris warheads out of,' he said enthusiastically.

'Just throwing them out the back?' I asked.

'Yep. No detonation, just rolling them out. They won't go off, but might just spill out a bit of radioactivity,' he replied.

'When are they going?' I asked.

'The Hercules are already on their way. Should be over Peking in about,' - with this, he looked at his watch - 'Four hours. Everything is being refuelled overhead Moscow and Kazakhstan both outbound and on the way back,' he said.

'No more bombs?' said Anna.

'None,' said Maurice. And then he coughed. Not just a throat clearance. It was deep and it sounded horrible. He wiped his mouth with a handkerchief and rolled his eyes skyward.

'Radiation eh?' he said.

We then travelled to Exeter Airport, and after lunch in the restaurant in the terminal building, we returned to watch the bombed up TSR2s blast off from the runway. They looked particularly magnificent with their White Shadows under their wings.

When they were just specks on the horizon, we all returned to the College. Anna and I were in the mess bar when Maurice came in and sat down with us.

'The Hercules have dropped the Polaris missiles and are coming home,' he said gleefully.

'Everything went okay?' I asked.

'Seemingly. All sort of on target, I'm told,' he said.

'What about the rest?' asked Anna.

'The TSR2s and Mirages will be on target at around about 1 a.m our time and they will all launch simultaneously. Then they're going to bimble about a bit to get some good film for the archives and the history films. When they've fired off their live rounds, they'll turn for home. Once they've landed and had a quick cuppa, the crews of all the aeroplanes will take off again and do some flypasts for us. So we're getting everyone up to the airport for around four tomorrow afternoon to welcome them back and enjoy a full RAF airshow as well,' he said

'What about your submarine then?' I enquired.

'Oh, Vanguard's been on station for over a week. She's going to send up a couple of remote controlled aeroplanes to try and capture the Trident launches from above,' he said.

'Will they be armed?' I asked.

'Nope, they'll be sent up on the missiles like great big chunks of metal and dump down on China to be blown up by your bombers,' Maurice replied

The rest of that day was quite tense and we saw nothing more of Maurice until around nine when he popped in to say he was getting an early night.

The following morning, Anna and skipped breakfast in favour of a cup of tea and went straight to the library. The morning paper's headline was one I thought I would never see.

THE LAST DAY OF A NUCLEAR WORLD'

That was followed by information on the timings of the flypast. Everyone who could possibly make it was invited to attend.

Maurice's Adjutant came into the library at about eleven and told us that our cars would be ready to take us to Exeter Airport at one. We were waiting on the College steps when Maurice came out in his full uniform, and he looked magnificent. 'The Hercules' were going to take bloody weeks to get home so they're stopping over in Norway for a short crew holiday on their way back. But by that time they will have set a record for the longest military flight in history, and by all accounts, they've got some great film and video footage of the missiles clanging into China and bursting open,' he enthused as we climbed into the staff car.

The roads were clogged with traffic, and all of it was converging on Exeter Airport. Maurice considered getting the motorcycle outriders to radio for a helicopter, but in the end we got through.

'I thought people were short of petrol?' I said as we finally swung into the airport car park.

'Yeah, they are. But since they can only drive one day week, they've all decided it's today,' he replied.

We pulled up in front of the terminal, got out of the car and were directed to the upper level by RAF police. The whole building had been closed off to the public for the day so we had the viewing platform, which overlooked the runway, all to ourselves. The TriStars and TSR2s from the 'last raid' were sitting on the apron in front of us with ground crews busily getting them ready for the flypast. The remainder of the Royal Air Force was on the opposite side of the field.

'The PM and some others are joining us later, and there'll be drinkies and nibbles later. The good news is the bar's open. Can I get anyone anything?' Maurice asked.

So we sat in the low afternoon sunshine, sipping very large gins and tonics until there was a bit of a commotion and the PM and his retinue turned up. After lots of handshaking and back slapping, we all settled down for the main event. There were no more than thirty of us on the balcony but there were literally thousands clinging to the fence and sitting on car roofs and up step ladders all around the airport's perimeter fence. Inside the fence, were dozens, if not hundreds of soldiers and policemen and all were facing outwards. We could hear the various aircraft engines starting, but it wasn't until just gone four that all of them started to make their way to the runway for take off. In order of departure, there were six TSR2s, thirty four Hawks, the two 146s, six VC10s, two Tristars, seven Hercules, eight Chinooks, seven Pumas, fifteen Gazelles and lastly, the seven Hunters. It was an utterly thrilling spectacle and Anna was soon clapping as each aircraft put on the power and accelerated down the runway. The Prime Minister spent most of the time on his feet. The rather feeble public address system that had been hastily set up around the airport announced that the display aircraft were on their way in from the right. The tannoy told us that the first aircraft were the helicopters who flew past in a huge formation. The rear two Gazelles were flying backwards throughout. Next were the remaining TriStars and the two 146s, closely followed by three waves of Hawks.

The chap on the PA, who, by now I liked very much, then announced that the next aircraft were the 'Saviours of the world.' The RAF's six airworthy VC10s streaked down the centreline at about a hundred feet on full power. It was mightily impressive. Next were the Hercules,' followed in quick succession by six of the Hunters. The announcer then informed us that the two TSR2s that had completed the world's last ever nuclear bombing raid were coming in fast, and by God were they low and fast. They couldn't have been more than forty feet above the ground. There was a huge roar of appreciation from the crowd.

I looked across at Maurice. His shoulders were heaving and he was coughing madly into a bunched up hankie. I went over and put my arm around him. He turned, smiled and buried his face in my shoulder.

The two TSR2s then came back for their final run, and I could see the occasional puff of black exhaust smoke from the jet pipes. They screamed past at near supersonic speed and then pulled up into a vertical climb and shot up until they disappeared into the clouds. Even as they vanished from view, you could still hear the crackle of their engines. I very nearly cried.

Once everything had landed, and after the last aircraft had shut down, the public began to disperse and the military types all headed down to the ground floor of the terminal for a reception with the crews of the TriStars and TSR2s that had completed the last nuclear mission. I don't know if Anna and I were invited, but we rather felt that we'd had our time, and now it was for the new boys and Maurice to bask in the glory.

We went to the bar and got a couple of drinks, and then went down to the perimeter fence and sat and watched a variety of birds as they returned to a nice quiet airport, looking for food. Obviously the drinks had helped, and probably the warm sunshine, but we were soon both fast asleep. When Maurice came over and woke us it was decidedly cool and dark.

'Come on you two old codgers. Let's get you home,' he said and we made our way back to the front of the terminal and to the staff car. 'Wasn't that great?' he said as we got underway.

'It was a magnificent sight, Maurice,' I said. I meant it too.

We were detained briefly as the Hawks and Hunters took off for their bases, followed immediately by the TriStars and the C130s.

Once back at the College, Anna and I made it known that even though we had had an absolutely wonderful time, we needed to leave the next day.

Maurice said, 'I'll arrange a car.'

We turned him down. The train was more relaxing and we really didn't feel that we should be tying up much needed staff for old duffer transportation purposes. That evening in the mess bar, we chatted about the day's events and then I asked Maurice about his plans for his submarines now that the need for a nuclear deterrent was passed. He told us that HMS Vanguard would be retained as she was, but rearmed with many more torpedoes. Victorious would only sail when Vanguard was in dock for major servicing or refurbishment. Essentially, she was mothballed for five years. When it was obvious that we were all running out of steam, Maurice said, 'I'm going to hand over the reins to Rich Fitzjohn when he gets back in a couple of weeks'

'He's going to be the Chief?' I asked.

'Yeah. I can't do this any more you two. I'm done in. I know it's my own fault, so don't feel sorry for me,' he said.

'Oh Maurice. You stupid bloody sod,' said Anna and she brushed her hand gently onto his cheek.

'Thanks,' he said and reached across and squeezed her hand.

'Once Richard's back, why don't you come and stay with us?' I suggested. 'You can stay as long as you like.

'Please come down,' added Anna.

We got back to the house really late because of delays with the train and it was well past midnight when the taxi dropped us at home. Anna had gone straight to bed, but I couldn't sleep, so I sipped some cider, then some whiskey, and was making a fire by half past five. By the time Anna came down at seven thirty, the paper had arrived. The headline said it all. I believe it's quite famous now.

7th FEBRUARY 1991   A NUCLEAR FREE WORLD

There wasn't much else in it, apart from some updates on the whereabouts of HMS Vanguard and a bit of sport at the back.

Maurice rang a few weeks later and did his usual thing of asking if he could come down. I didn't even bother to remind him that he was always welcome.

He arrived in a staff car this time, telling us that he didn't really feel up to the train journey any more. He told us that Vanguard was back and that an initially furious Richard Fitzjohn was soon to be inaugurated as the next Chief of the Defence Staff. Fitzjohn had calmed down somewhat when Maurice had explained the circumstances of his appointment. The entire crew of Victorious would now take Vanguard out on her next patrol. Her first as a conventionally armed submarine.

Maurice had brought us some fantastic video film to watch. There were shots of Vanguard launching her SLBMs, taken from about five hundred feet by the radio controlled model; the dumping out the back of Hercules' of the Polaris missiles, and the best of the lot, the TSR2s and Mirages launching their missiles at the Polaris dumping ground, taken from cameras in the nose and on the wing of both types. The last two missiles launched by us and the French exploded rather beautifully, and seemingly right in the middle of the smoke left by the rest. It was a sobering sight. We were privileged to see the film, as it wasn't being released to the TV stations for another two weeks.

Maurice told us he was handing over to Fitzjohn on the 10th of April and that it couldn't come soon enough. He explained, 'There won't be a ceremony or a dinner or any sort of official handover'

'Nice and quiet then,' Anna had said.

'Yes. So I can't really invite you as there'll be nothing to see,' he added.

'That's fine, chum. Just take it easy, eh,' I said.

'I don't think they'll be any more Chiefs of Staff appointed by recommendation any more after him. I reckon the government will decide who's next after Richard's finished his term. But it's fitting though. He's one of the war heroes right?'

I nodded in agreement.

And then he went quiet. Within a few minutes, he was asleep. Anna covered him with a blanket and then went into the kitchen. I disappeared off to the barn to check the presses.

Anna came out to see me a little while later. She grabbed my arm. 'He looks awful Ollie. I think we should call the doctor,' she suggested.

'He said not to. He said the pills he's on made him very drowsy. That's all it is. Just drowsiness,' I said.

'And terminal cancer,' said Anna as she returned to the house.

Maurice had perked up quite a bit by the time I got back and he and Anna were chatting away discussing the merits of apple varieties. He stayed for another whole day and then left early the following morning. As he got into the staff car, he looked quite frail and didn't even turn to wave goodbye. Anna cried for most of the morning and I felt very down. We were watching our best friend drift away, and there was absolutely nothing that could be done.

In the paper on the 11th of April, there was a column on the third page about the appointment of Fitzjohn to the post of Chief of the Defence Staff.

Maurice Bowen, the Admiral of the Fleet and a VC, famously commanded the Polaris submarine HMS Valiant during the war, and was captain of one of only three surviving allied subs that hammered the enemy on Sakhalin Island. He has been forced to retire because of ill health. In the accompanying photo, where he was shaking hands with Fitzjohn, Maurice looked like a sick old man.

I showed the article to Anna, but as soon as she saw the picture, she threw the paper onto the table.

CHAPTER SEVENTEEN

Maurice started coming to see us more often over the next few months, and during one visit asked if he could come down every weekend. Of course we said he could.

One evening, at the end of July, he said he was returning to his 'grace and favour' apartment at Dartmouth College the next day.

Anna said, 'No you're not. You're bloody well staying here from now on.'

And so, he became our house guest. He was looking ever frailer and I urged him to let me call the doctor or even to get him admitted to the Bristol Infirmary. He said he couldn't be bothered as he knew it wasn't going to get better, so he was just going to live out his life until his time came.

By the middle of September, his cheeks were sunken and he had a yellowish pallor about him. It was awful to see, but in the finest traditions of the British stiff upper lip, we didn't talk about it much. I hadn't witnessed slow, creeping sickness before, so his deterioration shocked both of us intensely. Everything he did was slow but precise. Every mouthful of food was cut meticulously into tiny pieces and chewed relentlessly. When he drank, his hand shook alarmingly. But it didn't stop him. He loved our cider and drank copious amounts. I rather thought it didn't matter now how much he drank.

One mid-October morning, I woke at seven because my nostrils detected frying bacon. I went downstairs and there was Maurice cooking up a fantastic breakfast. He was chatting away with Anna and seemed to be in fine fettle. He presented us with eggs, bacon, sausage, black pudding, mushrooms and fried bread. It was a magical morning and he seemed to have a new lease of life. He was vibrant, funny and extraordinarily articulate. By the evening, he had slipped back into a terrible silence. His skin looked paper thin and was grey at the eye sockets and the lips. He barely spoke. We called the doctor the next day and he eventually turned up. He took one look at Maurice and said, 'I know who you are Mr Marsden and I also know this gentleman. From his war record, I can assume that this is the result of radiation poisoning,' he said.

'Yes, that's right.'

'I don't wish to appear harsh or unsympathetic to his plight, but I am more concerned for your welfare and that of your wife after he has gone. There is potential for contamination, you see,' he explained.

I knew he was right. I thanked him for his time and promised I would call when the time came. That same evening, we sat and watched a bit of television and Maurice fell asleep on the sofa. I curled up on the chair opposite. Anna asked me if I wanted her to stay too, but I told her to go up and I would call her if necessary.

I woke with a start and a sense of terrible, crushing dread. Maurice was sitting there staring at me.

'Morning,' he said.

'Oh my God! Morning,' I replied with great relief.

On the night of November 3rd, Maurice said he wanted to sleep in the bed. Anna and I helped him upstairs and he thanked us. He didn't want anything to eat, just a glass of water for the night.

As we turned to leave his room, he said, 'Will you stay with me for a while?'

'Of course I will, old man,' I replied.

I looked at Anna and she went over to his bed and kissed Maurice on the forehead. 'Goodnight Maurice,' she said. She was crying as she left the room.

'Night night Anna,' he said with a smile.

At first, I sat on the edge of the bed, but eventually I lay down next to him. Then, at some point during the night, I grasped his little frail hand. I think I had terrible dreams through the night, because when I woke,

I felt an all consuming misery. It only took a second to realise why. Maurice's mouth was slightly open and his eyes were staring ahead and were glassy and grey. I pulled the blanket up to his neck and then I went and told Anna. She said she would like to sit with him for a while. I went out into the garden and wept.

It was on Thursday 4th November 1991 that Maurice Wade Bowen RN VC, Chief of the Defence Staff died. He was sixty eight years old.

I guess Maurice could have lived until he was my dad's age if we hadn't had a war and probably to eighty if he hadn't gone out into the radiation. But to be honest, once I had got over the initial shock and sadness of losing him, I reflected that he had had a pretty bloody marvellous life. He was as great a hero as had ever lived. He was unflappable, funny and charming. He didn't shout and scream like some senior ranks and he was measured in all his strategic decisions.

Now he was gone, and Anna and I had to make the journey to Dartmouth, knowing that it was probably the last time we would go there and also that it was under the worst of circumstances. The service was held in the college chapel and the congregation included the King, the Prime Minister and the heads of each of the Services. Richard Fitzjohn was there too. We had taken the train up, and as we were approaching Kingswear, the vast bulk of Valiant hove into view. She didn't look very different. Her repaint and tidy up had made her look very presentable. But I could barely look at her. It was too painful. Maurice was to be cremated, and his ashes scattered over the fore planes of HMS Valiant in a ceremony led by Richard Fitzjohn. Anna and I chose not to attend that bit. So, immediately after the funeral, we said our goodbyes and headed back to the station via the foot ferry. A fair few other mourners had the same idea and the little vessel was jam packed. As we bobbed our way across the river, I looked towards the front of the boat and caught sight of someone who I was sure I recognised. She was looking back at me.

'Excuse me darling,' I said to Anna, 'There's someone here I know. Won't be a minute.'

Dr Helen Flint looked as wonderful as I had always remembered her and she smiled beautifully as I approached.

'Hello, sir,' she said.

'It was always Oliver and now it's definitely Oliver,' I replied.

'It's lovely to see you, and you're looking so well,' she said, moving just a little closer.

'How come you're here, Helen?'

'Maurice had been my patient for some time, since I was posted here to Dartmouth,' she said.

'You were treating him for his cancer?' I asked.

'No, for his mental wellbeing,' she replied.

'I had no idea. If I had, I would have come to see you.'

'But you're married Oliver!' she said smiling.

'I didn't mean it like that. Well yes, actually, I did,' I admitted. The schoolboy Marsden again.

'Look, I knew you would be here today and I just wanted to tell you that I really was going to join you for dinner in the mess at Predannack that evening, but I got called down to St. Mawgan overnight'

I just looked at her. She smiled again and I melted like an absolute arse. As the boat neared the shore, she gently grabbed my hand and said, 'It really is lovely to see you. Goodbye Oliver.' Then she turned as we docked.

I walked back to Anna who said, 'Who was that, Ollie?'

'Maurice's doctor. I first met her when I got back from my Russian trip.'

'She's lovely,' said Anna, and left it at that. I deliberately chose a seat on the right hand side of the train carriage so that I wouldn't have to see Valiant again as we left. She was Maurice's boat and always would be.

The journey home was a sombre affair, not least because of Maurice's passing but also for my own strange thoughts about Helen.

When we got home, I realised that that was that. The last vestiges of my relationship with the Services had gone. I was now Ollie Marsden, cider producer. And that's precisely what I spent most of my time doing.

About a week after the funeral, Richard Fitzjohn telephoned and thanked Anna and I for attending. He added that we were both welcome to come up and badger him, or force him into the mess for drinks at a moment's notice. I didn't doubt for a minute that he meant it, but I told him that he was very kind and we'd think about it. I think he guessed from my tone that we would never go up there again.

I realised then that my retirement had started in earnest. I felt a bit down about it because I was sure that there were other things that I either could do, or should do. I just couldn't work out what they were. I fact, there were quite a few things that I couldn't remember any more. The details of my war day bombing flight were becoming very misty. The raid on Sakhalin was less vague, and whilst I had fairly clear recollections of my aircraft going down, the train ride and bits of our flight home, I couldn't always remember the names of my crew. Yet, I remembered every damn detail of my flight over France on the day I was shot down. I could picture that stupid pig in the upturned boat, the family in the shelter, and Huber capturing me. I could almost taste that pint in the pub in Hastings, and the annoying face of that irritating army intelligence officer. But I couldn't remember what I'd had for dinner last night. Anna said it was because I had spent almost my entire adult life putting my life at risk and now that I could finally relax, my brain simply wouldn't let me. Maybe she was right. When my publisher first got in touch about two years ago, they took away all my scribblings, and notes and the few bits I had managed to knock out on a typewriter. And it's just as well, because if you asked me now to tell you what I was doing in 1952 or 1986, I wouldn't really have the foggiest. When they recently sent me a proof copy to examine, most of the bits from the end of WWII onwards could have been written about someone else. Aside from the mentions of Anna and cider making, I didn't honestly think it was me until I had read them a few times and then it would all come back. Yet, I can remember Huber's face as though it was yesterday.

After the apples had been harvested in September 1992, I contacted Richard Fitzjohn's Adjutant at Dartmouth, and asked if he would be kind enough to get his boss to call me at some point, when he wasn't too busy. He promised that he would.

It was only a couple of days later when I received the call, and it was very good to hear from him again. I told him that I thought I was being a little presumptuous, but the reason for my call was to discover how all my crew members were doing after all this time. He said that he didn't think it was at all unusual, and once I had given him all the names, as best as I could, he promised to let me know as soon as he was able. True to his word, he gave me what I had asked for, but not in the way I had expected.

On November the 5th, a big black car pulled up outside the house as I was watering the plants on the window sill. Richard Fitzjohn climbed out and we hugged each rather warmly.

'God, it's good to see you Richard,' I said genuinely taken aback by his arrival.

'And you, Oliver, and you,' he replied.

I told him that as we were now planning to sell the house at Chew Valley, Anna was over there clearing out a few of our things, but I hoped she would be back before he left. We went inside and he sampled a few of my cider varieties before handing me a few pages of paper with my crew's circumstances nicely typed out.

Nicholas Clarke, my copilot from my first war mission had been medically retired, all as a result of his injuries on that fateful day, and now ran a bookshop in Looe. He was 52 years old and lived with a war widow who was a little younger than him. He was stepfather to her two teenage children.

My Bombardier, Steven Thorpe was 53, and still in the RAF. He was now a Squadron Leader, and chief weapons instructor at St. Mawgan.

Paul Maybury, my trusty and magnificent Adjutant was happily retired and lived alone in Ilfracombe, where he passed the time painting pictures of the surrounding coast. Apparently, they were quite highly regarded, and he did rather well out of their sales. I was very glad, he was a truly splendid chap.

I then moved on to my crew from the Sakhalin mission. My Flight Engineer Geoff Staples, was now forty and was in hospital in Plymouth suffering from an unspecified cancer. Whilst it couldn't be said for sure, it was almost certainly because of his exposure to radiation. It was deeply shocking to read and I asked if I perhaps ought to go and see him. Fitzjohn shook his head.

At that point, and to change the subject somewhat, I decided to show him around the house and the orchard garden. After that was done, we popped over to the pub for a bite to eat, and during lunch he told me about a day in the life of the Chief of the Defence Staff. 'It really isn't anything like you would remember it, Oliver. We don't need to send the ships out or the aeroplanes up, but we do, because it keeps the guys current, and it's good training for them. For me, it's just a round of visits to units and then reams of paperwork and persistent government interference.'

The new fighter-bomber that Maurice had been so enthusiastic about was way behind schedule, and was still over five years' away from service. And even when it happened, we were only going to take twenty of them. In the meantime, he had had to make some swingeing cuts to the RAF because of serviceability issues. Our once proud and magnificent air force now consisted of eight Hercules, twenty four Hawks, just four VC10s, six Chinooks, six Pumas, twelve Gazelles and only five Hunters.

'If we needed to bomb anything, then we would have to do it with the Hawks,' Fitzjohn said.

'So, the TSR2s finally conked out?' I asked. And he nodded.

'We'll be down to only three VC10s by next year, and another will be done in twelve months after that. We've pretty much run out of spares. We're desperately trying to keep two airworthy for as long as possible, but I don't know if we can,' he said.

'You won't have any transport capability at all if they go,' I replied, feeling truly sad that my wonderful bomber would soon be consigned to the history books.

'There are a couple of rays of hope. The French have said that we can have two BA 757s that are sitting around at Nantes, and some of your old colleagues have been up to Valley to see if they could get your Russian jet working,' he said.

'Good luck with that. I thought it was going to get used as target practice?, I queried.

'Couldn't afford to waste the bombs,' he said.

'How's the navy then?' I asked.

'Only in slightly better shape,' he added.

'What have you got now?' I asked.

'Two big RFAs, a decent destroyer, two frigates, and quite a few patrol boats and minesweepers. We're thinking of putting Victorious out of service and just keeping Vanguard as insurance, and sending Superb, the SSN out on patrols,' he said.

'Blimey,' was all I could think of to say.

I then asked Richard about the other allied countries. 'All doing okay really. Norway has got a lot of very happy refugees, and some people even made it to New Zealand in the end,' he said.

'Not Chinese ones, though.'

'No, not Chinese,' he answered.

'Good,' I said.

He continued enthusiastically, 'We sent a lot of our troops out to help the other NATO forces in north eastern Russia, and they are essentially travelling across the length and breadth of the enemy countries looking for pockets of survivors or resistance.'

'Won't that take decades to complete?' I asked, amazed that we were still worried about our former foe.

'No, not at all. There are over sixty thousand soldiers out there, Oliver. Ours, French, Norwegians, Icelandics, some Canadians, Chilean, Sicilians and Moroccans. I've only got about a thousand troops actually left here, all the rest are either traipsing north through China or west across Russia,' he added. 'They'll be done and dusted by the spring. We're pulling out of Asia after that. Leaving the place to the insects and the wild boars and wolves.'

It seemed that the radiation levels were still very high, but with the right protective equipment and vehicles, progress had been swift.

'And was there resistance?' I asked

'No, not really. A few skirmishes, but mostly just cave-dwelling zombies wandering around who had somehow not yet been killed by the radiation,' he explained.

'And what do the boys do with them,' I enquired.

'They shoot them, Oliver.'

Back at the house, and against my better judgement, I continued reading the notes on my crew.

My Comms officer Spike Finch was 35 years old and was still a Flight Lieutenant, although this was by choice apparently. He was based at Chivenor. His entry also included his actual first name. In the end, I think I preferred Spike to Gary.

Chris Griffith, my Weapons Systems Operator was fifty three years old, and had remarried after losing his wife to cancer a few years earlier. He now worked with Steven Thorpe at St. Mawgan.

Colin Edgecombe, my copilot; a superb flyer, and great friend, had been successfully treated for throat cancer but had now been diagnosed with lung cancer. I almost tore the paper up there and then, but there was one more name.

Rollo Geary, my chief engineer, and as fine a fellow as you ever hope to meet, had died six months earlier of complications following surgery for the removal of a variety of tumours.

I looked up at Richard and his expression said it all. 'Wish I hadn't come eh?' he said ruefully.

'They were all so well when I last saw them,' I replied.

'That's it though, Oliver. They were. It doesn't seem to take very long once they're diagnosed with it,' he said. He said that overall, the predictions of the UN had been pretty well spot on. People were dying sooner than they should have, but in a very random way. There weren't any particular towns or even areas where you had a greater or lesser chance of surviving through to your dotage. Plenty of service personnel who had been around aircraft, airfields, ports and ships during and after the war, and the Sakhalin mission, showed no signs of radiation sickness at all. Others who had been in exactly the same places at exactly the same times were dead or were ill.

'There is no sense to it, Oliver. And what's more, in the future, nobody will believe that we could have been so very bloody stupid,' said Richard.

His car returned at six, and after we had said our goodbyes, he left. I was still at the front door, and his car was barely out of sight, when Anna came around the corner from Bath.

By Christmas of 1992, I had developed a cough which I couldn't shift. I supposed it might have been my years of smoking cigarettes or equally, I could be next in line for the reaper. I did my best to keep it secret from Anna, but eventually she realised, and got the doctor over. I was astonished when he told me that it was just an infection, and that it would go in time with the help of a few antibiotics. By the summertime, Anna and I had settled into a blissful routine of watching our fit young employees bring in the early harvest, pulp them and then present us with the fruits of their labour. The cider still tasted very good, just not quite as good as when I used to squeeze it myself in the garden shed in the early years.

As Anna and I sat on the veranda sipping our drinks, I reflected on a wonderful and fulfilling life, most of which I wouldn't have missed for the world. The thrill of going to war, the wonderful comradeship of my fellow crewmen, and the glorious satisfaction of knowing that you have done a job well. There were plenty of parts that I could have done without, though. Anything to do with the last war and the terrible losses that it caused. And all my friends and colleagues who didn't deserve to have their lives cut short by insane political decisions.

But in the end, as lives go, mine has been a pretty good one.

Chief of the Defence Staff, Marshall of the Royal Air Force, Sir Oliver Marsden VC died of cancer in August 1995

Glossary

GHQ General Headquarters

CO Commanding Officer

LDV Local Defence Volunteers

NCO Non-commissioned Officer

Air Officer C in C Air Officer Commanding-in-Chief

A/C Aircraft

NATO North Atlantic Treaty Organisation

SAC Strategic Air Command

RFA Royal Fleet Auxiliary

SSBN Subsurface Ballistic Nuclear (submarine)

AFV Armoured Fighting Vehicle

BRDM Russian-built four-wheeled amphibious Combat
Reconnaissance Patrol Vehicle

121.5 The emergency frequency used throughout civil aviation

CFO Chief Flying Instructor

NSA U. S. National Security Agency

OCU Operational Conversion Unit

SSN Sub-Surface Nuclear (submarine)

Printed in Great Britain
by Amazon

33945230R00136